Matinee

A NOVEL BY

ROBERT STEINER

Fiction Collective Two
Boulder • Normal • Brooklyn

Fiction Collective Two, English Department Publications Center, Campus Box 494, University of Colorado at Boulder, Boulder, CO 80309-0494.

First printing, 1989.

Library of Congress Cataloging in Publication Data

Steiner, Robert, 1948–
Matinee: a novel/by Robert Steiner. — 1st ed.
I. Title 88-18061
PS3569.T376M3 1988 CIP
813'.54—dc19
ISBN: 0-932511-13-9
ISBN: 0-932511-14-7 (pbk.)

Published by the Fiction Collective Two with assistance from The New York State Council on the Arts, and the Publications Center of the University of Colorado at Boulder, and with the support of Brooklyn College, Illinois State University, Teachers & Writers Collaborative, and BACA/the Brooklyn Arts Council.

Grateful acknowledgment is also made to the Graduate School, the School of Arts and Sciences, and the President's Fund of the University of Colorado at Boulder.

The author wishes to thank the National Endowment for the Arts and the University of Colorado Committee on Research and Creative Work for their generous support. Also, thanks to typist Carolyn Dameron, and special gratitude to Janet Hard and Ralph Berry.

The Publisher acknowledges generous permission to reproduce the following works of art: Reclining Girl (Mademoiselle O'Murphy) *by Francois Boucher, Wallraf-Richartz Museum, Cologne; photo of Venice © 1988 by Mary Tanner;* A Lady Writing *by Jan Vermeer, National Gallery of Art, Washington, D.C., (Gift of Harry Waldron Havemeyer and Horace Havemeyer, Jr., in memory of their father, Horace Havemeyer); others © 1988 Robert Steiner.*

Manufactured in the United States of America.
Typeset by Fisher Composition Inc.
Typography by Abe Lerner.

FOR

JOHN HAWKES

MATINEE

——————'s?, etc.

WHERE do you go from here? ——— asked T[illegible]irling the ice in his drink with a pencil lifted fron[illegible]sk in Theo's study, a study suffused by austere m[illegible] with louvered windows, blood-wood walls, rugs bl[illegible] blue, a poster of El Greco's Toledo in the year 161[illegible] being near the death of Don Quijote and the birth o[illegible]on Juan both in the same country though different provinces, provinces which centuries later would strike observers as the source of modern painting from El Greco and Velásquez say to Miró, Gris, and Pablo Ruiz Picass[illegible] Picasso however removed from Theo's study walls a[illegible] though Theo wanted before him nothing but the saturni[illegible]e eyeful of the melancholic ones, ones like Goya, Fuseli, and Piranesi, copies of whom were pinned and curling at the edges, and such as Bosch and Bellini who'd figured in the ms., the ms. ——— continued to hold in his right hand shaking it at Theo, Theo himself listening to his favorite Mozart, Mozart his favorite genius, so that ———'s disappointment was acknowledged only by the spectacles and wineglass which flamed in the shadows of the study if he adjusted or tilted the disposition of his wrist or head, a head which in sunlight would have been white hair cropped close as though against vermin, a head round and soft like a ripe cantaloupe a peach tennis ball anything soft and round at the same time, a head appointed with large hazardous ears the ears of a klipspringer, and pale lips overhung by a balcony of mustache as white as the hair, soft as the peach, hazardous as the ears and waiting to be stroked by Theo's bony fingers, a head retiring even farther into the shadows where with the ms. in his right hand ——— could see still only the wineglass and the rim of the spectacles so as to keep an eye on Theo while he asked with impatience and growing anger where Theo planned to go from here, not meaning How will this novel continue since it could indefinitely or as long as Theo's life if he wanted to achieve that sort of thing but what did he plan to do now with the muzzle of the pistol he'd been fixing on ——— for hours: squeeze off one round during his own summer party?

And so the party that summer Saturday was under way—bleaching pastures ghost white while headlights nursed curves in the road, cars roared for hours. The lights scattered bats from the roof of a rotting barn, lured moths the size of fists into grilles windshields and onto the party where when they landed formed letters of the alphabet in everyone's hair. Gates of iron opened and shut as often as the doors of screen pine and metal, each of them creaking or banged. Among the guests friends kissed, acquaintances hugged, intimates nodded, adversaries grinned, enemies coughed, and strangers with drinks perspiring in their hands felt awful at the solitude. Guitars harmonicas flutes, trumpets bongos kongas gamelan, the stereo's roofed speakers smothered the crickets' rasp and loads of laughter; the laughter, like the conversation causing it, spavined out into the darkness heading high and low for tall grass, woods, a brook, the stable, the road. Fireflies bigger than toes wooed matches, hot coals and cigarettes, and mosquitoes fertilized millions of eggs on moist arms, legs and foreheads. There were cats peering, owls hooting, dogs barking, dogs snuffling their own and people's genitals, Theo's lone bull snorting in the pen behind the warning B SHARP OR B FLAT! A burst of joke ate much of the talk, skidding tires swallowed the joke, a shriek in the night consumed the tires, the slam of a door deflated the shriek, cries savaged the slam, a howling retriever inhaled the cries, the shatter of glass pierced the howl, rock 'n' roll sliced pied and treed everything so that from high oak limbs shaped *W* Theo's wife JJ could not hear herself sobbing.

She could however reconnoiter the acreage, elevated thirty feet as she was, from the stable where by the gray of the sky guests fondled Casanova, Theo's aging sorrel, to the crowd hunting grub in the kitchen, to the bedrooms opposite her perch where she saw napping drunks and grunting lovers and all those folks too shy to whiz in the woods queuing before the bathroom. God JJ was miserable! Her legs that had gotten bruised and lacerated in the climb were numb from not moving, her spine ached from moving too fast, her hand she'd sliced with the cheese, her feet blistered their toes bunioned, her rump she felt wenning, soon it would be her period and sooner, JJ thought with dread, it would be the end of her marriage to Theo.

Yes the party was on.

Lights! Lights! above eaters laminated against insects to the crust of their elbows, who leaned toward clouds of smoke and grilling flesh before the theatre of music headlights fires and noise. Spunks that flamed in the meadow halfway up the hill drowned as soon as they surfaced. A murmur punctured the sound barrier the dark provided. Nicole, Nicole's neighbor Henriette said, How well I remember Theo plopping down on my divan at rue Casanova Neuf looking wretched to tell me he loved you, undoing his silly little necktie and of course hugging the briefcase for fear I think that someone might actually want to swipe his first novel—anyway he praised you to the ceiling my dear to the ceiling. The party listened talked munched nuts and quarrelled, neither to nor about these women but in surges over serious things, groping too at shadows that might have been food or other hands, even bugs. But you did not see each other often after Paris did you? Sometimes by chance we met, Nicole mumbled. Here and there? Mostly there. Was that, I don't recall, before Munich and Marie or after? Come along Henriette, we both know what happened to Theo and me as well as to Theo and you and you and me too so how much of it do you think I'd tell you now. Legs crossed, uncrossed, the smoke, the moisture in the air, the music grinding down nerves, waves of unease agitating everyone who wasn't drunk or drugged or out of his or her mind from fame or sex. If a torchlight fell from the woods eyes leapt to it, toes curled and fingers felt on and under tables. What's more, heat lightning to the west! The gala is like touring a castle or viewing birth, the party itself a cause for celebration, eaters celebrating with briskets and breasts, flanks and loins, some settling for cheese in blocks, beer in cans, wine in cups, or the incidental burger passing by. Nicole, Theo's Paris lover over ten years earlier, tugged Henriette's shawl to unmask an oyster-colored throat and a vaccination mark big as a quarter. Her husband sincerely kissed her shoulder blade. *Vous êtes trés m[illegible]lant vous savez.* Yes the party was on!

Gravel paths forming *X* a fragrant meter wide and the length of seven more before each path meets the other at the marble-seated junction of mums, nightshade and mignonettes quaintly called the grove. It is Theo's garden. Asphodels abound, a bird bath, an arbor, a statue of Orpheus propped and chicken-wired because it's missing a left ear a lyre and a foot. One graffito has been crayoned across the buttocks by Theo's grandson who resides in Italy with his mother not in London with his father, Theo's son Paul who while promising to appear by train from Brooklyn where he's visiting his mother Gretl was forgotten by his father at the station, nothing but a country crossing really, out in the middle of nothing but rye and corn and melons. Having trained and taxi'd and walked to the farm Paul's entered secretly by the pasture cursing the literal and other sorts of bullshit and poises by now sweaty overheated overdressed against a hazelnut tree in the grove where drawing hard on his cigar, booting acorns into the pond waiting as though for a nut to conk him he gazes blank with anger at the crippled statue in the dark.

Ashing his fat leafy smoke Theo's son dramatically saluted the eyeless chinless demigod. Fractured truth he murmured. When he blew smoky coils that dissolved into lazy half notes a look of grave satisfaction strained his face. Paul was drunk. Moreover fed up. Fed up drunk philosophical a wad of shit on the thin sole of his shoe the jacket of his summer suit over one arm in hand a pint of bourbon (can't see the label in the dark) really fed up just to think of it all and still drunk but getting less and less philosophical maybe edging toward the mawkish even the murderous only time would tell yet he was able to stand though not much more yet wanting nothing else deep down after all was said and done but to take a solid poke at someone. As drunk as that. Certainly too drunk to expect to discover at his father's loud pig fry or fish roast whatever the hell the old bastard'd called it this time a woman. It could happen, it's that kind of party.

In fact Paul had only finished retching into the pond when he heard her crunch stones and weeds under her sandals then shortly heard her zip something whether up or down he could only hope. Seeing with surprise this woman emerge from among the azaleas and hollyhocks righting her jeans with a great twist at the waist. Too tight. Trying to stuff a few years out of sight. Lo said Paul to keep her from fainting at the surprise she was about to have in the dark in the grove at the broken belly of the green Orpheus. Still she sucked air when she saw the shadow in the path and worse thought whatever the hell it was it smelled like a wolf den. Lo then Paul said. Fucking Christ she cried out nearly falling over her own feet to lurch back toward the hollyhocks. Taking a leak were you Theo's son asked in an effort to normalize the situation. Zat booze in your fist or somebody's dick? Nobody's dick Paul replied passing the pint delicately over. She pulled at the bottle without spitting a drop. Afterward she sighed, like a heroine Paul thought. His head was clearing, he thought the zipping sound did it, but on second thought his head wasn't all that clear though he made it to the stone bench. Paul sat at one end rather than in the middle and the invitation, the woman mumbled at him, was irresistible. She sighed again, he asked her was a lung punctured or what but she answered Every time I get home without being fucked I feel like a bus accident just missed me. This woman needs a name Paul decided. He started calling her Eddie though her name was Nicole, and when she didn't object he tagged it onto everything he asked asserted or defended. I'll bet in daylight you've got the sweet pinched face of a crêpe. Slow the beat Casanova Eddie warned him with an elbow I may be easy but I ain't fast.

At the barbecue pit the only light comes from smoldering coals that spit when pig fat falls. Otherwise it's darker than inside a boot and where it's dark are the mosquitoes so the crowd has circled the reamed pig despite the fiery heat and the viscous snout. With the beer the wine the liquor and the steamy night it's already too hot to touch or to be touched. All those faces redden and glow in the snap of the flames above which now and again someone rips out/off a fistful of pork. Someone else commences a song that doesn't get to the chorus but mostly at the pit the crowd is hungry drunk and teasing each other about the nearby undergrowth the dense black weeds the sudden movement like a tracer in the grass or the porcupine everybody saw when they drove in as well as the wind's hot breath the belch of frogs the eerie stillness just this far from the house and why nobody wants to follow the deer at the top of the rise. Meanwhile the pig is finishing, if not quite golden at least not pink and though not succulent not puckered either. What's better than a keg of Pabst barrowing from the house sounding in the dark like a Conestoga traversing a ravine?

At the same time the couples trios and quartets who've been scattered like birdshot throughout the acreage start drifting in down and up toward the food if not to overrun the tables then to grab a plate to refresh their drinks to ask after Theo before lighting out again for the private party *mise-en-abymed* in the big public one. Watch 'em snakes! some asshole calls out. Of course they're there but ugly not harmful, not half as harmful as assholes, just coiled in the grass of the night you wouldn't know them from a string of fossilized dogshits. What next but that the pig here and there starts popping so that the ashes fly the moths crisscross to their deaths one or two drunks cascade the hill downward threatening each other with repartees of a grosser and grosser rudeness which makes the dogs howl and race up and back toward more ashes more popping skin splitting the pig along the breastbone while all those faces go moist alert and purple in the fire everyone eyeing the cooked pig and wondering who's in charge here. In the gray of the quarter moon boulders go white and start to move, they look like rhinos for Chrissake, the trees come walking out of the woods like it's a fairy tale. The swine's hide is coming away like a jacket. Its tripe oozing. Whaddyamean tripe??! Goddamnit stop scaring us somebody yells. The night starts whistling on its own, insects fiercen, the fire crackles, the beers warm, the love hesitates, the porcus not only browns it blacks, Jack's picking his Martin and his hooter at the same time. The barbecue pit's jammed and smells. The pig hits the coals with a thud then flakes into hundreds of fingers of delicious dinner. Everybody cheers the fallen swine, the party's in full swing.

A party featured in or even sprung from the ms. ——— was holding, one that from inside the confine of the portentous study would have to be termed *going on outside* not only the huge rambling house in the yards front and back and the garden at the bottom of the yard as well as the veranda enclosing the house but all three storys excluding the attic though not the cellar to say nothing of the blacktop of the winding country road or the hillside west the wood south or a brook more south, and most importantly *going on outside* the study isolated as it is by closed doors closed windows the grave mood Mozart notwithstanding or intended perhaps even to conceal heated conversation or to muffle noises like pop pop pop pop, added to which ———'s recent experience, itself exhausting, of reading the ms. Theo had either left unfinished or finished inconclusively, Open Ended was the way ——— put it to Theo, Theo not impressed but squeaking the hide of his armchair in the dark where he sat aiming the equalizer still at ———'s midriff. Open Ended ——— repeated thinking through the sobriquets of small weaponry then pointing from the ms. in his quivering right hand to the invisible barrel of the widowmaker in Theo's and finally to his own recessed navel which was naked like much of him except what was covered by seersucker swim trunks, trunks he'd been wearing for the heat of the summer night which the scotch he'd been swilling in the study for more than three hours had only made hotter more claustrophobic and unbearable, Open Ended Theo —— was saying nervously indicating the ms. the muzzle his bellybutton unable to think of anything else anything better anything more appropriate, really obsessed suddenly by the words Open and Ended and so trying various contexts out on them the way someone sitting in the dentist's chair is fascinated with a crack in the ceiling or a particularly flagrant hair in the dentist's nose, conceiving what might happen in the next few seconds, what might happen to postpone it, what might happen to prevent it. Your best book to date ——— came up with hoping to prevent it, wagging the ms. lifting the scotch glass with studied casualness to his lips Just the sort of book I wish I could write but of course couldn't in a million years ——— added encouraging Theo to converse to get Theo's mind off what might happen in the next few seconds to distract him should a sudden great jump at him or out the window or to the door be necessary what with the dark the Mozart (what is that the *Requiem* oh shit) the isolation that piece that iron the scotch the party *going on outside* Come on Theo say something ——— demanded not sure where he was getting the courage from, maybe the anger at being that afraid This has gone on long enough I'm about to leave you alone in here if you keep this up Leave you to it if you know what I mean Assuming you want to punish everybody who cares about you Who loves you A good book though I really mean that Even if you squeeze one off at me it's good With some work of course But a terrif first draft No maybe a second Okay let's say a third Just a few polishing strokes actually Obviously a heap of work's gone on here So that's what you've been at squirreled away while I've been . . . You'll see though It'll come together Sooner or later what difference does it make So what it's a bit discontinuous So's life Theo I really mean this whatever happens Really If chutzpah was genius you'd be greater than Cervantes Come to think of it to Cervantes chutzpah probably was In that case Theo In that case as good as As good as who Theo Who? Me?

"Grivois. *You know, racy. It's how they speak in Paris.*"

The Death of Don Quijote

AFTER which Sancho Panza walked in heavy grief out of the Don's gate into the streets of the nameless village where the heat and dust, though unusually fierce, did not exist for him anymore than for his dead master. He walked with the misery of many things in his pockets, and on his shoulders all the troubles of the future, so that his sagging body traveled only a few steps before it needed rest. Village life was returning to normal, since it was to be a hundred years or more before museums, chapels, and voyages to La Mancha made the townspeople reconsider their opinion of the austere daring Don who'd lived such a foolish existence.

A man of immense faith (now), patience, and wit (earlier), of renown and holy virtue, Sancho Panza entered his mud home to find his wife squaring debts and squandering the inheritance that was passing from Don Quijote to her family. Viewing his wife's radiant eyes, and his daughter's sudden vanity in light of her new position, Sancho Panza recognized the gravity of his own transformation and fortune. He sighed and sat on a rock outside the door, suffering to express his heart's confusion to his wife and daughter. Before all these things, Sancho Panza had seen to the care of Rocinante, the Don's brave steed, and spent an hour or two among the other middle-aging men at the village well, in the vineyard, at the tavern in the plaza; in each place trying to paint the more recent occurrences of his life into the complete and final picture of the adventures of his late master. But for all his proverbial wisdom

Sancho Panza had always proven especially inept as a storyteller and so efforts to lift his spirits were on these occasions dismal failures, if only because his tales had to be too full of digression, explanation, definition, and windy exploration of insignificant details. Failing to rekindle the past, Sancho Panza had ambled home. "My dears—" Sancho began, when the two women of his life had paused in their pleasant scheming to hear of his grief and were kneeling at his knees in the dust, "—my dears, now that my master is no more I feel a terrible curse has fallen onto our heads." Here he observed his wife make the sign of the crucifix against her tiny bosom, and say, "It is only the grief, my husband and one-time governor, that seems to you a curse. The heart aches, they say—that is not an example of poetry when you have it happen to you."

Yes and no, pondered Sancho Panza—of course the bereavement was mighty, like a fall into the night from a heavenly tower, yet a fall which was inevitable because the tip of the tower had always been the size of a pinhead and no one could balance there forever; but no, *not* grief on the other hand. "After all the wisdom I attained travailing behind the fabulous Don Quijote, I am suddenly a relic and buffoon to my own people. They rightfully look straight through me!" His wife and daughter began to weep that Sancho should be feeling the loss of his master so keenly. "You need sleep, my husband who was once a squire," his wife said. "*Lie unconscious?*" Sancho cried. "I should sacrifice my exciting life simply to forget a horrid pain? Do you not see it, my humble wife? And you neither, my sweet though not especially ravishing daughter? The fact is, my dears, that my lord set forth toward everything and concluded nothing. Yet he himself concluded, which is enough for any man. But Sancho did not, only *the Story of Sancho,* as if by the Don's death he died too." Now the women shouted that Sancho Panza, their husband and father respectively, was not to wish himself dead, and forbade him this unhealthy mask of gloom. They recalled to him that Don Quijote's notoriety was a madman's, and that most everybody who'd met him on their journeys recognized the pathetic state of his senses, either humoring, assailing or taking advantage of the world's final authentic knight-errant. These last words, sharply barbed, pinked Sancho's heart, increasing the earlier ache he'd felt there, so that he had to move away from the screeching voices which echoed, a part of him knew, the very same truth his master had disclosed at the end of his life.

As he wandered the village in the hottest part of the day, brushing flies from his sleeve, growling at the flea-ridden dogs and smacking the rumps of erstwhile donkeys—doing, that is, what a disgruntled Manchegan villager would be expected to do—Sancho struggled to rekindle the wit and flourish he had developed over the miles and months with Don Quijote. While it was impossible for him to be clever in the absence of his master, Sancho wanted to say something like this: though squires of chivalry remained poor and silent, Sancho Panza made himself famous as a wise funny peasant and came home rich. The Don, on the other hand, resembled nothing so much as a very tall skeletal darkness, a brooding blackism against the white light of the Spanish plain. While his shape, size and travel had made the Don readable, it was impossible to say which made the difference, his gaunt determined figure or the whiteness against which it was set in motion. Thanks to his discursive nag he could wander the whiteness, remaining distinct like an especially rumpled spider limping across a table; yet this also condemned him to stay *within* the margins of his known frontier—the Quijote was never more than a few days from home! But (and here the former squire's unhappy thoughts had been tending from the beginning, when he'd confessed to being as dead as the Don) Sancho was on the one hand, like his master, within the margins, and yet by virtue of the death of Don Quijote, left behind as well—and he not only a sane squire to a mad knight but a *gracioso,* a zany whose greatest performances were staged for no one and therefore for all!

Thus did Sancho Panza want to brood on the horrible fate of outliving Don Quijote. And brooding as faithfully as to get him sobbing now and again or kicking stones at a cat or swearing at the young boys who taunted him, Sancho momentarly feared that if he tried to speak to anyone or tried to touch them they would ignore him as if he were not there, and feared too that standing among the vagrants and bravos he would hear them talk of his own untimely death. No manner of shouting or pulling at their whiskers would get them to take notice of him or of the fact that he himself, though the dead knight's squire, was very much alive! "What next?" Sancho managed to reduce all these significant ideas to, having lost his wit and wisdom. What next for the likes of him? Retirement was out of the question for there was nothing to retire from—a peasant remained a peasant forever, and a squire became a peasant overnight, as he'd discovered. He could move his family into the castle of the Duke and Duchess (Cf. *Part II,* Chaps. XXX-LVII) where only weeks before so many strange events had taken place that surely they could find a way to turn Sancho the peasant into something greater again. If the worst came, of course, and he felt the boredom of this death-like trance becoming intolerable, he could always learn to read—though how dreadful things might have to be to come to that he dared not imagine. As he meandered the village, booting the occasional scorpion or snake out of the roadway, Sancho was led again and again to the outskirts of town where finally near suppertime he discovered himself before a familiar plain. Here Don Quijote and his squire had encountered giants, had tangled with monks, massacred sheep, liberated corpses, and rescued ladies. It was too terrible to remember, so Sancho turned from the plain of past glories and headed into a wood in the midst of which he could hear the running of a stream (in the old days one needed to stroll only a little way before the neighborhood grew as foreign as jungle). In despair, longinquous from his village as if it were the moon, and dressed as unlike an isle governor as possible, the well-known oft-discussed Sancho Panza, once called Sancho Vanca, exited the *GOLDEN AGE* of squire-and-knighthood to enter, by nudging aside the thorny stems in a thicket, an epoch of *SENSUOUS AMORAL PASSION*—from acorn to twisted oak!

His infallible nose sensed the forest: "I smell something feminine." And upon those very words, the abracadabra of stone rolling, Sancho Panza, who had come to believe in miracles against all evidence, heard a young man's voice rise out of the rocks that scarfed a stream. "Would to God, my sweet Tisbea, my fishgirl, that I had drowned in the sea, so that I would have ended sane instead of driven to madness by you. The sea could engulf me in its silvery waves that crash beyond their bounds but it could not set me aflame." Pretty speech! It gathered the miserable Sancho toward it, pulling him like a grizzled fish toward the speaking river; for a moment he feared his mind was luring him to death or that the enchanters had appeared again but that this time, as with Don Quijote, they would exact the price of his life. The voice did not express the ardor of the Don, who had desired only, who had forever held in his overheated brain the image of his beloved (no cameo was ever so permanently impressed!), though it drove him to melancholy. And yet this sounded like Quijote himself speaking, except for the overstatement, of course, and the vulgarity of confessing so baldly without bending to one knee. For now Sancho Panza could view the pair—no conjurers' trick they!—as the young man touched the throat of a girl who was the age of the squire's own daughter. In this bravo's eyes was the fire of animal heat, the new impulsiveness Sancho had been hearing of since his return to the village. "What is there to fear?" the fellow was saying, to the young girl's dismay, "unless you would have me despise you?" At that she began to crawl from him toward the bush behind which Sancho stood, but her suitor gripped her fetlock and quickly let a hand disappear into the darkness of her simple dress; this halted her escape, caused her to catch her sparrow's breath, turn on one hip to permit greater access, and slowly close her eyes in the direction of the former squire who observed the scene from the safety of his thicket. Her camisole undone, the bodice slipped down, the fisher girl lay back while the seducer regaled his success, causing meanwhile his victim to moan, groan and frog out her eyes with disbelief. Sancho Panza stood in the protection of his wooded redoubt watching the child his daughter's age being ravished, and thinking, Ah! Master Quijote, how swiftly you'd have impaled this twice-backed animal!

He cleared his throat gigantically, making olympian noises with his boots so as to make certain that were he caught leaving the river bank he could not be mistaken for a spy. He never expected to be greeted warmly, as the young traveler did when he called to him, "Come over, fellow there. Let's have a look at your shaggy figure." The intrusion seemed unbearable for the deflowered child, who fought back tears and tried to hide her face until—unable to bear the shame (or the cool air on her blush)—fled into the woods like a rabbit, her waist entirely bare, though in no way furry, the hare comparison ending with the speed of her retreat. Her lover laughed at the embarrassment and held into the light for Sancho to see a stocking that appeared carefully knitted. "A boy with a tongue," he said, "dreams of growing up to many languages but the tongue itself dreams of mouths."

"Ha, ha, ha, ha!" Sancho replied angrily, "A man without a tongue is not alway tasteless!" While this was puzzling in the extreme, the young man jumped to his feet roaring with laughter, slapped Sancho stoutly on the back, grinned his white teeth like windows, and claimed he had been very fairly bested. He offered up his sack of wine. Handsome, sturdy, careless, brassy, a kerchief tied across his head, a breed of danger Sancho had not the power to recall even from his travels, the young man with the ruby earring was the strangest act of magic Sancho had ever seen. Was he a bandit? There was no fear to him, only a largeness that might mean he was boastful. Was he a nobleman's black sheep? But his clothes were no finer than Sancho's, and the wine possessed the bitter nutty quality of little more than one week's aging.

"What is your name, brother?" the fellow asked, and Sancho Panza could not help speaking it, if only to inquire of this younger generation whether it knew its famous dead. The seducer had to think for a moment, muttering to himself that the name was familiar.

"Perhaps it will help if I tell you that I am of that village yonder and that my master is only recently deceased into legend." The young notable gazed leftward, seeing nothing but forest, and acknowledged that a village lay beyond only to humor his guest, while Sancho began to itch with nervousness, worried that he was indeed invisible.

"Of course," said the traveler, "I know the place," which considerably eased Sancho's burden.

"Even if you did not" Sancho said with irritation and swelling pride, "you will have heard of my lord Don Quijote!"

The young man was now sure of Sancho's peculiarity. "Are you talking about the book with the looney in it?"

In this manner Sancho had his worst fears confirmed, and for such a reason as hadn't occurred to him; it was one thing to *feel* dead because one's "other half" actually *was*, but very much another to be told one had never existed in the first place—had never had, in effect, the opportunity of dying. Here then was the testament Don Quijote left to his squire Sancho Panza (as though the money were for the wife and daughter only, and *this* legacy reserved to the one who could use it least): that because of their success together as a book they were nothing to the world but characters in a fiction—and Panza illiterate no less, so that he could not even read the story of his life but must instead live after it. Yet how could he live if he was said not to exist? So when the youth with the maid made his cruel and careless remark Sancho sat himself on a large squat stone overlooking the swift river's talking and contemplated that end which he assumed would either affirm his non-existence by not actually happening even though he would throw his plump odorous body into the river's throat, or prove that Sancho Panza *did* live by the fact that he had died. While either consequence would prove satisfactory, both would leave Sancho in the similar state of not being there, though on the one hand still believing he was, and on the other not able to know that he wasn't!

It was at this time, when Sancho Panza's intellect was exhausting him even more than his grief, that the traveler offered him a piece of cheese and a hunk of bread to sop up the wine; with these before him the squire recognized his favorite pastime in all the world. Together they ate, the man of the wood eyeing Sancho as if he were a spirit and Sancho staring into space like a lovesick horse across a fence. His stomach soon full, Sancho Panza began to suspect that he was after all as alive as anyone, though it wouldn't have surprised him to be told he felt full at this moment only because a book said he did. Gradually, his good senses recovering, Sancho Panza pieced together a plan for the future. But he needed also to justify this plan by announcing its origins and so, trusting his companion's patience if not his experience in such matters, spoke the following: "My master could not die during an adventure, for that would have proved the false books to be true, and that knights-errant exist in the world doing heroic deeds. No, by dying in bed and renouncing the madness of his belief in knights-errant my lord Don Quijote made the noblest sacrifice any knight-errant could. To prove the truth of his commitment he offered up his armor, his helmet and sword, even retiring the sweetly disposed Rocinante who does nothing now but munch oats and dream battle. My lord himself disenchanted Dulcinea del Toboso! And he did so by becoming sane, relieving her therefore of the spell he himself had placed! Was any knight ever so *bueno*?!"

Well, thought the youth by the river when Sancho had finished, here is a live one who may well suit my needs—he is unreasonable, insensible, perhaps looney, too, believing that what doesn't exist does, and vice-versa; in short, he's topsy-turvy and therefore may view me as right when I am wrong. "An excellent speech, my friend Sancho Panza. Of course I recognized you at once but was too amazed to let myself believe it was really you." (The traveler hoped he'd got the name right.)

However, Sancho's mind was at work too. It had come to the deserted squire like a stroke of genius, and yet it also felt as though a grain of sand had been imbedded somewhere sometime earlier and had by now dug out a gaping hole, an arch in Sancho Panza. "Then you admit you know me?" he cried.

"Like myself," was the answer.

"And so you know of my adventures with Don Quijote?"

"Do I remember my own parents?"

There was something insufferable about the interlocutor's method of agreeing. "Then you can recall the many occasions in *Part II* of our book when my lord and I came upon certain people, such as Don Alvaro Tarfe, who spoke of *another* Don Quijote and Sancho Panza?" Having never before met the one pair the traveler saw no reason to deny the second, nor did he. "And do you recall if at any time in our book of adventures, which at times went on and on worse even than the life we were leading, the mystery of that pair was explained?" Here, for fear of being revealed, the interlocutor stayed mute, instead shrugging, at which Sancho Panza raised himself from the stone on the river, thanked his host, and set off in still another direction.

"Where do you go now?" cried the youth, not eager to lose his gullible companion.

"To unmask Sancho Panza!" Sancho Panza replied.

"The other one?" the traveler asked, bewildered.

"The same."

Though this was all the traveler heard, and so could only judge Sancho as hopelessly insane, here is what the former squire concluded as he began his way out of the forest, before the youth could catch him up to introduce himself: What is left me now is my errant task of finding those other errants so many people have seen—I mean the Quijote and the Sancho who were sighted in Saragossa while we were at Barcelona, and who combatted the Knight of the Wood even as we slept in the comfort of the Duke's castle. My master and I have seen the world *TRANSFORMED* many times but no one has explained to me who the *others* were, or how to account for them, or what manner of madmen might have read of our exploits and by reading, like my master, believed they were what they read. It is not enough any longer that I have a document signed by a mayor to prove I am the true Sancho, because my master had drawn a document to say he was Alonso Quijano and *not* Don Quijote (though I recall too that before we ever sallied forth he was called

Quexana, and not Quijano! A trick? A jest? An enchantment at the last minute?). So it would seem that with the death of my master, *whoever he was,* our adventures are both true and false; and is that any different from the adventures of those others that I know to be false, and those others perhaps to be true? I must find then that other Sancho Panza to see if, when I lift my right hand, he will raise his. Or perhaps it would be his left if he is a Squire of Mirrors as there was once, according to the story of my experiences, a Knight of Mirrors. Or is it possible that when he raises an arm I will feel mine lifting? It seems as though my fame were so great I must sally again to undo my success before I can feel I've accomplished my life—which, if that be sense, makes of me my own enchanter, turning *me* into *not-me*!

But by now the traveler has blocked Sancho's retreat, cutting off his ponderous thoughts as well as his path. He smiles, flicks forth a wet tongue blue with wine, embraces the slightly confused, preoccupied former squire, offers him a stave of cedar limb to match his own, and says, "Squire, I can help you. My name is *(me llama)* Don Juan and I am new to these regions but I am full of energy, eager and willing to risk all at a moment's notice. Surely I am no *hidalgo* but the era of courteous gentlemen is more or less behind us, and while I do not see giants in the world I see plenty of danger, which I face constantly and with a smile. Let us go together, then, and rather let me introduce you to the new world. Though we will be seeking these others you speak of, whose existence I do not doubt for a minute, let us also travel for pleasure."

Here Sancho pauses, unable to understand, squinting his eyes, fingering his ears, scratching his nose. "What do you mean, travel for *pleasure*?"

Don Juan laughs again loudly, a trait which already has begun to annoy the formerly hilarious squire and make him wonder if his own reputation for laughter is based solely on a comparison with his late melancholy and oft-exhausted master. "It is all the rage, Sancho—it is called *el turismo*!"

"And you just go looking at things?"

"Exactly—there is a master, and a valet who tends the master's needs. Since I have never been a master before but intend to be, it stands to reason that I need an experienced valet to teach me what it is to be the master. And what greater experience of service than that of squire? What greater experience of squire than Sancho Panza! Let us leave the forest here, return for your chamois and farthingale, then hitch your horse . . ."

"Mine is an ass, or have you forgot?"

". . . your ass to a cart, at least, that will carry us on our first tour of what is left of the world. Who knows but that we may encounter your others in a day or two, or may learn that one or both of them has gone the way of your master . . ."

"And of his squire."

". . . his squire, yes, that too, so that in either case we may be able to hold the mirror to their mouths for signs of breath." Though he does not bother to say it Sancho Panza thinks that there will never be more than one

DEATH OF DON QUIJOTE!

Still they depart the wood together, having forgot the deflowered Tisbea, and turn in the direction of the village. Whether Sancho will choose to accompany Don Juan after the death of his master is a question he cannot yet answer. Though on the subject of women, touring, and endless laughter Sancho feels compelled to disagree with Don Juan's points of view. As the sun is setting in La Mancha, misting the nameless village in a haze of yellow, red, and memory, Don Juan and Sancho Panza walk quietly to town, speaking softly, the young Don recalling a story with a snap of his fingers that he is certain the former squire must delight in, despite the few parts that are a bit *grivois* . . .

"A bit WHAT?!" shouts Sancho, exhausted now by the sheer perplexity of his problems, his decisions, his future.

"*Grivois.* You know, racy. It's how they speak in Paris!"

Dirty stories! moans Sancho to himself before crying aloud to his companion, then to the purple sky—

IT'S a party Bengal lights around the roof Venetian lanterns strung on clothesline Someone's got to ride the horse Somebody else wants to film the night Not the party just the night Cut off his drugs he can't afford the film his wife says We'll be broke for months The film's in Theo's fridge Been there for a week Waiting to be a cool movie of the night   Casanova is saddled Quijote the retriever nipping his hooves Neck to toe in bibs the color of liver Marie from Munich (Theo's second or third wife) strokes the sorrel's knotty flesh tracing the wide blue rivers along his heaving chest His ears flick blowflies His tail wasps His mane nets burrs Marie can't help gandering at the extended pizzle when he lowers it to piss

Out of the dark somewhere up the hill a voice calls out through cupped hands Centurions to the Right! Weeping women Left! Peonies daisies black-eyed susans are trampled without warning Someone's lost a contact in the grass Six people no seven crawl on their fours using matches to come up with roaches a condom an address crumpled and tossed away but no contact Great the owner of the missing lens gripes Just great Jew no wot jew con do jes? drums in Jawal the mdanga player who knows Theo through Paul at the Juilliard Jew can kees dem gooby Since it's a party something like eighteen people are on their knees combing the grass Stoned drunk half-naked giggling they part each clump like its hair and put an eye down into the center   Wuz is? Berkeley Bill wants to know since he's arrived late Wut sorta game you freaks? From the kitchen the yard with eighteen people nineteen counting Bill on their knees and the barbecue pit with another twenty tearing pig and the hillside where Jean-Paul's shouldered his Eclair switched on the sungun and is shooting the moon From the kitchen these places appear positively reasonable because here's where the acrimony's brewing the smoke's choking the fridge buzzes and everybody seems to be making pancakes While outside they're toying with sex inside they've not got there yet Right now it's politics so there's war civil rights therapy to get through in order to get to old movies trivia Disney Leopold Stokowski before he and Theo fell out and the assassinations where the room gets mad then teary then quiet tired depressed After depressed horny Horny at a summer party in the night in the country when you're drunk but not too and a strange person is actually finding you attractive It's no dream He She wants to touch your private parts in the bushes upstairs on the floor on the table bending over the toilet absolutely anywhere Let's go

When all who're left in the kitchen are the dialecticians and the Buddhists Somehow the feminist spillover heads for the road to sit in a circle under the moon Smoke some drugs Pass a bottle Check out each other's welfare A circle several bearded men in droopy jeans are uninvited to Not nastily just firmly And so they either stand around trying to hear their wives lovers and friends mention their names or they form their own square to discuss their sons their divorces their points of view their new lives They nod in the direction of the circle when they say that Trying to pulverize the past and realizing that what one looks for in this life is a good neurotic to share it with Just not a bad neurotic That's what they've learned That's a lot Let's drink to that   With help from Jack the guitarist who does everything strapped into the Martin and from an Asian named Phoenix Marie from Munich wraps the reins around her fist adjusts her bibbed breasts buttocks and boots then brushes Casanova's red flank with her cheek and alley-oops her way not only high enough to the saddle but with four hands to push nearly over the top and onto the other side Anyhow she's up and the crowd here and there applauds She threatens to do a trick such as staying in the saddle for an entire minute if the horse doesn't move The whole bunch at the barbecue pit and scattered along the hillside start calling Whoa when Casanova stamps a hoof Looks like he's counting to ten or something He casts one of those cyclopean long-necked muscular moody looks of contempt over his shoulder when he sees who's up When he sneezes Marie massages his rump He sneezes again Phoenix finds feathers from a crashed crow and plants them in the horse's halter remarking on the scab on the thing's nose The thing starts stamping again Real slow Worse Jack puts an oil funnel from his Chevy onto Casanova's forehead but the horse agitates it off Keeps stamping Keeps counting Fud zee hell! Marie cries angrily You tink is a unicorn? You gonna ride him Jack says Or get your picture taken?   One of those forever incapable of holding an opinion without giving equal justice to the other side no matter how otiose irrational and downright destructive Actually mealymouthed Such a person in whom (JJ was thinking of Theo from her tree limb thirty feet above the party) wonderful and dreadful ideas exist side by side like that ms. An affirmed neutralism about everything Even us Toward life generally With no integrity left except for that so-called relativity which he understands as an absolute and uses like a gun The kind that leads him to ask all his old girlfriends over Is it a reunion Is he dying or something No he's just feeling sentimental Sentimental my ass Moody secretive injurious self-absorbed Time is short he says Life fleets like a snowshoe rabbit he says Everything he says is an advertisement of his restlessness That's it Even so what are they doing in there so long?

While the party's still Schlitz flapjacks hunting contacts and sniffing orifices hither and thither and clamant politics and good books and sizing up Theo's collections of rugs lithos metals gems records and friends Jean-Paul's filming a bush Tina's carrying the battery-pack like she knows what it's about J-P's wife Lil's crying about the cost of the footage if he really intends to shoot the night but actually it's striking her as she watches her husband and Tina work so well together Eclair and sungun that they're balling behind her back That's why she's crying in fact Who cares about a few hundred bucks of 1748 in the face of this news! Her father warned her Frogs he said That was all he said too Where'd Tina learn to do that We've broken bread and ice together Lil says to herself of Tina   Henriette swallows a drug   Paul and Eddie stop talking dirty in the grove   Jack picks out "Moonshadow" on the Martin   A porcupine wanders into the kitchen from the road smelling the garbage with ecstasy   Berkeley Bill keeps thinking he's found the missing contact but it's always only dew   Husbands whose wives are drinking in the road start sliding under one another's cars to look for rust   The pond shimmers from the legs of the fruit flies   Wives in the road envy the singles beside them but recall the loneliness the need for some sort of attachment   Casanova Theo's sorrel has just about had it with the poking prodding and prettifying   Bertrand Russell's logical atomism is being atomized in the kitchen by three anti-positivist post-Wittgensteinian linguists

Nicole's husband keeps watching his watch and thinking fondly of the little inn they're rooming at though it isn't Provence by any means   One of the Munich sculptors is making an aluminum something or other in the stable with several damaged bicycles he's taken apart and begun to solder according to a glyph he's lately seen The pig is looking less and less like one The grass itches The owls blink No worm turns In her tree JJ mutters gravitating lust okay desire okay passion okay okay deep deep need which cannot be helped can it Another auto crunches Theo's stones on the way in nearly creaming two pairs of male legs poking from under a Corvette

Upstairs the house the john's exhausted and a squad of couples is scouting TV's in case like everybody else Theo keeps his hidden out of shame The pancake batter's gone sorry Quijote the dog continually gets shouted at out of the darkness to get the fuck away he's got eczema which is true and it's because of his nerves so the rejection only makes it worse

Jamal confesses he's sick and tired of the mdanga and wants to play the sax in the Village at least once before he's pyred Theo's bull snores so loudly that anyone nearby thinks he's a swarm of bees which Theo for some reason has fenced in Someone out there can't believe the size of it whatever it is Form yourself another drink Theo suggests to ——— in the amber of the secluded study At the top of the rise the deer dream of hunters All these things so that when Marie bolts by the barbecue pit atop and spread-eagling Casanova she does so screaming and warning everyone out of the way The throng at the pig scatters The horse gallops by The gang on its knees freezes at the obscure sight of rampaging hooves heading for their brains Casanova flies across and through What's left of the kitchen squeals laughs and yells Whoa you wicked bastard Casanova snorts past From upstairs the house people call out ideas to Marie Marie hangs on Marie screams Shtop I fill pee killed Casanova lathers on The road's cleared of feminists before the beast arrives There's a corn-field on the other side JJ screams out Shit Jean-Paul comes running from the bush to shoot but too fast for Tina who stands holding the cord and the battery-pack thirty feet behind him That means the lights are out Casanova's rump clears the ditch Marie's calling out something in Bavarian Jack's picking the song of it all like a troubadour

Merde and double-*merde* the film-maker moans Lil smiles Wuzzat Bill asks nobody in particular Hey I found the lens nobody in particular replies Woof woof woof barks Quijote into the dark of the cornfield from the edge of the ditch Some party Nicole's husband mumbles to his empty wine glass Look at this chick here she's out cold So where do you go from here? ——— asks Theo more times than he can count or remember CUT! J-P shrieks. CUT!

The Death of Venice

Love, waxed Amerigo, is the hope of a schoolboy who writes tragedies. Leaping from bed using a hand to hold closed the rear of his nightgown, he had been swept away—hours railing against love, pacing the stone floor with a squirming cat in his hand, chasing out servants who attempted to keep the fire roaring while narrowly skirting the upraised toe of Amerigo's boot (he had tossed too many slim volumes of love lyric into the capacious fireplace for the blaze to die down). "Listen to this:" he cried, drawing from his dressing gown another unposted letter. "Erotic genius is a music of human spheres—never, like number, vertical but always horizontal, always curvaceous." The agony of unrequited desire rippled his face until his countenance resembled the crushed words he tore between his fists and for a change of routine tossed out the window rather than into the fire. Swallows gliding by grasped the scraps in their beaks, catching the sounds *ero, mus* and *sph* in their throats.

"I mean," he tried to speak reasonably, "I cannot send this sort of drivel into the world?"—here he gestured broadly, both arms casting out like east and west on a compass—"it will convince her that I am a lunatic." He studied among the bedclothes the embroidered silk pillows and fragrant quilts, hoping to raise the attention of a motionless silent lump hidden there. "And yet," he quoted from another letter that magically appeared in the center of his palm, "I am committed to that fate of all fleshly passion which demands that love be triangular, as geometric as the fertile and furry plain which in my feverish moments rushes to the back of my eyes like a forbidden tapestry moved by a breeze; triangular if only because true love demands an obstacle or great stone to be rolled aside if it is to be for both lovers a love worth knowing. And so, just as I am thrilled to discover the jealousy I feel upon seeing your father take your arm in the street—reminding me thus of my need for your proximity—so too should you rejoice the fortunate—yes, I say, fortunate—occurrence of yesterday in the boiserie when you discovered the depth of your own affection simply by observing the harmless manner in which I accidentally brushed that young woman's thigh with my forefinger. She was of course my sister and it was a caterpillar I was removing from the arena of her garter. . . ."

The bed had not stirred and therefore Amerigo lifted the sleeping cat from the warm fireplace mantle and threw it screeching at the pillows. Europa peeked an eye over the edge of the quilt, glimpsing the cat (rapier-metal blue) thrashing on its back for gravity, and said in a squeaky voice fresh from slumber, "Even a happy love affair will not see you leave me."

Assaulting erubescence with erubescence, Amerigo mournfully replied, "I blush because I cannot blush anymore."

"Make *me* blush" Europa murmured with the unimpeachable voice of her sexual authority, tossing away the kilos of quilt to reveal an uplifted fulcrum of knees and in doing so entangling the scratching cat in the bedding where, suffocated, it would be found hours later by the faithful and virtuous chambermaid Felicité. (In the meantime the cat would struggle in the dark against thick knots of silk that enclosed its bony neck or bugged its eyes and with each frantic movement for freedom were engorging its pink throat so that it could only hear the cries in the four-poster, only feel the muscular seasick weight of the violent bodies that were tossing, snarling, biting—the dying cat believing these were the sounds of its calling mate.)

"I thought," laughed Europa meanwhile, "that I had taught you to graze and not to gobble."

Amerigo adopted the screech of a guinea fowl and buried his head in the flesh of his sister's leg, dreaming however of Therese who was modest, austere and educated by nuns. "Be expressive," Amerigo concluded with his nose sniffing his sister's ear, his teeth pecking the twin nose, "but be also discreet."

On Europa's insistent whim after this conflagration of perilous rapture, brother and sister enjoyed a full-dress oyster breakfast. Their parents were quiet and dull, father bewigged, mother behind a morning mask of sturdy cloth around which it was difficult as well as noisy for her to eat her gray porridge. "Then I shall bathe," remarked Europa to the air of silence, "for I have upon me a sweet familiar, very *familiar,* stench." Amerigo ceased to chew as he always did when his sister alluded to their relations but their father, fortunately, was occupied reading a letter he concealed within another that had to do with business: Ninety barrels of salt by trans Ven/Dov the fifteen Avril in this year of Pourquoi ne pas déguster ton amour? What would be more naturelle than de lécher ton amie et de goûter à l'essence délicieusement salée de sa féminité? Splendide! Transfer overland (faire l'amour dehors) is how best the bulk can be delivered (n'est-ce pas ainsi que l'amour devrait être libre et sans honte?) without being tumbled (dans les spasmes) or for that matter somehow spoiled (baiser) or worse, and so forth. That is, between the folds of the mercantile directive there was secreted a string of obscenities quilled by a woman whose profession it was to write pornographs. Mother glanced through her gauzy mask at her husband's clenched jaw, her son's purpling neck, her daughter's fixation with some middle distance as she sucked a berry, and recalled that she might have married the young soldier whom everyone expected to die of fever on Corfu but who managed instead to distinguish himself against Turks and return decorated to marry a cousin of the Doge no less, so that now after these years of unredeemed habit Mother frequently retreated into the reeds of romantic lagoons where that soldier, ceasing to row, once remarked on the delicacy of her earlobes and exposed a golden tooth in his smile. Of the four at breakfast none, in short, could avoid thoughts of a private nature, the sorts which if revealed would constitute a quartet of scandals. They remained seated until their obsessions—Amerigo's Therese, Europa's Amerigo, Father's pseudonymous libertina, Mother's chivalrous antiquity—left them frozen before their plates, hearts quaking, imaginations quibbling, consciences retreating like pinpoints of light to the blind. Meanwhile, outside the windows of the small palazzo, the activity of Venice had begun.

It was not the gondolas skimming the oild suface of the Grand Canal that mattered, nor the languorous riggings strewn along docks and decks waiting to be drawn to the attention of the wind, nor an unexpected chamber group commencing to play a concerto, but in fact a couple that had stepped from one of the gondolas only to stroll past the standing ships from the north, and to light parasol, hats and gloves at a cafe in the Piazza San Marco. The young man smiled his endearment as if some word recently spoken by his companion had charmed him to distraction—tears filled the wells of his gray eyes. Suddenly the pair laughed. She continued her story, this porcelain-skinned eighteen year old, on condition that her escort buy her an ice. They sat, removing their accoutrements for the *cammina,* and leaned close to each other in order to savor the tale's intimate evidence. At this point, the teller related, the boy still believes . . .

"You mean no one has told him that you are. . . ?"

"No one."

"No?"

"He knows no one who knows."

"Oh, this is rich."

"You agree then that it would have to make a difference to him?"

"It's a good one. I agree with everything." For a time the couple laughed, he fully, she more guarded, unburdened of an obvious tension that often played between them because he had been at one time in love with her and had had to "see" what the boy of the tale had not. Laughing then, the pair went on loudly and long enough to disturb others in the piazza, including the cathedral musicians, one of whom immediately ceased stroking his violin and pointed his bow in the direction of the rude young couple. One, then another, then another of the remaining musicians discovered he could not carry on without the others so that soon all the musicians, listeners, strollers, and waiters were focussing on the pair of storytellers, themselves oblivious to the offense. In the silence brought about by the abrupt break in the musicians' music, the waiters' patter, and the strollers' murmurs, the laughter of the couple rose into the morning breeze, crossed the nearby rooftops and began to flutter the lace curtains in the breakfast room of the small palace owned by Amerigo's parents.

Like a hunting hound the young man lifted his nose to the air, crinkled it as if he might smell his lady's perfume—in fact her raucous voice entered, throaty, hoarse, and unique, coursing through the lobby to settle like a pet around the statuary in Amerigo's ear. Only he of course recognized the spontaneous sibilant outbursts taking place two streets away and, relishing the noise of Therese's harmless joy, managed to catch in his machinery the low polite chuckle of a man as well. "Ah, God!"

Amerigo wailed, rising from the breakfast chair and placing a hand across his heart as though to squeeze the agony from it, before he collapsed across a wheel of cheese. His parents glanced once, nodded at the sight, then at each other, and returned to their reveries; Europa grasped the jealous occasion by tossing her napkin tearfully upon her brother's skull and departing the room with a cry of disgust.

It so happened at this time that one of the more famous galantuomi of Spain was visiting, having traveled for years in the north of Africa, bringing with him a large book full of adventures recounting daring feats, exotic caves, magical occurrences, and libidinous stories featuring the mind's most beautiful possible women. Nose against the page, this gentleman was strolling the quay at the scarf of the piazza when he was interrupted by a shrill piercing laugh. He raised his eyes; his brow furrowed into a terrifying look of malice. Across the square, where the musicians pointed and the various couples were staring, sat the young female in question, whose head continued to bob, roll, and shake itself long after the joke had left the eyes of her companion, the young man grown embarrassed by what seemed his friend's hysteria. Furious, the galantuomo marched across the piazza, shrugging off vendors, brushing aside a sniffing pup and, arriving at the table, cleared his throat so vigorously it hurt. "Does the signorina know that any of the women in this book here are worth ten the likes of her?" Of course there was a row at the foreigner's unforgivable remarks but, as it has often been noted, reading can be a holy office, and being interrupted at it remarkably like disturbing a prayer.

Even so, the row got out of hand very quickly, despite the efforts of waiters and musicians to explain the customs of Venice and the virtues of printed matter. In the midst of so much clamorous speech the young lady's outraged companion saw no choice but to challenge the

Spaniard, which he did with a suddenness that might have made a less worldly recipient shake in his footwear. Alas, gloves across the cheek notwithstanding, galantuomi are the ablest of men, and this one in particular had already survived innumerable adversaries. "But what if you are killed?" Therese whispered to her friend as they left the piazza to the bookish galantuomo and him to the devouring eyes of the crowd.

At her words of warning the young man paled, soon needing to sit beside a fountain, and while he did he saw, as if for the first time, the beauty that was around him—the swooping sparrows, the bright-eyed squirrels, the plashing water that arced from the fish's mouth in the fountain where they rested. He could not die! Seeing the illness that had overtaken him, Therese said quietly that his fear was nothing to be ashamed of. "Is that all you have to say?" he replied, annoyed by now at his foolishness and therefore in search of someone else to blame. Therese's lowered glance was sufficient. On both their minds, after a moment, was the problem of Therese's secret—it could become unpleasant, really awkward! "But if I were to go away," the companion said, "and had sworn myself to silence, then one other in the know would not be too dreadful, if as a gentleman this Spaniard could be trusted."

"You mean that *he* should be told?" Therese asked with shock.

"Not told, *shown,* for only the sight would be convincing."

"Would that, do you suppose, make such a difference?" asked the sorry girl, in her voice already the tone of resignation that relieved her friend with the wet mustaches. But she was trembling, sick at heart, this whole affair had gone too far!

"But of course," said the friend. "Once he would see your unfortunate condition he could not help but be moved. He must then not only renounce the duel but beg your public forgiveness. It would be only human, seeing that I would otherwise have to risk my life under false pretenses." Therese saw the logic of the argument and agreed to append her signature to a note that would draw the galantuomo to the grove beyond the Accademia; there—Therese shuddered to imagine it—he would be shown what few others had seen, or could hope to in three lifetimes.

As irony would have such matters, and irony usually will, both the galantuomo and Amerigo were lying abed when messengers arrived at their respective apartments. Our gentleman from Iberia continued on with his episodic comedy, laughing until the tears ran, barely remembering the duel reserved for the next morning, while Amerigo, on the other hand, lay cringing and whining as he read and revised the miserable *billets-doux* that he felt for some reason were more urgent than ever before. A servant brought the message on a plate; noting the color, aroma, and delicacy of the envelope Amerigo could not help but imagine it was from Therese. "My dearest," it began, "I too have shared . . . but discretion in these matters is the uttermost. Meet me tonight before ten in the grove. But do not let yourself be seen or it will be . . . discretion, again, I am afraid. Yours, T." While Amerigo is left to leap again out of bed, and to call out for a bath to be prepared ("One with bubbles!"), the Spaniard has been discourteously abandoned, an unpleasant way to treat a foreign visitor. So there he is again, having resisted laughter over his book long enough to respond to the knock at the door. He too had a messenger but with a different though equally tempting word to convey: "Dear Sir," the messenger began. "As there should be no misunderstanding concerning the serious occurrence of this morning, nor the uncommon difficulty regarding the excellent offices of my companion, I think it essential and, under the circumstances, decorous that you and I meet privately this evening to discuss the issue of honor. Shall we say the grove, just after ten. Please do not fail me, or yourself . . . La Signorina della Bocca.

Since the discovery of the dead cat has earlier been revealed we shall overlook the grisly details and relate only that Felicité the maid screamed at the sight so as to draw to her side the entire household but that when they came—servants, neighbors, master and mistress—Amerigo and Europa were missing. It was past nine-thirty in the evening when Felicité, unable to wait any longer, settled for the audience she had gathered, and fainted. (Thus concludes the significance of the cat to this story, or almost.)

The verdant orchard lay behind the Accademia where such artists as Tintoretto, Botticelli, Giotto (and soon Piranesi) have worked and taught. In the grove things grew in a chaotic claustrophobic manner, providing secrecy out of the labyrinth and pleasure in the smells and the fruit that one (or two) might pick. At night the grove was a wild place, ghostly, full of unnamable sounds and unholy acts verified by mornings which cast light on the debris of eaten fruit and on the impressions made in the grass the night before by the diseased bodies of the undead. There were owls at night. There were numerous crawling bugs. Fortunately the snakes walked upright . . .

"Signorina, I fail to see the value of our meeting like this since I know perfectly that your young man has encouraged it, and that you with your ill breeding do not know cowardly behavior even when it has placed your honor in question," he said.

"Are all things human so simple and uncomplicated to a man of your obvious experience and knowledge?" out of the dark, she said. Surrounding them were leafy bowers and enthickening moist vines that crept like reptiles along the ground and about the trees.

"You are too forward in your speech," the galantuomo chided. "Young ladies, if they wish to remain so, are advised to keep their sharpest words to themselves, though best of all they should not think them in the first place." (It should be noted that the galantuomo, despite his glossy surface of liveries and manner, looked from his dour expression and wrinkled face as if for all the world he were gravely ill; this grim aspect many take for worldliness when others know that real experience cuts through the misanthropic, leaving one more appealing to look at and surely more refined, more tolerant in one's dispositions.)

"Sir," said the quavery voice at the conclusion of the scene's interruption, "I'll not trade glibnesses on such a damp and chill evening." For *punto,* Therese sneezed.

"Have you taken ill then like your defender? Has the prospect of that pup's death sickened you so?"

"Sir," Therese answered wearily, "he and I, who are mere good friends, have been reconciled to each of our fates."

"And how," cried the frustrated Spaniard, used to action and not all this talk, surprised in fact at his own vocabulary for it, "is your unseemly fate to be reflected in this necessary if soon-to-be-outmoded form of settling differences? You will merely be known as a woman worth dying for, though in my own younger years such would have hardly been the case. Women were once worthy of it; that is all I'll say of women this night."

Plaintive, struggling to sound vulnerable, even provincial, attempting to touch the galantuomo's happier past, Therese cried out to him, "Why? Why is this? Why should a gentleman of obvious and certain education, experience, much traveled and well-booted, overhear the giggling of a maiden—for that is what I am—and instantly find it so unbearable, as you certainly do?"

"Obvious? Certain? Another good reason for running through your companion."

"Ah! I see!" wailed Therese under cover of the night, of the heavy soughing boughs of a mimosa and of a lemon tree. "I see that you are finally nothing other than a woman-hater!" There was no reply. Therese hid a sneeze in the sudden singing of a nightingale. "As most of your profession are, I suspect," she continued. "You are a decaying species then, you galantuomi. How tedious it must be escorting and seducing the unfortunate dullards whose tables feed you and whose beds . . . well, certain things are better left unsaid."

The galantuomo cleared his throat and, circling his shoulders more closely with his damask cloak, felt his feet grow heavy and wet. As the moon bit through the clouds he began to interrogate the young woman's silhouette, a meter or two distant. The night would see frost; already a fog was lifting off the lagoons, and as it did the Spaniard realized Therese's intention in meeting him. He said, "There is no noble love but that which recognizes itself to be both short-lived and exceptional." In the pause that followed Therese felt pity for the man's tired monologue but knew she must stand her ground; though she had a desire to laugh in his face she remained silent, allowing the silence to speak for her, so that indeed the galantuomo, receiving no warning against his approach, stepped forward until he could hear the breath in Therese's lungs rush at the touch of his hand. She had been standing there in the shadows with her mantle open, exposing her naked body to him all the time.

"It must be dreadful," Therese whispered.

"You must be kidding," the galantuomo answered, plunging his teeth into her neck.

"I mean," Therese continued, "that trying to be everything to everybody you are no thing to any, many things to most and nothing for very long." (Her words were the sort that would have sounded excellent in Latin.)

"If you say so," groaned the experienced gentleman

who, dropping to his knees in the wet soil, negogiated the lambent surface of Therese's belly, loins, etc.

But the grove, like a deceptively conceived story or the naturally deceptive human body, had several entrances and exits, so that nearby there were similar adventures taking place. Among them was that concerning Amerigo, who had confined himself at the last moment to his most refined plumage, a small linen cap in the shape of a capsized sailboat—white, clean, boasting a single tasteful feather. Under this cap Amerigo stood in a leather doublet and breeches of satin, silk hose, and boots that were as felt as slippers and had come from China. His heart had been throbbing ever since he received the message from Therese, and by now he feared two things: first, that she would not appear as promised, and second, that she would. If she failed to arrive he would of course be obliged to kill himself and so had, on the way over, selected the very spot on the sea wall over which he would hove himself, his wrist tied to a stone; if she did not fail him and instead appeared as her missive insisted, then it was quite possible his poor heart would burst from too much joy.

Fortunately it was very dark in this part of the grove and Amerigo was spending his time adjusting his eyes. When his love did suddenly emerge from between two great gnarled trees he could not look clearly into her face and so, like she, was suffering more from eye strain and embarrassment than from overweening need. *That beauty, mine? All mine?* This he would have plenty of opportunity to consider in her presence before the actual beauty might be viewable; in short, though she stood a foot or two away she might have been the man in the moon. Neither could see the other but Amerigo at least saw something. *All mine?* love said to him. But how had it come about? By what spirit had both of them been touched? In all the city, in all the world, for these two to be brought together by natural forces, when he already loved her so! In fact, it was too much; Amerigo fainted, but briefly, waking himself up at the sound of his own thudding body; for a moment he lay in the grass wondering why love caused him to lose consciousness so often. When he was himself again, shivering among the frogs that were painstakingly covering his body with leaves, he looked up at a cloaked figure searching the near distance, peering into the denser wood for someone and blinking at voices carrying on a sober conversation a few arbors away. "Yoo hoo," Amerigo said softly so as to avoid being stepped upon.

"Ah!" the cloak screamed, stepping ahead in fear and thereby planting a heavy boot against the soft flesh of Amerigo's inner thigh.

"Yie!" he cried, pulling himself at last to his feet.

"Yah!" the shadow screamed, now jumping back as it might have done a moment before.

"Therese?"

"Amerigo?" Each moaned at the recognition, then laughed at the manner of their first actual physical contact. "I fell" said the one, "I stepped" the other, and "we shouldn't," they said together.

"It's so dark," Amerigo complained, "that I cannot see to the foot you may have injured when you stepped on me with those great knobby boots."

"That is so," the shadow murmured, "but it is also true that the darkness aids me in seeing to your injured thigh."

"How is that, surely?" Amerigo found the life to ask.

"Ma bocca, mio caro. You may have it. But don't tell my Papa."

With that she knelt until her eyes met the rope of his breeches, and only then did Amerigo shut his eyes, no longer needing to see the depth of Therese's beauty. "This is no painting," he thought with amazement.

Were the point of this tale already implanted, as it would appear other points have been raised and are nowhere near being lowered, we might relax here and now, content to have proven that pleasure is symmetrical. As the poet said to his mistress's father, "It may be obscene but it's writ in alexandrine." And surely we can be pleased imagining the grove smelling of sauces five hours off—were this the direction the tale was wagging. But *sshh! Ecco, ora, lì*—even now the borders have been altered, the tone is near its change, the lovers have had their dreams upended, and you, among all listeners, bear witness to their ends, befitting, moral, strange . . .

"My little stone guest!" the cloaked figure laughed in the protected dark. Amerigo, despite his near death by shock at the very touch of his lady's lips upon those tiniest lips of his own, smelled a very pungent aroma of sourness. He was, the woman on her knees knew, nearing his time, because the guest had grown fat in her mouth, insinuating himself with more vehemence; had suddenly become one of those intoxicated intruders who must have his opinion not only noted at dinner but memorized by all, and so will repeat himself a dozen times, slapping the table, pounding his boot, sloshing the wine around in its goblet. Like that the guest reiterated his tale, and it was while in that frothing aggressive state that Amerigo, sensing all the fruition soon to be aborted between his lover's lips (and in an orchard no less!), felt as well a vague unrest, as though the maiden were fearful, had perhaps not fed a guest so fully before and were now at a loss what to do when the feaster must relieve his burden. Yes, a palpable grating of divine teeth across the swollen skin! Oh, there was a danger now of destroying the ideal moment, of undoing the hospitality the mouth's mistress had so far shown, and of bringing the party to the unhappiest conclusion possible. Oh, my! It was true then that she had bit off more than could be chewed, and were now trying to chew her way back to safety's sake! Dear God, no! She's biting it off!!

And it might have concluded that way too, with one assertive stone guest losing the power of speech in the first real rhetorical binge of a promising career and a hostess kneeling astonished to discover that the stone had come unfastened. But the guest, though ruffled, remained seated in the soft fur of its place and the hostess, also ruffled, was not and could not have been astonished, in part because she had meant to do just what she did, only completely, though whether she'd have lost her nerve (or he his many) was a moot point (as his soon became, you can well imagine!), because the fact is that at the precise moment when Amerigo realized the situation below his waist and the mantled maiden was deciding how profound her jealousy could go, there arose from another fruity slice of the grove a cry remarkably kin to the one which was about to escape Amerigo's lips. At the instant of this unearthly wolfish call, the rustling grove everywhere else fell silent—squirrels, owls, lovers, voyeurs, voyants, paid spies, furious fathers, watchful brothers and uncles, exercising rabbits, all these froze in their postures. The fog continued to move, encircling all, with the moon between the clouds seeming to travel no farther but lighting the scene just staged, which was a theatre wonderfully symmetrical: Therese kneeling before Amerigo stage left, the galantuomo doing the same in front of Therese stage right . . . But wait! WAIT!? How is this possible? Even Therese, ambiguous as she is proving to be, cannot be enjoying both a tail on her tongue and a tongue on her tail in two different parts of the grove at the same time. And unless the ghostly tales attending the grove's medieval history are accounting for the enchantment of this already ambivalent maiden, it must be that either the story is fatally flawed, the anatomy of humans absurdly plastic, OR . . . neither, which demands therefore an immediate explanation.

It is memorable that the galantuomo, understanding the

nature of this secret meeting, pressed his case (among other things) in the direction of Therese. Discovering the mantle flung wide and the bare flesh beneath, he proceeded to fondle the young woman's pert tenacious breasts, palming them sternly, tweaking each chilled nipple standing the length of a thumb, and otherwise unguarding himself to the "obvious and certain"—to regurgitate, he thought, the poor bitch's own words upon her. At the same time elsewhere in the grove, behind the Accademia where at that hour perhaps a great genius was burning a midnight candle, Amerigo had been met by a young lady, too, with both gentlemen very near to discovering mysteries with shattering enlightenment. The cry was the galantuomo whose lips were descending Therese's personal landscape even while not-Therese absorbed Amerigo's; both, all four, however it can be counted in the imagination, arrived at their appointed experiences at exactly the same moment. Amerigo knew this was not-Therese but an imitation of Therese, missing in her mimicry Therese's gap-tooth, bearing instead his sister's eyeteeth fangs; while the Spaniard, on his knees like not-Therese, discovered the stone guest *of* Therese which she was *certainly* and *obviously* not supposed to possess but rather a gap! He howled his bewilderment, shouted his disgust, cried aloud at the horror and, all three revised within the book of his experience, boomed to the wood before him his bitter recognition.

Birds stilled. "And so you see that my gentleman cannot in truth be fighting on behalf of a lady, and that I cannot defend myself as a gentleman against your insult." These were Therese's words amid the natural silence.

In the galantuomo's confused mind it was somehow all too neat, though the more he curried the hackles of the past the less smooth the way seemed. "I am not even sure," he said a little breathlessly, "that I can believe what I've touched. It may be an attachment, ox-tail as is used by widows, spinsters and the occasional honest nun."

Now humiliated past caring, and weeping heartily into the ruff of her mantle, Therese stepped forward boldly, took the Spaniard's gloved hand and thrust it between her legs. "It is some seven inches, and all mine," Therese said with sudden pride. Now the galantuomo was struck dumb: he had heard of such creatures of course, had acquaintances whose mutual acquaintances among others had known travelers who had intimately known etc., etc., but here before him stood not only an example but a beautiful one (suddenly he felt very tired, very old, not well at all), and then there was the matter of an affair of honor. And also. And so forth. Oh, it was all a mess! His reputation!

"Won't you be the fool and wretch if you kill a man because of me?"

"What would you have then?" the tempered gentleman muttered.

"Your public apology."

"What? I am to apologize for calling to accounts a loud, couthless, barely-classed young lady who happens to be only young and not even the other? You are hardly more than a child, and queer at that."

"I am also injured" Therese said.

"Well," said the galantuomo softly, "I've hit upon a solution anyhow. Tomorrow morning"—he paced as he talked, stroking his chin—"when I meet your scurrilous defender I shall kill him only by half, as warrants your own connection to womanhood."

The cruel logic of the solution rent Therese's heart so violently that s/he did not remain to hear the Spaniard's further boasting. The shame, the humiliation, the risk—all had been realized and none proved worthwhile. At dawn the defender of Therese's honor would undoubtedly die. Wrapped tightly in the wool mantle, face hidden by the headpiece and weeping bitterly, sneezing along the way, Therese fled the grove and hastened to her friend's lodgings not far from La Fenice and the theatre district. Exactly what s/he would do for him Therese could not imagine, beyond informing him of the latest debacle. Containing a tearful outburst until s/he could reach the privacy of his rooms, and needing to remain anonymous, Therese skulked like a thief through the foggy streets. A dog had to be shooed away, a rat crossed the moonlit path on the heels of a small furred animal.

Once within the shell of her protector's safety Therese discovered an empty pair of rooms and an old valet sealing a trunk. "Where is he?" Therese asked nervously, ignoring or forgetting entirely the need for discretion.

"My master, do you mean?"

"Of course, Pietro. You know me, do you not?"

"I suppose I do," the valet said quietly, with regret.

"Well, then, where has he gone?"

"Rejoined the regiment, signorina. I'm to follow *subito.*"

The horror of the situation now pinioned poor Therese fully: s/he had revealed herself to be half man, half woman, had pleaded with a worldly and dangerous traveler whom s/he had been forced to allow to fondle both her precious parts, and had been abandoned to the humiliation of a public recognition, which surely would be the galantuomo's recourse once her defender failed to appear, since the galantuomo could claim to know the secret. It would have been better to have done nothing, for then Therese herself would have been merely insulted by the foreigner and deserted by her friend; as it was those things had happened, and worse was about to. How many people knew the truth? How many *thought* they knew? Who, at this late desperate hour, could be trusted to come to Therese's aid?

Amerigo, once he had recovered himself enough to seal

his breeches and flee the grove, found himself wandering the theatre district—the glitter, the clatter, his anonymity among the tourist trade, these would calm his heart and perhaps even ease the pain in his vitals, which was considerable. There was before him in the street the intermission crowd of some opera, a new frivolity in which actors sang at each other, nose to nose, spraying themselves and the nearest audience with their frenetic musical juices. For a time Amerigo passed through the elegantly dressed audience, circulating among them, wondering what life must be like as a galantuomo, and did such men have the bitter experience he had just known under their belts, so to speak? There was a great beauty in the center, and an apparently famous gentleman speaking to her in Russian. No sooner did the crowd and the musings they gave rise to begin to comfort Amerigo than the intermission ended and the audience of shimmering handsome foreigners vanished, leaving the street silent and lonely. And then it was that Amerigo, crossing the narrow alley, saw Therese—he'd have known her in any light!—slinking and shrinking along the wall, and that at the same time Therese, wishing s/he had never been born, or at least had never adopted such a cumbersome silly rôle (which will soon become clear), noted Amerigo, whose face and name had unfortunately not occurred to her in her distress. Such a handsome boy, Therese thought. Too bad about his crazy sister. Ah! God! thought Amerigo. Can it be that tonight of all nights in this eternity of dark gloomy evenings I should come upon this lady, miserable in mind and sore in the pants as I am, and all on account of my love for her and the vengeance of my sister?

In brief, they accidentally met, he prised out of her a modicum of the relevant facts, those being the insult and the cowardly desertion, so that Amerigo saw Therese's defense as the great offer of his lifetime to dramatize his love and as well to repudiate once and for all his decadent sister. "But I cannot allow it," Therese protested. "We have only once been introduced." There followed a long impassioned speech containing what highlights from his unsent letters Amerigo could recall at the moment. So moved was Therese by his inability to rise above cliché and the crudest sort of sentiment that s/he could not doubt his earnestness. After some time of Amerigo's voice bursting against the silence of the heavy night Therese stopped him, a little exhausted, and said: "*Va bene,* you can do the dueling." Elated and overwhelmed by the honor Amerigo could not sleep that night—or what of it remained, since a gray pallor was replacing the fog even before they reached Therese's modest home—but rather passed it below Therese's own shutters, watching for dawn, listening for the cock to bring her to the balcony. Meanwhile he honed his sword between his knees, flint in one hand, polish in the other.

The sun behaved as expected, one of the few elements of this story that does. So without hope of some natural catastrophe to postpone what must be someone's private apocalypse all the participants in the drama appeared at the agreed hour. The galantuomo, in need of a second, had bothered a passing cloaked figure as he'd left the grove the night before. This turned out to be Europa herself departing the grove and choosing to pretend a gruff voice, her face hidden in order to be mistaken for a man; she had only to hear the name La Signorina Therese to offer herself as a member of the party. Amerigo too required a second but had forgot this until the last moment, not thinking of sharing any moment of the honor he was about to receive. So in his case it was Therese who realized the error in protocol and, despite her defender's complaints, dressed the part, hoping as well that her presence even in disguise might prevent the worst. And thus to the grove we go, just after dawn, with the dew steaming, the birds alive with fearful warning cries, the duellists stiff and anxious, hungry yet too agitated to think of food.

Wearing the cloak of a short frail friar Europa, when she saw her brother enter the tiny circle of meadow that was the hub of the grove's wheel, very nearly cried aloud her spite. For her, fortune was too good to be true! "But this is not the man I saw yesterday," the galantuomo insisted, by now totally nonplussed at the events of the past day, becoming uncertain of just about everything. "Who are you, boy, that you should join this circus?"

Amerigo raised up on his toes like a long thin bird readying to fly. "I am that man who will cut out your gut and feed it to the cat," a remark so ill-advised and *dégouté* that all the other members of both parties turned their heads in dismay to groan their displeasure.

The galantuomo shortly regained his composure, studied Amerigo, shrugged his shoulders, then sighed while unfastening the hasp of his cape. His clothes that day were the finest and most unusual anyone there had ever seen, each layer a more delicate material, and each from a more distant land. "Don't worry," the Spaniard said when he noticed the young man's tense jaw, "thread never killed anyone."

"Nor *half-killed* either," said Amerigo's second loudly enough to be heard.

The galantuomo hesitated, then remembered his solution of the night before. "Quite right. Not that either."

"Still," called out the Spaniard's second from beside a tree, "a man in such finery must have survived a long life, many adventures, perhaps a dozen challenges or more. He is much travelled in the world's neighborhoods."

The galantuomo frowned at his man. "Or his tailor is" he replied sharply.

True, the sight of so professional a duellist turned Amerigo's courage cold but the other sight, of Therese concealed in the clothes of a man, stiffened his resolve, heating his ardor if not his armaments. "Come, sir" he said abruptly. "Let us do it!" With that he flung his cloak to the ground. The Spaniard unsheathed his sword, displaying a jeweled handle of Indian ivory, a curvature to the blade suggesting it was uniquely designed for evisceration and, if one looked closely, bearing the slightest discoloration that was either blood improperly removed or rust. The duellists stepped forward. However, having spent the damp hour in the grove the night before, the galantuomo's feet were aching with arthritis so that when he caught his toe in a rodent's hole he twisted his weak ankle, falling then to the ground. When they attempted to lift him to his feet to begin the duel, Amerigo, Therese, and Europa discovered that he had fallen on the edge of his extraordinary sword and cut a depth into his chest and belly the length of both. Upon seeing the wounded man's rolling eyes and unwinding intestines, the three survivors surveyed each other and of course each recognized another's hidden identity. At that instant the Spaniard rolled over, his bearded face thrust toward the sun, his fingers gripping Amerigo's collar as if he wanted to tell him something of great import. The trio leaned down to hear but the galantuomo very ungallantly burbled a pint of blood, shook his head, and lay still. It was as if an epoch had passed to see the beautifully dressed, elegantly coiffed, but on close inspection sodden figure suddenly give up breath, taking with him decades of wild existence, innumerable friendships in myriad tongues, women that had been either cultured or brazen or both. The very sight of him so near and still brought tears to the eyes of Amerigo and Therese but it was Europa who first ran from the dreadful scene. Therese and Amerigo remained a few moments longer over the body, looking now at him, now at each other, oblivious to the yellowing day and blue sky.

We have committed murder, their eyes said. The birds, the birds, in the grove there were always so many birds . . .

Years passed.

Amerigo, a merchant, became rich; Europa, mad as a virgin, imagined she was not; and Therese became a convent resident, living outside Fiesole. One day Amerigo returned to Venice for the purpose of buying and rigging several new ships—a galley and three galleons—with the plan of sailing forever to Cathay. Still the arch-romancer. Before he left he visited his family, each of whom were yet living in some dreamy realm where no real action need ever be taken and no opinion became a conviction—in short Amerigo easily saw how he himself had got the way he had. The sorry case of his sister was of course the worst: Europa thought her brother was an enchanter; she had, she insisted, been transformed into a constellation and though she therefore could be seen by everyone everywhere, could not be touched by anyone anywhere. Her brother listened with great chagrin, saying finally in a quiet forgiving voice, "Your brother will always be with you in spirit," to which Europa replied, beyond a point of hysteria, with her usual song of change:

THE
WEAVING
QUEEN OF HAN

transverse flute in C: Pim! Pom! If I stayed beside you in the green reeds on the shore, your basket, your pretty basket hanging from your arm, we would miss our duties, we would spend all our time away from my seeds, away from your loom, & lost in the crimson maple leaves, not doing what we are told, swimming daily in rivers that would turn gray, would run to the Lethe & turn the reeds to brown. What would you ask me to do?

If the clouds rolled & the sky gave rain, you say you would still stay beside me. Pom! Is this what you ask me to do? Pumm! Pommm?

harp lyre: Sing! Sing to the daughter of the Firmament, the Weaving Lady who sits on the stars at her loom spinning the future of the world. Sing! Sing out! Sing!

pianoforte: She was once a queen on earth who had been fair in her features & faithful in love. But she had committed a crime! Queen to the King, a round & handsome ruler, but she committed a crime! Their kingdom was Han & their castle mounted on a mountain top; it oversaw the city. But she had sinned! She sinned by luring her husband from his ox to pass the afternoon in her bed. Being still the young groom, her King was anxious & in turn had led his Queen by the hand—the hand of the Queen of Han!

cello: Outside, the ox wandered aimless, graceless, lumbering to the nearby dense wood which no man had tried to penetrate.

pianoforte: Late that night, as the King & Queen played whist within royal sheets, a mournful bellow was heard, heard from the wood through Han, through Han to the castle of the King & Queen where they played under crimson sheets.

quartet: Soldiers searched to the ringing of the bell master—the bellman in his cassock ringing the bell of Han, which was made of mirror—but found nothing, not a trace of the royal ox, not a tail's thin hair. Up, up, above the wood the bellow came again, beyond the limbs of the soldiers & the limbs of the trees. Up went the eyes of the people of Han, the King clutching the cold hand of the Queen! & the royal house was watching for the lost, the neglected ox.

harp lyre: Sing! Sing out! The Weaving Lady is sitting at her loom. There! There! Sing out!

quartet: Up where the eyes of Han looked moved the

stars of the darkest night in the history of Han. A shape formed there where everyone looked, & the bellow was deafening! The bell master rang louder, then the form of the stars' making grew clear &

cello: A million stars! Spread a million miles apart! & still the King could see it was his ox who stood in the sky with a heavy throat hanging and its scrawny curved back.

harp lyre: Sing! Sing out!

quartet: The loyal Queen's hand, cold hand of Han, turned like iron &, with the King a million miles away, she fell across his naked lap. She clutched her sore breasts as if she were milking, she gripped the King's hand in hers. Up! Up where the eyes of Han looked, had been looking, & will ever look, moved the stars in the blackest night Han had seen & a shape came out with a cry, and another disappeared—the ox walked as though nothing had ever happened out of the wood to the bridge before the castle. The eyes of the King were drawn up as were those of the city, & the castle, & the world. Up!

harp lyre: Sing out! The daughter of the firmament! Sing, the Lady in the stars! Sing, the Weaver of the world! Sing, sing out, the dead and living Queen of Han!

transverse flute in C: Pom! Pom! If you were with me in the weeded sand, without any near shore, your trowel, with your little trowel, we would dig the holes where we could hide, you who awe me: I see what you want me to do. If no thunder drummed & the sun stayed round & the world turned black, just ask me the way you do, & I'll stay beside you—this is what you want me to do. Pumm! Pumm! Pumm!

harp lyre: Sing the song of the King of Han, the lonely King! Sing the game of cards of the King of Han, the game King! The starred King of Han watching the stars!

quartet: In those stars there! The China stars! The Grecian Stars! The Egypt stars! From over the treetops, in those there, those glistening butter lights, she lies. The Queen of Han, the Weaving Lady of the City, spinning the fortunes of the world. This is how life splits, how it flies to the sky, etherized! This is the Weaving Lady over the village of Han:

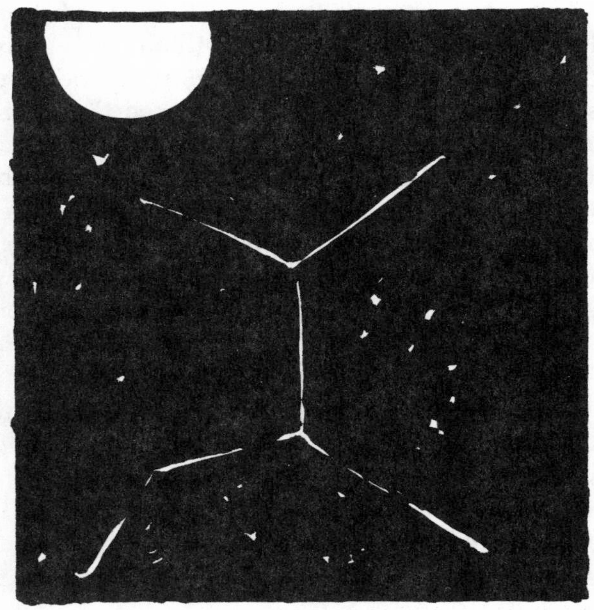

Such a frightening performance exhausted Europa and caused her disbelieving brother to sit for a moment at the edge of her bed. Only when he realized the state of her misery did he waken himself enough to rise suddenly from his sister's sheets. Her madness stunned him: how had she managed to learn to sound like all those musical instruments at once?!

He rode by horseback to Fiesole on a glorious day for a final glimpse of Mediterranean life before the decades of Asia would become his habit. When, after a long anguishing wait in the shade of olive trees, he was brought within the convent, Amerigo could not help but memorize each nook and niche of the blue-walled place; here a deep well down which one could throw oneself if need be, there a cellar that could easily be locked from inside where one could suffocate slowly, like the cat of years past that had strangled in the lustful bed. And during this time of musing and recollection Amerigo relived in his imagination all that had passed years ago between himself and Therese. It was not that much when one really thought about it; a few words, vague glances, certainly no laying on of hands to heal Amerigo's pangs. Still they shared more than most young couples, and would at least have the memory of the secret death of the galantuomo to carry with them to their own graves. Then with great suddenness he was taken to a private interview with Therese, and began to weep halfway down the corridor. The years had changed them; he had grown dapper and she stood plain, without eyebrows. They longed to embrace, but a certain and obvious modesty prevented it. Finally they faced each other long after each realized he/she knew nothing whatever of her/him.

"I'm rich," Amerigo began, tastefully enough.

"I am extremely poor."

His guilt and awkwardness, her austerity and calm—these were enough to terrify them both. Amerigo turned to leave, thinking they no longer had anything in common except a tragic moment in a tragic history of the whole of humankind. He could not wait to be in China! But as he turned Amerigo recalled what it was he wanted to show the only person he could trust with such a fact. So turning yet again, in a circle, and with his arm in a haversack, Amerigo was about to make Therese a present when the simple nun lifted her shift and bared her still extraordinary thighs. It was morning, the light was strong and cool, the room bathed in whitewash, empty of furniture but for the two chairs. Upon one of these Therese had hefted a meaty leg, separating her right from the left so that her protector and defender of years earlier could not help but have an unobstructed view.

The skin hung down as stiff as a statue but pulsing with a palpable blue tint of life. Its rubbery gelatinous tube and nozzle drove Amerigo to the wall where he stood transfixed, toad-eyed, salivating with shock, his knuckles cutting into the plaster behind him. His breath came hard in his chest. No longer fearful or ashamed Therese undid the sack cloth bosom of her robe and showed herself fully naked to this man who would at least no longer live in melancholy over her, but in anger. Her breasts were fuller than on that night when the galantuomo had suckled them toward womanhood and the skin between her legs was another two inches long! "So you see," Therese began in the voice that would have been familiar were Amerigo not overawed, "that you fought for no woman, my poor merchant, but for a grotesque hideous thing. The wolf in wool, you might say."

Of course Amerigo, despite the experiences of the last several years, remained in shock, and could have passed for dead were his chest not frantically pounding. Nor could he remove his blazing eyes from those of the person he had loved for so long, had dreamt of every night; and in that powerful moment of knowing both the freak and the same person he had loved, Amerigo matured, recognizing the melodrama of his past life. "Your affliction does not matter," he said wisely. "It's you I've loved and not some part of you I neither saw nor thought often of in the first place. Besides, thanks to my sister I now have an affliction too, and what is more my imperfection is in the same place as yours. My stone guest has been stone dead since the night before the duel."

Therese paled and seemed to need aid; Amerigo, thinking she was about to faint (and thereby remove from him the stigma of being the only lover in this story to pass out), was instantly beside her, grasping her elbow and easing her to one of the chairs, forgetting completely what he had just seen. But Therese was not ill, at least not vexedly; rather she had hoped to witness the display of fellow feeling that she just had. It was for his sincerity again that Therese noted Amerigo, though on this occasion there was more to it than mere bravery in the face of death. "Come closer," Therese therefore said. He did, though a little juberous at the prospect. "Now kneel, my merchant, and look close at what your goodness has purchased." Amerigo was prepared to draw away, even to flee, thinking that this one too had gone mad and belonged in that same firmament with his sister. But Therese was calm in her insistence, and at the last smiling too. "Look," she ordered him, "and tell me what you think that is."

Amerigo then recalled the power of the sentiment he had always held toward Therese, and with the faith of his earlier love to guide him knelt down on the stone floor, gazing upward between Therese's fuzzy legs, looking past the nun's robes straight at the organ that nearly touched his nose. So concerned with Therese's request was he that he had the courage to examine the area using the lorgnette that had only recently been invented; holding them to his eyes he studied the flesh as if under a microscope, which had also recently been invented. "It is nothing like my own," he casually remarked.

Not a very convincing *religieuse* from where he could see her, Therese held her hands on her hips, one leg thrust across Amerigo's forehead and a girlish foot on the chair. "And you say it makes no difference if I am a man down there?" Therese asked to hear the reassurance.

"It changes many things," Amerigo replied to Therese's abrupt change of color, "but not one of them is my love." The blush returned to the nun's cheeks and she saw the earnestness in the merchant's face—it was the same look of truth that she remembered seeing the night he offered to risk his life for her. Seeing that truth, Therese gripped Amerigo's ears in her hands and lifted him from the floor like a puppy; her face was beaming, her small body fairly leaping with joy. All of which puzzled Amerigo a great deal for while he retained the nobility of his affection for Therese he could not imagine how things could be said to have taken a good turn.

"Why are you depressing me?" he asked. "Yes, I am faithful to my feelings, but obviously and certainly we are more or less doomed."

Therese jumped even higher, this time clapping her hands overhead. "And yet you love me still?"

"I have said I do, and it is, I think, no more hopeless now than years ago when I merely believed I was not good enough for you. So I suppose I have lost nothing in the long run."

"Indeed you have lost nothing," reiterated Therese with a sly look in her eye. "What a lover you are!" she cried with laughter. "Don't you know the look of a woman's most pleasurable flesh, even if it has grown unusually large and sensitive? As you will see while the years between us go on and on, it becomes longer yet, my merchant, more swollen and ruby red, in need of your constant purchase. And I gather that in your travels you have learned a new language or two? And having learned a few of the theological mysteries during my stay here among these curious sisters, perhaps I have learned enough to raise the dead—"

It was hours later, after they were on the road to Venice upon Amerigo's horse, that he regained his composure sufficiently to recall the haversack around his neck. Even so his eyes were glazed, his jaw slack, and his appetite gone, as he continued to mumble, "I've never seen anything like it," and Therese replied, "It's all yours, my brave earnest husband-to-be!" Setting aside for the privacy of the imagination the afternoons and nights of bliss these two will share, we may conclude on a higher plane of moral, though not, I think, of mystery. What Amerigo at last handed to Therese from the haversack was a book he had found in the galantuomo's Venetian lodging, where he had visited before his sudden departure to foreign lands. The Spaniard had carefully shut his trunk, fastened papers with ribbon, and dictated a number of letters—standard acts before an affair of honor. He had, however, passed the night apparently in reading still this book which had caused all the trouble in the first place and which Amerigo had taken up when he entered the dead man's rooms to learn the name of his victim. The book was neatly open on a desk, a leather marker separating the seen from the to-be-seen, or the reader's past from his future. While not at first reading the words at all, Amerigo wished only to know the name of the book and of its author, since it was the sole sign of learning in the place. What created Amerigo's astonishment, and later his great grief, was discovering, as he flipped the bright pages, that the book was an illustrated version of all that had taken place prior to that moment; and as he turned yet another page he viewed himself in the galantuomo's room viewing himself! It was terrifying, since he feared turning the next page to find himself arrested and imprisoned, perhaps hanged! It was also impossible not to peek, and when he did Amerigo learned that he would learn that the man who had died that dewy dawn in the grove behind the Accademia was none other than Don Juan himself, long a wanderer in a decayed manner and unable of course to separate himself from the volumes of books concerning him in his later years. Were the books being produced rapidly enough to keep up with Don Juan's life?

"It was a famous man, Therese, whom we saw die those years ago. A member, in his own earlier days, of a great profession."

Therese observed the page before her carefully, then deliberately slammed the book shut; it contained nothing but illustrations. Therese cried, "If he allowed a hack to dream his death for him then it was nothing but poetic justice." Riding behind Amerigo in the saddle, Therese bore down on the horse's flanks, rubbed her thighs against the leather, sighed, and tossed the forgery to the ground.

"Feels like we're waiting for somebody to make a dash for it, Jack says chording his Martin."

So THAT's where you go, ——— said with puzzlement, indicating the pages Theo had pointed to on his desk with the barrel of the pistol. Not only was he terrified that Theo had gone beyond outraged reason and jealousy, increasing the possibility that Theo after all intended to shoot ———, himself or both of them, but ——— was starting to dizzy from the lack of air as well. As for the music, it was the music he could expect—etherized sopranos pursuing higher and higher visions, spectres of death, Mozart's own even. He had to get out! He needed air, needed food, needed to see living people not totally twisted by fury, booze, and senility. Tears sluiced his eyes. Why didn't someone knock? That noise? he asked Theo and in the meantime leaned his body doorward. Not distracted, the hollow eye of Theo's weapon followed ———'s torso. The noise? ——— tried again, sliding this time on his sweaty soles. Marie, Theo mumbled without stirring. My second. Or is it third? Trying to ride Casanova. My sorrel. *Siddown!* Oh God! thought ———. I suppose the door is, ——— wondered. Tight, Theo replied. The chances, ——— said, of simply strolling away from all this, say disappear out of the valley, are. Not very, was the answer. Noticing the glossy new latch on the door, ——— realized this was not a whim and he no arbitrary victim; this nothing impulsive like he'd hoped, nothing he might expect would pass like pigeons in Theo's head. Had he intended it for weeks? Was the party to celebrate it? Had Theo gathered around him all the people of his past or present to say to all the memories that even after fifty years of failed emotion he could still feel alive enough to kill? Theo moved forward in the creaky leather chair to take sharper aim, as though he'd read ———'s mind. He aimed at ———'s exposed flesh which with a muffled whimper ——— could not help but fold in toward his heart, covering instinctively the most vulnerable spots to violence, namely the face, the chest, the scrotum, all of which he tried to conceal with an open hand across his turned jaw, his forearm latticing his nipples and the free hand palming his crotch. Like this, contorted, constricted, yet fixed as a statue, ——— emitted an inhuman whine that he muddied as soon as he recognized it had escaped his throat. He awaited the flash of gunfire. Okay desire, okay passion, said Theo, things that can't be helped and are therefore somehow not serious either, just necessary like sleep like scotch like eating certain things for a while instead of others, knowing certain things as a phase of life. You thought this was only your phase, ———. It's mine too, Theo informed him, waving the gun. Pretty soon ———, bang bang ———. No new paragraph. Death of you, death of the book. When next ——— looked up, the floor was close to him, his hands were clasped, and his barrelly chest heaved. Stupid, was all he could think to say but he didn't say it. Stupid! Stupid!

What ho! Berkeley Bill whooped. I hear pussy! He snapped the tab of a Bud. One man's bow-wow, groaned Jack the guitar player. *Naaioo!* growled Bill, not *that* kind, I mean the meowing one, stands on fences fer chrissake and guts birds in the morning, pukes furballs and such. C'mon Jack you know what I mean. Thought I heard one somewhere. Jack went on flapping jacks in the pan and wiping Bill's spit from his eye. Ja hear it too? Bill asked. Sounds in pain. Man, I do pancakes, whaddo I know from meat with a tail and whiskers?! Hey!! wailed Berkeley

Bill. You freaks shaddup a minute! Who else heard the squallin pussy? This is serious. Have a drink Bill, someone says, stealing the beer from his palm. Yeah thanks, says Bill, cupping the air in front of him. Bill, says Jack, go get Lil, they're ready. Bill crushes the imaginary can. Imo find the wounded cat, you get Lil, who's Lil anyway, Imo find dat pussy. You're drunk Bill, a woman told him. Yeah, he said, well you're Winston Churchill. He left the kitchen in triumph, slithering the halls of the house calling Puss Puss Yo Puss! Puss Puss Yo! with one of those uncanny senses that something is wrong somewhere. Nearby someone told a Marxist joke, someone else refused to discuss the Kennedy killings, flashing a butt an inch from Bill's eye. He was breathing heavy, his eyes were too. Even though a few of us, she went on, have done voluminous research, one or two here at this party might even have a line on who. Yo Puss Puss! Bill lost his balance and hit the door of the study with his shoulder, both of them going pop but Bill alone sighing Mutha as he slid to the floor. Imo pass out, he said softly. And unless you've done the work you don't know jackshit which is why I never discuss it. Have you done the work? You have? I didn't know that. I refuse to pass out, determined Berkeley Bill. I passed out *last* night. He felt hot ash singe the hair on his head. He looked up. Hey lady shit do I look like an urn fer chrissake, yer burnin my ears off! Tsokay, a man said to her, Bill's just shitface, go on, who d'ya think did it? Fucking pussy, Bill moaned. The woman turned around, bent down into a squat and stuck the tip of her finger into Bill's upper lip saying, If I ever catch you call me that again I'll rip out your asshole. Get it? Got it? Rrmpfh! Berkeley Bill said. Get it? Mmpff! Got it? Aarph, he tried to answer through his crushed lip where the spike of her nail was bringing tears to his eyes. She eased up to let someone walk Bill's arm to the second floor. He started to crawl away, telling the woman that the pussy he was after had an even rougher tongue than she did. Sheesh! he said heading for the verandah.

Eddie, was it as good for you as it was for me? Better, she said. It couldna been, he answered. Sure it could cause I'm a dried out dead cow. You're wonderful, Paul mused. I'm dry. No, no, not at all. Look, she said, let's not lie to each other after the little we've been through together. I was dry and I apologize. But Eddie . . . No buts, I stay dry. Well, only a little maybe, I could hardly notice it. But then it musta hurt you, he realized, so I had the better time so I'm the one to be sorry. How about if we're neither sorry, Eddie said. And we both had it better? Paul added. Still naked they stretched themselves at the foot of the green chipping Orpheus, passing the remains of the bottle and Eddie's cigarettes, now and then grazing each other's flesh with fingers that tickled and palms whose grips caused them to suck air at the erogeny. I feel like a million, Paul couldn't help saying. If I don't, Eddie replied, it isn't because of you. Thanks to you I won't go home unfucked. Listen, Paul said, you don't have to go home at all. You got a room nearby or something? Eddie asked. As near as the house. By the way, how do you know my father? Who's your father? Eddie asked, picking gravel from a buttock and only half listening. Theo, Paul said quietly. Who? Stone Theo Stone whose shindig this is. Eddie stopped scraping her rump. This is a joke right? If there had been moonlight under the dense black foliage the lovers would have looked into each other's eyes. As it was Eddie lit a match close to Paul's face, giving him the idea to do the same close to her's. Maybe from now on you should call me Nicole, Eddie said. Their chests whomped for a while, each quietly deciding what to do next. Who'd believe it? Eddie suggested. Dad'd shit, Paul announced. With the crickets grating, bullfrogs chafing, and tree boughs huffing lightly they sized each other up by matchlight before, a little self-conscious, they started in all over again. You go here, Eddie ordered. You, there, Paul did too. They were laughing. Hey, Paul hollered. You're wet!

Time was Theo wanted me, JJ knew, sitting in the tree. Now he explains everything, me to myself for instance, not even once but twice, twice in my life I've fallen in love, love is never worthwhile, while he's making me guilty for ———, ——— means nothing, nothing works with Theo, Theo's hopeless and fucked in the head, head out is what I should do tonight, tonight at least I should pack, pack it in like it feels I should feel. Shee-it! JJ concluded beginning to ease down the tree.

Once she had gotten the hang of it after years out of the saddle, Marie from Munich managed to like it, coaxing Casanova to a canter, a trot, a slow lazy walk through the cornfields which itched, then out and around the highway back toward the house from the hills where the deer could almost be heard spreading themselves out in the brush, and not quite sure where she was she was entering the grove just south of the brook, not actually Theo's land anymore but ———'s, whom she'd met once and figured would be at the party though so far he wasn't, a man she had felt must always be doing things he shouldn't. One look at Theo's latest, the frumpy one with the initials, and Marie knew there was trouble all over her. Poor Theo! Again! Casanova stopped for a pee and at first Marie was afraid because it was dark and leafy, in fact she kept her hand in front of her eyes to protect them from the trees. And she was also nervous because the great horse just stood there hotting up, snorting and now and then swiping his tail at something or other, a whole sequence of manners that scared her into thinking something was wrong all around. What is it boy? she whispered. Was ist das? Casanova coughed and moved on. Wo ist the party? Marie now wondered. At the low skyline of the treetops she was able to glimpse, in one direction at least, the gaseous yellow haze of either a UFO or the barbecue pit. She tried to be nonchalant about steering Casanova toward whatever it was but he halted again, stamping a hoof into the dirt. This time Marie said nothing but watched the horse's ears prick up. There was definitely something out in front of her, maybe even lying in the path on purpose. She tried to draw Casanova back and was figuring another way out and around these woods without crossing the brook again. Not only was it something stretched out in the path but some*one*—that was a leg wasn't it that was moving? Casanova refused to budge, Marie refused to force him, or try to, so they stood in the pitch of the forest tracing the anatomy of the body ahead. Not only stretched out but prone and not only that but trying to be still flatter, as flush with the earth as possible. Casanova crapped. Marie peered through the dark, cursing her vision and squeezing her eyes so tight she felt a headache. He wasn't just bellied down to the ground asleep or dead, his arms were working in front of his face, and what they were doing was, what he was up to was—say, this fellow on his stomach was parting a cluster of ferns or whatnot so he could look at the space he made. Say, not look at the space, look *through* it! This fellow is looking at something, Marie realized. She rubbed Casanova's neck to reassure herself he was warm strong flesh beneath her. It was clear now that that man was seeing something he didn't want to be caught seeing. Casanova stopped crapping and started ahead. Nein! Nein! Marie whispered, but either the horse didn't care or it didn't know German because no sooner did he start clumping along the path than the man on the ground growled out his surprise and scampered off. Och! Marie moaned to the horse. He flinched at the sharp sound piercing his earflap.

Giddap, she murmured then. That stopped him in the road, nobody's said that to him in years, not since he'd first learned to ride under people's thighs. It made him take another look at his rider, who though not as young as the new mistress of his old master was firm in the saddle and erect. Casanova headed for moonlight where he could take a better look. Whoa! Marie called from above. That too is charming, he thought.

I haven't pulled the trigger yet, Theo remarked. Just some idiot bumping the door. As for last words ———, you wait until I've finished mine. Though she's my fifth one my wife, JJ, means alot. True I've fallen in and out many times, like other people don't you think, but just not everyone does much in the face of all that emoting. Well I do. Or have done. That's over now. This was the time, ——— knew, when instead of listening to this old sot he should be reconstituting his own life, it being threatened with an end and all, just the way Theo was doing half in and half out of the dark, thinking things through. I think I think I am, ——— said aloud, not realizing it. And what sorta name is that, Theo continued. I oughta plug ya just for that. When you are going to shoot, thought ——— very seriously, you don't talk you shoot. This washed over him like the chorus in Mozart he both heard and didn't, and like the moonlight he knew was there but couldn't reach. The trouble is, he began nervously but with courage, the trouble is, Theo, life is always both too short and too long. You know how when we need to solve something, make a decision and generally overcome diffidence or inertia—well isn't it the truth that we either say Life is long to justify our decision or we say Life is short? For example. Eh? said Theo waving his weapon. For example, ——— went on, we have a million bucks which we decide to spend extravagantly, on something that will bring us only brief venal joy. Being prodigal we rationalize pumping our simoleons down the toilet by saying Life is short. Same million, different decision. Life is long, we say, let's stash our loot for a rainy day when we'll spend wisely. Not only this, but get this, Theo. Same million, first decision—let's splurge because life is long and we can always get more. Go figure, Theo. We seem to have a similar problem here tonight. Don't we. When Theo cocked the hammer ——— lost his voice, remaining however on his knees to squeeze the bones of them hard in his hands. Suddenly, out of nowhere, it meant a great deal to ———, perhaps as a novelist himself, to know the kind of pistol Theo was about to use. He wanted to be able to visualize the name and caliber, to speak of it in his head at the very end. Moreover, if possible he wanted to look at the bullet that would do the job. Rather than think things through as he ought to be doing at such a time ——— wanted to see, feel, and become otherwise intimate with the mechanism of his death. Forget his kids, forget the ex-wife, forget his mother, forget JJ for God's sake over whom this was happening. ——— bit his lip and sighed. The pistol seemed to be growing bigger every second. Okay, said Theo, presumably finished with his speech. Anything you want to say ———? ——— hesitated. You're not gonna believe this, he said.

Though the landscape was lush it was also flat as far as the eye could see, and beyond the Autobahn a forest thickened by shadows and by what appeared to be shadows but were in fact troops fanned out to search the brushy terrain. The far distance intimated hills, behind these a pink glow vanishing to purple and yellow and last to white, even past white, to the absence of white, all these hues inclining as the eye moved upward, as it was directed overhead. It was the kind of sky, illuminating the fields and forest as though before a storm, out of which one might expect to see angels descend. And still one might ask: Sunrise or sunset? After the soldiers approached, the eye viewed the clogged Autobahn where cars rested bumper to bumper with ignitions off and where their owners strolled between them gesticulating, questioning, complaining, smoking in each other's faces, ambling down ravines to relieve themselves. Police were marshaled everywhere, holding back the dogs and resting sten guns on their hips. The line was formed at the Bavarian border and it extended ten kilometres north. With the eye the southern hills could dimly be seen because of cloud cover; in Austria it might even be snowing already. Those men, they're government agents, yes, agents in dress suits and neckties, but the same leather longcoats we've come to identify with Gestapo. These agents, with badges pinned to their lapels and fists carefully pocketed, these agents move from auto to auto waving passengers out, informing each that the delay may be as long as four hours, that that's how long it will take to search even superficially all these cars halted on the Autobahn and packed six abreast like a parking lot. Much of the luggage must be opened for inspection, and since it is August it isn't only foreigners traveling but Germans too, heading south to Austria and Yugoslavia and Greece and, God forbid, Turkey. And unfortunately families with small children will not be exempt from search. A file of young men is frisked in a ditch, their arms lifted behind their heads, a machine gun lazily scanning the horizon. Two armed police, uniformed like local constabulary, pass among the gathered drivers holding large hounds by chokers and leading the way for the agents to examine identity papers and passports. Radios are requested off; autos must not be unattended; tourists are asked if, at their latest hotel, they did their own packing or were there servants. Feels like we're waiting for somebody to make a dash for it, Jack says, chording his Martin. What kinda movie? Berkeley Bill wants to know, coming in late. Who they lookin for, those Nazis? Get outa the way, Bill, Lil says, slumped across the floor, her t-shirt riding high on her ribs, exposing her belly, her belly's long down, crinkling to disfigurement the face of Alfred Hitchcock that's been baked into the shirt front where Lil's wide pendulous breasts tend to make the famous director even more jowly than usual. Bill can't figure whose face for the creases in it so he keeps turning his head over her chest until Lil frowns. My tits, she says brusquely. Huh? replies Bill. Everyone looks at him, he's in front of the TV screen, busy being oafish and curious. Outa the way! Bill gets the idea and stands in the doorway watching the screen. Sheesh, he thinks, a rough bunch. Not sure if he means the men in the leather coats rummaging through people's lives or this rude crowd at Theo's party. Hey Theo, Berkeley Bill thinks. Imo find Theo. He backs out, nobody cares, he feels he's lost an argument. An old guy with handlebars over his lip and a beret cocked left nudges him, cornered by several young women between TV room and balusters. Bill flounces through feeling like a truck, glancing back though when the geezer says, Among women such as yourselves I prefer to feel vulnerable, even a trifle shallow. Bill halts in mid-step, not so stinking yet that he can't tell piss from champagne.

Robert Steiner

☞

"AND here is the book, which my father retrieved after Mother consigned it to the dust." She held it aloft for him to feel, having produced the soft worn leather volume from under her pillow like a surprise end to her story. But no hand reached for it. When Henriette turned toward Monsieur de Farussi she discovered him soundly asleep, his mouth open but his eyes closed and his large head facing the window. She spent the time examining his features: his angular prominent nose was not one of those *fin de siecle* protrusions, some moist tiny button; no, neither finicky nor faggoty but as subtle as it was long, prodding, searching, sportive with inquiry, curious as a cat's paw—the bump on the nose's bridge she especially liked to nibble. Farussi's exceptionally high forehead bespoke an early baldness as well as a high degree of wit, but Henriette would not be knowing him when both of these took firm root. Lips, ears, eyes—all were formed idiosyncratically so that each offered its own character, like little beasts, not so much handsome as compelling, and the whole then was more a matter of *style* than of beauty. Having described her lover to herself, as though for the benefit of some sightless onlooker peering through a window, Henriette carefully slipped her hand under the bedding to graze Farussi's thigh before plunging her fingers between his legs where—entirely for the benefit of her future memory—she gripped him as if she were drowning.

"It's a fake!" Monsieur cried with laughter, sitting up suddenly and shocking Henriette so that she screamed loudly enough to awaken the entire hotel. He was on her in seconds, this large powdered gentleman, straddling her and holding her arms tight against the pillow with only one of his immense hands. Try as she might, or feigned trying, she could neither budge nor evade his unsheathed * * * * which swelled before her eyes and purpled above her head, hovering, looming and throbbing toward her. She saw the immense furry XXXXX behind it, observed the chickenflesh as it squirmed with Monsieur's excitement. Together ----- and ——— cast a shadow across her chin and throat, a silhouette which she pretended to resist the more it prodded, though she finally accepted it on her tongue with its pearled moisture, its musky odor, its skin moving like a nervous creature caught in the trap of her cupped ††††††. With a single act of resignation she inhaled, succumbing to the insistent turgid exploration, breathing bullishly through her nose. No sooner had she succeeded in regulating her snorts than the !!!! began to thump against her delicate tonsils. The musculature of her tongue was aching; her jaws creaked, they strained; her lungs craved like a ship's canvas the clean bite of fresh air. It was thundering in earnest then, bobbing in the dark salt lake of her mouth over tidal waves of spittle—and her teeth fought an urge to chomp down, her great puffy tongue twisted to get out of the way, *her throat!* her throat spasmed to grow wide, wider, as wide as the entrance to a thieves' cavern! Now it seemed that everything was out of control, the frothing &&&& and its shaggy 00000, which continued growing and squirming, continued to stuff themselves farther into Henriette's stretched vowel, galloping along the veins of her cheeks and under her palate toward the inevitable deadly precipice of the black abyss. Oh, the shoving and the searching! Yes, the plummet toward stomach that made both of them groan, the sure sign that his ???? was larruping toward a conclusion! Her face was jammed with pregnant blue flesh, her tongue gone flaccid for comfort, if there was such, and her jaws, despite the sound of wood splitting at the center of them, were yet being prised further. Her eyes too had swelled, round and lensy as planets, watching Monsieur's face strain and coil as though he were trying to give birth to a new set of ears. Henriette fastened herself to him while a hand squeezed his ##### and another his = = = =, all in the hope of bringing on the finale before she choked or drowned, or spat the whole wedge and wad onto her chest when his relief finally arrived. The sound of his pain was awful; hers was muffled; and if she glanced quickly at the driving :::: it too was sore and raw, and so engorged with blood that it might well burst at the sides or that thick seam along the center that made it look like a stuffed penguin before it ever did so out of the little mouth on top. He made the noise of a falling horse, she of a sinking sailor, his $$$$ went on like hissing metal—until she drew her finger along a thin line from his IIII to his BBBBB and then back even farther to the purse of his QQQ, which set him rocking onward furiously, crushing her bruised U U, lifting himself from his knees to his feet for leverage, overriding her to a 90 degree angle. Was it never going to end?! she and he thought. Hair drifted from his '''''''''', powder from his periwig, she caught as well a fetid odor escaping him and drove her hand deeper where he urged it. *"Je viens! Je viens!"* he whinnied, turning to stone, his neck craned, his head flung back, the sweat dripping from his chest. Already his reply was congealing, roping her teeth and tongue, sinking into her belly with the weight of its journey.

And then the sea was calm, when Henriette managed to extricate the ¼¼¼¼ with her lips alone, pouting it away from her as a child rejects its porridge. Only then did she catch her breath and smile; only then remember what he'd said earlier. "What's a fake?" she asked of his remark, laughing.

THE FOX, THE COCK, THE DOG THE SLY ARE EVENTUALLY OUTFOXED

Before he replied M. Farussi glanced rightward, across the spacious room to the screen picturing doves, a lake, bathers under a tree, and called out, "You may cease now!" The music stopped; the sequestered players coughed and shuffled their feet; someone dropped his bow, another complained of hunger. "Someday," Monsieur said to Henriette, "everyone's going to have music in the boudoir. I predict it."

"But so many players then?" objected Henriette. "If everyone's fiddling," she said, "then who's fiddling?" He preferred to praise her conundrum than to answer her earlier question, but this she would not allow. "We've learned what is *not* fake between us," Henriette insisted, "and surely under the circumstances you will not suggest that my mother's divine affliction was a lie. I am here as her replica to prove the truth; your eyes can do the rest."

He had an aversion to the answer he must give. Better to pretend he had slept through it all than to admit he had hung on each word as if by his nails. Henriette-wise, Farussi was as smitten as Amerigo, as lusty as Don Juan. "Come on! What's fake? Tell me so I can disagree!"

Slowly, bemused, cautious he said, "Everything *but* your mother's affliction."

Henriette straightened herself, sitting up against the pillows in the canopied bed to take in her lover like a mother scrutinizing a cowardly child. "Why do stories of Don Juan trouble you? Men most especially find him totally absorbing."

Here Monsieur paused again, gathering his wits since their sexcapade, and by now querulous at the conversation Henriette pursued. "First," he insisted with impatience, "let us agree that none of these figures among your Quijotes and Juans Don rubs me actually wrong simply because none has ever existed, would, or could, or shall as well. But do not expect proof of what isn't there: I cannot produce, even to verify your *maman* her story and life, non-existent corpses, and even less can I *not* produce non-existent corpses convincingly!" Henriette enjoyed his squirming; she snuggled down amid the doeskin, listening wistfully to the ardent speech, and gradually eased her body into a lascivious hithering pose not unlike that of the Weaving Lady in the Night Sky.

Stretched, warm, and ample, she learned from her distracted lover that Don Juan was a bore because he accentuated his masculinity and fought on behalf of it—"All libidinous energy, charm, wit, and virility are spent in the social activity of seduction. In the sheets he's nothing."

"*Mais* wait—" interrupted the provocative Henriette. "What of those who view him as a lover who for an hour or two makes a woman for the first time feel like an animal, *une femme comme une femme.*"

With ease Monsieur tackled this: "These are not antagonistic positions since a woman, like the animal, is most a woman, and the animal the animal, when she is being pursued."

A good reply but not quite worthy of an interrogator and debator of the steel of Henriette, who accused the remark of being the male's defined female condition and so led Farussi to wonder on the instant about her education. "What's worse," she added, he was presuming to speak for the view of women that they preferred the niggling, the bragadoccio, the insipid fawning which men considered seducing. Moreover, "and certainly the worst" was her faultless logic that placed her lover in the position of being himself mistaken or not being himself a wonderful lover. "Take your pick."

Hrumph, internalized Farussi. That greasy foreigner, he stated vehemently, "merely reflects the sexual conventions he violates, which constitute a social competence much like successful dining, opera watching or ballroom dance."

To which the sturdy splayed Henriette replied, "*You,* you really want nothing but novelty while I need intensity! And speaking, Monsieur, of *ball* room—"

THE TWO COCKS
(THE MEEK INHERIT EARTH)

Had M. de Farussi, aged twenty-three, not been traveling incognito according to his mother's maiden name, he would have been at a better vantage to clarify himself and refute the lady beneath him. As it was, his fear of discovery and arrest were greater than his distaste for defeat, and since Henriette had become more than a conquest these past months of constant tourism (*being on the run,* he didn't want to call it), it cost him no pride to be bested by her. He had already begun to think that he loved Henriette precisely because she possessed more wit more quickly than he. "Do not you sometimes feel *like* Don Juan, Farussi comme Juan?" Henriette asked.

"I do not collect women," he heatedly said. "I do not feed off the weakness of others, nor provide a problem for morality or geometry." "Every healthy creature tends to multiply itself," quipped his lover in the light of what sounded rehearsed and more than a little insincere.

"It is myself I reproduce in the arms of a woman, and yet I am an ordinary lover really—merely a conscious one." Henriette enwrapped his waist in her downy legs until he felt the prickly fur of her XXXX as she ground her hips against him. "Play, maestri, play!" Monsieur called to the screen.

At the first tap of a boot on the floor and of a bow against strings Farussi and Henriette joined, quickly entering the rhythm both had become familiar with (*oom pa pa oom pa pa oom pa,* or some teutonic timing like that), soon finding that their pleasure brought them to tears, and concluded that life must be a cruel bandit (though they themselves were far from concluding). "I'm so jealous" Henriette murmured, "that I don't even want *me* touching you!" At which point Monsieur was so moved that he very nearly confessed his identity, a name not yet as evocative as Don Juan but already notorious in more than a few cities—and to what could have proved his eternal consternation Henriette, who also was concealing her true name, might never know that not only had she spent several happy months in the arms of such a famous personage but that had she been, or put herself, at liberty he might have married her, settling in a small city of the world where he was *not* in danger of arrest. In the meantime the musicians had begun a more melodic movement, freeing Farussi from that twisted German syntax into which his body and his monologue had fallen. "Ahhh!" whispered Henriette, "That's better!"

And she?—coursing through her brain while her lover provoked her center again and again, and she rose to meet the provocation, was the simple tragedy of this splendid romance, the fact that it was only hours from coming to an end, when she would have to say to him, as she departed in a barouche or curricle at the appointed moment, "we must never see each other in the future. If by chance we meet in a public place you must not acknowledge me but act rather as if I am invisible, as if I were that Sancho Panza after his lord's death. For that is what I will feel, and you of course, being the closest thing to my one true lord (though in truth I'm unfree enough already), must seem as dead to me, even if the idea sick-makes. Promise! Promise me you will never reveal our relations to anyone ever!"

In his *Histoire de ma vie,* begun at the age of seventy-two, or forty-nine years after the Henriette "episode," though not published for yet another twenty-nine years (the chronology, alas, is complexly thus: Henriette in 1748 at Parma, Genoa, and Geneva; the memoirs composed 1797 at Dux near Tiepole in Bohemia; and published 1826-38, twelve volumes, in Leipzig in a bowdlerized unauthenticated version, deleting several volumes that either were, or were purported to have been, lost!), the lover and memoirist herein calling himself Farussi will report this "affair" in a manner representing at once the pure bravura of a *fabliaux* (Henriette first appears dressed as a soldier in the company of an aged Hungarian captain who is visiting Italy under the ridiculous assumption that Latin is spoken there!) but ends, as we shall see, with a dose of human pathos that, frankly, is an even grosser example of romancing the real than either the Sancho or Don Juan or Amerigo story.

Fleeing the Inquisition for fraud, necromancy, and corrupting children, he believed he was in love with Henriette. She offered him the intelligence and immodesty of a mature woman, though she'd have been still a few years his younger. While there are facts to prove the encounter occurred, and its apparent significance to both (e.g., their false signatures in the real guest book of the Hotel des Balances, the famous phrase scratched into the window, the report of Farussi's fresh finances, his subsequent effort at starvation), it remains likely that it was *in retrospect* and not some lover's *ab ovo* when Henriette occupied the picric place of this great lover's ONE GREAT LOVE simply because the affair ended without either of them sated. In any case it is most certain that he *memorized* his emotions for later use, and that the process alone made him feel much better. This is not to imply that Farussi had any distance on the matter while he and Henriette were close; on the contrary, the very same obsession with losing himself in his own reflection, otherwise known as Writing An Autobiography, characterized his understanding of love.

Even so poor Henriette, well lathered and galloping to one cliff after another, began to experience the imminence of their separation which made every thrust painful as a dagger, every moan they shared the mournful cry of grief. He stabbed at her, she embraced the weapon; he withdrew it, she clamped on; they heaved together with the force and grunt and bluster of a horserace. Of a sudden the sadness embellished the sex, with the result that through her tears Henriette began to fear Farussi might resolve himself too soon, or that the musical players behind the screen conclude without warning and with one of those abrupt mincing finales that doesn't let you know it is time to applaud. Or of course her despicable cousin d'Antoine might arrive to fetch her home early. Or. Too many terrible possibilities for there not to be present at least one likelihood. To prolong therefore this last ecstatic agon Henriette said, throwing caution windward, splicing the musical measure of her companion's rhythmia, "If Don Juan was not really alive, that would make his possession of the book all the more poignant, *n'est-ce pas*? Ahh! Deeper!"

"Madame! *Ma*–dame!" replied the breathless lover, "Do not go on about your fictives under these circumflexes—they and I are trying enough without . . ."

"Imagine though," Henriette proceeded, slowing Monsieur with a finger to his hip, "the poor señor trying to appear to others as more than an idea in a head, more than the absence of someone else. *Très triste*!"

M slowed, tried to recover the meter behind the screen. "A bit like tracing you out, my dear," he said bitterly, "only to keep discovering I'm here by myself, doing all the work alone."

"Or worse," cried Henriette, committed now to holding her lover as long as possible between her legs, "since neither of us is using his or her true name to boot."

M halted unequivocally. "Thanks much. You back there can stop. Obviously. You want to play rough, I take it, do you? Well then, desire is the enemy of freedom, which must lead to a greater awareness of both, because each of us remains *inadequate* to the terrible demands of desire's design."

"Such as not blundering one's buss too soon?!"

"Exactement, cheri! Precieuse!"

"And surely not *failing* to shoot once the quarry has exposed itself?!"

"That is out of the question!" He remounted immediately, and with a simple slap of his hand upon her thigh caused the bows to fly again:

"Then," asked Henriette, grave with triumph and certain of an extraordinary experience on the horizon, "what—oh God! oh Sir! oh PAPA!—what, what, *what, WHAT* is this inadequacy you are speaking of! if not the man's trouble of either finishing of a sudden or not at all?"

Farussi, under his aliases that were already as long as his * * * *, looked heavily and forlornly into the eyes of Mme de ———, alias Henriette, alias Corporal de ——— and, contemplating their mutual need for secrecy even from each other as well as the inevitable sorrowful end, saw no hope really for the future of their episode—more exposition and mood than high drama (of climax he was not now so sure!), and all of it out of order anyhow—and therefore chose with regret to minimize both their despairs by cruelly answering, "The inadequacy is our eventual recognition that we need not love rarely or singly in order to love much and well. I am able to love many women, as I love you, *greatly,* because I love the *effect* of myself upon them, you. *None* of you, them, is interchangeable and *all* of you reflect my need to please. I am nothing if not the pleasure I provide." This sort of feckless sordid conversation was just what both of them required.

"Then you must be the same to all of us" cried Henriette with the highest blush in her cheeks and nose, lifting her hips frantically toward the ceiling, dragging her lover up with her, luring the musicians (or they her), "if not utterly PERFECT, at least utterly equitable. Oh! La! My love, la, la, la! I am coming to the edge again . . . and again . . . Ach Och Ech!!! Give me ****! *Donnez-moi votre #####*! *Me gebe das ¼½l!*"

THE COCK AND THE PEARL (ONE MAN'S MEAT IS SOMEONE ELSE'S POISON)

He was delighted to give to Henriette more and more ****, *#####,* and ¼½l, and felt as well the diverting discussion had done its job, preventing him from giving too much too soon. She of course could give too much only when they both began to experience an unfortunate scratching pain—Henriette said, with comic disappointment, that her ---- felt as dry as a biscuit. "Stop the music!" she called. Again her lover slackened his pace and groaned his displeasure at still being on the far side of near, but laughed at the difference when Henriette complained of her stiffness and he of his. "And my muscles ache! And I'm exhausted!" she added.

"Hungry?"

"That too!" She feared the effect of her innocent reply and kept her mouth closed.

But then said, "Didn't any little bit of my story appeal to you—not the foreigners at the opera or the ubiquitous confessions of love?" Indeed those were some of the worst moments, since Farussi was himself an opera-goer, and because the idea of confession, like that of incarceration, made him shudder.

He held Henriette by the thighs. "What I liked," he said softly into her kneecap, "was the obvious fact that you are unaware, like your mother before you, of the madman at the center of the book. The fake, my love and yum-yum, is *you,* who say you believe it when you knew and know that the man your mum and dad murdered was either himself *another* madman, or your pop was when he concluded what he did, or WORSE, your folks killed the *Author* of the Book Himself. Why the Author? you ask with that incredulous look on your face I'd expect from any old listener who happened along. . . . Say, the book *didn't make* things happen, as your parents thought, but was in fact enacted by the penman who was fulfilling his story by conforming his life to the word he wrote of it. If by imitating his own book of desires he imitated DQ or DJ it was himSELF and no book that authored it; enough imitation makes it real. Steal grandly enough, fraud enough, and you will be authentic—it's halfway that hurts. I'm pooped of this. Ask DQ."

Fearful suddenly that the man beside her was nothing other than a sequence of well–hung quotations Henriette withheld her gift—no, not that one, which at this point isn't all that sterling!—namely the moleskin book of her mother, father and the dead Don Juan. It was then and there, despite her passion and shamelessness, her pathetic condition and the imminence of her separation from him forever, that Henriette chose to keep the volume safely tucked under her pillow in order to will it years later to her son. While making this momentous decision she managed to burble out a leading question which she instantly forgot so that her lover's reply is all that remains: "No," answered Farussi with a smile, "but that is why Don Juan is a bore—it is *his* problem, being nothing other than the symptom of an illness. At my worst I am the illness itself, and no mere description or illustration. It would insult me were *I* to make myself the hero of a novel. I loath a hero's death! Strike up your arrows there! You behind the arras! This at least will not be mistook for a fraud! *Ecco, ora, lì*—Henriette!"

Yes, my unreliable, unreliable, and thrice unreliable listener, Henriette *thought*—but dared not say—I had planned to offer you some gift or other all along anyhow. Take it! What she *said* was: "I want you, my darling, to fill that space of me which no other man has yet mortified, and whose tenderness even at this instant astonishes me. It is not possible, I think, your sinking the length there, I cannot believe it will work, and yet you are already present, etched beyond description into my system, a poison I feel! Ignore the tears in my eyes! Do not stop the music, no matter how great the pain you cause or how foully I curse you! Push on until you burst, push on! Surely nothing else can remind you of yourself more than this!"

It would be recorded and then suppressed that on this occasion the twenty-three year old memoirst, futilely in love with a disguised woman, a woman married of wealth and childed, rolled his love onto her stomach while musicians were playing

and, applying the sharp point of his quill, wrote in mirror script into the lady's firm loaves of buttock his true identity. Lying amid the soaking pillows, the sweat drenched sweet sheets, and the pungency of their sexual acrobatics, Henriette bore her lover's love letters

as though they were ground glass or slivers of steel imbedded in her skin. The buttocks reddened and trembled, they tensed from the pain and pressure of the word. On he drove his quill, making it as painful as possible by tattooing himself permanently onto her globes. The name divided neatly in half, would have sounded melodically syllabic if spoken—imagine her exposing one melon alone, then the other, and an audience down front suddenly reading the message she carried wherever she went, even seated, even in the privacy of her evacuation. Blood beaded under his palm but he kissed it away; the lady moaned as he attempted to bite the slash mark of his middle A into one fleshy island. She nearly slapped him without meaning to when he traced with his point the circle of an *O* over and over again. With all her efforts in the midst of such torture, and the strain of the viola not twenty steps away—though twenty she'd never have been able to walk if he'd let her up—Henriette was unable to spell the word. "It's like a ham back here," he cried, "or a beef roast, the sort they give you in English towns where the rain is always falling and you can't get a place to stay for the night, and they have that warm beer . . ."

"OUCH."

"Oh my love! This must last a lifetime! Do not let me believe it!"

"Believe it, my darling," Henriette growled, biting the pillow.

"I cannot!"

"Do!"

"I do!"

"Yes, yes, yes! Write the agony out of your soul, my Farussi! Imprint it on me like a punishment for deserting you. Aiii!"

Her plaintive cries of pain, his morbid tears rolling onto the steamy congealed letters, the quartet's gloomy tune, the clack-clack of an arriving carriage below their window at the Hotel des Balances, the sharp rap at the door that silenced all of the above—in this lyrical mode did the episode of the married mother conclude, and thus did Casanova become a figure of speech for the first time.

Eager to foreshorten the dreaded farewell, Henriette dressed hurriedly, hoop skewed, bodice ajar, feeling numb but for the love notes on her quivering pink rump, and not affording either the risk or the time of reading her flesh in a mirror as she would in the leisured privacy of her chateau with the playful sounds of her children drifting up from the lawn—"Europa!" she would call to her daughter, "Don't tease your brother that way"—and all the time bare below the waist, admiring her departed love's handiwork. Now, though, she was content to feel the sting of the message and, while Monsieur arranged downstairs for her trunk to be removed, to leave behind her own sign for him. She cut it into the window with a bezel of her wedding ring. It was then too, as she heard his tearful voice warning her cousin Antoine to guard her safety against her husband lest Farussi himself hunt both husband and cousin and kill them, that Henriette placed the five hundred louis into the pocket of Casanova's waistcast. At the last minute before her swift departure, Henriette swung through the room with her parasol, peeking around the edge of the screen to thank the startled musicians in their formal attire by handing each a gold coin. "I'm sorry I won't be able to employ you at parties," she said. They shrugged their understanding. Then she hesitated before leaving, as if realizing how empty her life might now be. "I can't even give them a reference," she wept as the sun at last caught her in its full midday heat and carried her tender tale out into the light of day.

Casanova stood beside a tree some yards away; Henriette studied him yearningly and long, to the point where for an instant he believed she had changed her disposition and was prepared to humiliate herself, her family, and its hopes in order to be with him. But he was mistaken about her, for Henriette, which was not her name, accepted her cousin's gloved hand, which turned her gently toward the predictable future. Casanova observed the lady's life cross the Place Bel-Air and vanish over the bridge. The lake was gleaming, sailboats weaving like the fins of fish; the air was sweet and very hot. It seemed that everyone walked in pairs.

THE CAT AND THE COCK (NOTHING DETERS THE EVIL WILL)

When he discovered that Henriette had removed the moleskin notebook from under her pillow and taken it with her wherever she was going rather than leaving it behind for him to find, Casanova was furious. He chased the musicians from the room, conscious that Amerigo in the book had given a like boot to his family's servants when he was in a miserable state of heart. Henriette had left him nothing then to remember her by! Nor had Therese Amerigo, Tisbea Don Juan, DQ SP! Casanova railed and sobbed, locking himself in his room when the innkeeper appeared—a tired balding man searching out the disturbance and looking as though he had been awake all night. Dizzy, nauseous, trembling, breathless, his eyes on the rumpled bed, Casanova ran to the window with murder on his mind. If he could follow the carriage's escape from Geneva he could overtake it by horse and cut her throat in her cousin's presence; or he could kidnap her and torture her to death with leeches; or he could go down on his knees and beg her to run away with him. Resolved to decide a course of action when he learned which road she had taken, he sought the carriage. He found instead Henriette's souvenir to him (the money was still hidden in his coat). She had after all left him her own love letters, scratched into the splintered sun of the window.

When Casanova stared at the scratches in the window of the room he'd shared with Henriette in the Hotel des Balances, the angles and curves of each letter were to him a code of passion in an empire of desire; each sign intricate enough to be deciphered like an intensely secret, incredibly urgent message. On the instant of touching the vandalized window and feeling his way across the words as though he were blind, Casanova for the first time experienced life as a sequence of signatures and symbols. Though he failed to locate Henriette's departing carriage, his vision underwent a permanent change, so that the tree he could locate was meaningful, and the squirrel breaking a nut on the tree's branch made perfect sense. Down below there was a horse shifting its tail for a bowel movement—Casanova was touched. A milkmaid righting herself after a fall, her milk rivuleting toward the horse's gathering turds—the sight from his window caused Casanova to sigh with approval. The innkeeper's large doughy wife, hatchet in hand and screaming her fury at both the horse and the milkmaid, chasing both so that she was certain to catch and hammer neither—Casanova wept for the obvious coherent truth in the falls of a milk pail, a maid, a hatchet, a shit, all the while spelling out on his fingertips Henriette's farewell letters of love.

It was then that Casanova decided on a life of seduction and betrayal.

"Was it as good for you as it was for me Eddie? Better, she said."

THAT is one way of expressing passion. Another, Jean-Paul's for instance every time he hefts on his collarbone the camera and the artificial sun. He's not just shooting something he's already editing it which is a matter not only of cutting out the tripe and splicing in the heart but of setting them next to each other. Heart to heart. It is the film Jean-Paul wants to make and has been for a long time now. Tonight for instance he's feeling for one reason or another he's on to something and so in his head he's already putting heart up against heart, that is, Jean-Paul's dictating to some extent the mood and pattern of the night because he seems to be everywhere and no one wants to be a spoil sport, then too a lot of people are too drunk or stoned to care or in fact only feel involved at all when they look around and J-P's not far off. What they don't know is J-P *wants* them to be self-conscious like that, it's self-consciousness he wants to shoot and edit to see if it too has a heart. Or if it's only artifice.

What was that noise? Just the party, she said. Sounded like a bear in the bushes. *Allez les elephants!* she mocked. C'mere Lips, she ordered. Where the hell is that finger of yours. Piano player, right? I think we had better head back, he said. Paul was getting nervous for no reason he could think of as reasonable. But then Nicole gave it to him by saying, My husband's back there honey and I really can't stand the prick or the way he gets jealous all the time. Holy cow, called Paul. I don't believe this. You and me here and my father your ex-husband and your current husband back there. Holy mackerel! I'm heading to Brooklyn I think which is a shame since I ought to say hi to my old man. My earlier hubby, Eddie added. Mmm, Paul considered. He too was jealous to a fault Nicole and Eddie and Paul recalled. Let's just say, Eddie said, we never met okay? Mmm, Paul considered. I see, Eddie added, that you're ashamed. Mmm. I'll bet sober too huh? Mmmmmm. What gave both of them real cause for concern however was the fact that when she reached for them in the bushes Eddie's panties were gone. She was reaching thoroughly, with two hands, and soon so was Paul, groping as well for his shorts. Elephant my ass, Eddie said, trying hard not to grin at the distress obviously filling Theo's son's face even in the dark. My golly you're really worried, she remarked. Paul had just realized his shoes were missing too. Honey all we did was fuck a little! Suddenly Paul was angry at his ex-wife all over again. If she hadn't sent him packing in Venice, out of it actually, he wouldn't be going through this now. No shoes, he groaned. Eddie sighed and for an instant Paul thought this was where he'd come in, hearing her blow experienced breath in his direction. Wanton too, a notion that hadn't occurred to him in years. He was finished groping the bushes. He must've taken whatever was within reach, Nicole concluded. Who? asked Paul. My husband of course, who else? Saw it all probably, as usual. He must be nuts, Paul conceded, with the word wanton still stuck in his mind. It struck Eddie then that because of his father Paul worried more over craziness in people than over jealousy or vengeance. Poor guy can't handle spontaneity, she discovered. But darling, she whispered, if my husband was crazy he wouldna stole our stuff, he'd've blown out our brains. Let's walk calmly into the party, we'll separate just before we do, and when I hear a tune from the piano I'll know it's for me. How's that for a harmless end? Paul's face whitened. End? he said accusingly. Oh no, thought Eddie, he wants something more. Paul's shirt wasn't anywhere to be found. Mmmm, he moaned.

Meow!

A bloody mary!

One of her sisters!

Her mom!

What we say we pilots is twelve hours from bottle to throttle!

I told him he was the common denominator and he called me divisive.

Eve gives Adam a pair not an apple!

Women like yourself make me ashamed to be male.

Merchant of Venus we're calling it.

Ever see an E-flat through a phonoscope? *Bleh!*

Who said anything about rape? Seduction isn't rape yet is it?

Suddenment I'm not well. *Mal d'estomache je crois.*

L'absinthe makes his art glow fonder.

Meow!

——— had never seen a new bullet close up before. To his surprise he was more fascinated than afraid. It was like a lipstick, the polish wakened his pride. And this is called? he asked Theo. Point three eight, Theo replied softly. What's that mean exactly? Theo paused to scratch his chin and realized it had been days since he'd shaved. He looked at his hands, the knuckles were filthy, it must've been days since he'd washed. He could feel the soreness in his eyes, his joints creaking, a persistent ache to his skin—he hadn't slept for nearly a week. Means you get a donut for a gut, Theo remembered to answer ——. He sat back again, fatigued, this time tuckered from insomnia rather than the suspense of promoting the cold machine-gray of the weapon. —— observed his neighbor's body relax as it found the ruts of the armchair. Theo's knees protruded, catching light from the lamp on their pans and flooding it along his shins which were bare of hair, too much time in a room like this, —— concluded, airless, neck craned, grip clawed around a pencil, and those legs under the desk knotted painfully together in the stress of his labor. Rubbed hairless. Now that Theo's face faced the ceiling —— was comfortable on his knees, despite his sleeping foot, and took in the whole of Theo's spotted scarred body, unable to ignore completely the flaccid penis and the distended turkey-flesh ballocks. For the first time in hours —— relaxed. Holding the cartridge to the light he heard Theo snore to the Mozart. Naked buzzard, thought ——. Whose murder weapon is sliding into his crotch.

This is another way of expressing it, not Jean-Paul's way at all, nothing whatever to do with cameras, lenses, lights, or self-conscious citizens but rather a way that dignifies the history of sight prior to the invention not only of moving pictures but of photography as well. It looks like this:

Which wife was that? Jack asked his guitar while he waited for the painting to do something. None of the above, someone said who'd been looking longer at it. Jack strummed an anxious progress. Did you paint it? Jack said. Theo's was the sort of party where that sort of question was possible, if a bit innocent, irrelevant, and impolitic. No, the fellow replied and of course the strolling bard felt stupid. I just know Theo, that's all. So do I, said the guitarist defensively. Not really, the other concluded. Wowser, thought Jack as he ran his bass across the room.

This brief exchange took place in the large living room of O. T. Stone's clapboard farmhouse which, after years of additions built upward, to the sides and to the back (twice), was more a manor or chateau than a working farm. In fact over the years it had become a refuge for a variety of wayward souls, many of them artists, a few true artisans in jewelry, pottery, and ceramics, and dozens of poseurs. At times the house was so overrun by uninvited guests that the owner himself would pack and leave for a month just to get some work done. What was more, he hated parties, especially large ones, and rarely gave them, though in younger years he had attended many.

A fatty, Nicole said sidling up to the nude. She was still a bit breathless and at last a headache blossomed. Famous fatty, the stranger in the living room said. He was lean dark and uncomfortable, had folded his arms across his chest which made it appear that he might be actually studying the painting but in fact he stood that way for protection and for something to do with his arms. By the bathed look of him he'd newly arrived. Already the smoke noise and jostling disturbed him, opening up still wider and deeper the neurosis that usually made him regret any crowd he'd fall into, and usually led him to a quiet corner chair like an octogenarian, or abruptly home in a sweat. The wine in his hand was cold white and dry, and he'd brought it himself. So what's it doing up? Nicole wondered aloud. Not like Theo. I've always known him to hate anything porky—*that* looks like a pudgy naked teenager to me, she said. What it is, the man beside her said folding his wrists closer into his ribs, is a painting of a pudgy naked teenager. I'd never have guessed, Nicole surrendered before shuffling away and thinking with greater pleasure of her encounter with Paul than before she'd spoken to this boor. Now if she could mollify her husband and retrieve Paul's clothes. And thinking of Paul, she thought to herself, where after all is Theo?

Particularly from the front where Nicole strolled in search of both her present and her former husbands the glorified farmhouse exhibited the looming and luminous quality its owner had dreamed for it. Gabled, spired, turreted at the side, the house at night under the moon grew by turns ominous, morbid, sanctified, stalwart, at once scarred by and impervious to the vegetable life ascending its cheeks. That it hovered like a judgment merely suggested its owner had correctly named it Schloss, or castle, whose Germancy might be urging the viewer to understand it in the light of Franz Kafka's unfinished novel but was perhaps more privately motivated by the eerie (for Theo) connection between the two writers, namely that O. T. Stone was birthed the day Kafka died. 3 June 1924. Until one realized, however, that the house only looked like a manor and the manor a castle from the front on certain days and nights, and that from other perspectives on other days and nights it was what it was—a rambling thoughtless maze often drafty or smelly, half fallen, unkempt, shabbily furnished, and uniquely comfortable. As most of the guests, intruders, lovers, and wives had come to discover, the castle's terror and its attraction must be in its observers because the house itself was more a theatre, film set, or gothic sketch than the scourge and wrath of super-nature. After sufficient acquaintance with all three, Theo's house, his person, and his work afforded continuity among them, quite a surprise in the face of each on its own—formidable, disturbing, mannered, larger than life. Together, however, the uniformity harnessed all that grave power, reducing the individual achievements to a more human level; in fact people often remarked at Theo's weaknesses and flaws, at those in his work or in his house, once they gained access to all of them and could shape the phases as they wished. In their eyes the house diminished its owner and the diminished owner belittled his work. Everyone eventually sighed with relief.

This should not be construed to mean that the Jews killed Kennedy, the buff said demonstrating her cigarette. They probably did not even though Jack Rubinstein AKA Ruby was a Jew working for FBI, CIA, and Howard Hunt's, AKA Eduardo's, Alpha 66 *grupo* by shipping guns to Frank Fiorini AKA Frank Sturges in Havana. The fact that Alpha 66 AKA Fair Play for Cuba Committee shared the address with Oswald's cover ID clearly, too clearly, implicates just about everyone. This I suppose is why we never speak of the assassination. Several people around her posed questions, flung opinions, waved the theories away. It made them thirsty and sweat.

COMING THROUGH: the metal sculptor whose hair was nothing but thin ringlets the size of pinkie nails moved past the assassination team, looped through the spokes of three wheels, one each on his arms and the other a leg, wearing across the arc of his skull a rusty fender. He was *not* the final result he insisted but merely wanted to plug in his welding torch. Try the cellar, Henriette said wearily. Whose bicycles have you got there anyhow? Dunno, the sculptor answered disappearing with trepidation down the narrow black stairs off the kitchen. Jean-Paul, at his heels, helped to light the way. I'm not feeling especially well, Henriette mentioned then to Jawal whom she didn't know. Something I ate it feels like. Oh Jes? Jawal answered. Jew muss trow it op den. Bot hwere? he added surveying the living room in search of a place. Perhaps I'll go upstairs and lie down rather. No No No No, Miziz, trow it op I teld jew. I think I'll lie down rather, thanks much. Jokay. Jew no hwere? Dear man, Henriette said calmly, I used to live here. Once this was my house too. No sheet? Jawal asked. Number three, Henriette informed him with her fingers as she left. Jean-Paul was behind her, his sun flashing against the swell of her hips and buttocks.

Where's Henriette off to? JJ asked Jawal with tears in her eyes and her nose redder than a berry. A strawberry. She trow op. JJ sighed ruefully. Paul, having crept in barefoot and shirtless but wearing, thought Nicole, a swell suit, had broken his promise to keep a distance. Until he would look at himself later in a mirror Paul didn't know about the leaves in his hair, the swelling blueness of his lower lip, the scratches in his neck, or the mosquito welts that puffed and reddened his forehead. It only bothered him that his toes were dirty and that with naked feet and stomach even a good suit looks ridiculous. Then too he fumed sex which Jawal was the first to smell. Jew trow op too? Where's my old man? Paul asked him.

Yes, it was that time of the party when guests inescapably began to be curious about the absent host. While it wasn't unusual for Theo to disappear early from anything—a party, a dinner, a movie house, even a phone conversation—he only did so after recognizing the presence of others. He'd at least pass among them holding a glass of water in his hand, smiling and saying Hawaya, overhearing some anecdote before shoving on to the next enclave, and so on until he'd portioned himself around for an hour. Then he'd gloss the food and booze, either his own or somebody else's, and only then retreat either to his study or bedroom or to someone else's study or to his car where without disturbing anyone he would silently steal away. More than once while guesting elsewhere the host and hostess, about to serve dessert to twelve, would realize Theo had been away at the bathroom an awfully long time. A search ensuing for the sick perhaps dead author would end in the children's room where Theo, a child under each arm on the sofa or floor, would be transfixed by the blue glare of the TV. In a room otherwise pitch dark and full of teddies dolls and hobby-horses he'd just be one of the kids with potato chip crumbs on his chin rooting for the home team. Worse, he'd prefer vociferously to remain right where he was than to rejoin adult life even though he'd been unmasked and the sentiment of the picture concluded. All his wives had found this trait embarrassing, and particularly humiliating was the fact that when he'd be discovered his face bore the vacuous stupefied look of the TV viewer, mouth open, eyes like dinner plates, legs pretzeled under him like in a wigwam, and it would take several seconds to bring him around. Huh? he'd say in the meantime over and over again while the host, hostess, wife, and six or seven other guests would watch from the doorway at the wash of narcotic light and listen to the hubbubing cheers and boos inside the set. Sometimes he wouldn't come around at all, wouldn't really acknowledge that anyone but his fellow viewers—three and a half feet tall and in their pj's under his thick hairy wings—existed; then it was the gradual falling away of the other guests, their laughter subsiding into annoyance, their eventual retreat back to the dining or living room without him, last the host and hostess leaving whichever wife in the doorway with a supportive pat on the arm so that she had to study her transfixed man until her nostrils flared and vexation silenced her completely. Quietly she would close the door behind her.

Since it was true that Theo only liked to watch live transmissions on TV, those he saw as affirming the external world to people like himself who otherwise would frequently doubt it, it seemed likely to many of the party-goers that his absence meant something must be happening in the box. To others, who knew something was happening because they themselves were watching it from upstairs in the castle, the explanation for Theo's absence must be a second TV in a concealed room where the aging genius was holding a beer on his stomach, prising peanuts from their shells with his teeth, and ingesting real life framed and flattened into a movie. To Theo such events proved that the apocalypse had again been postponed. And so on this particular night Paul, Nicole, Marie, JJ, Bill, Jack, Jawal, Lil, Tina, Jean-Paul, to name but a few, went in search, each in his and her own good time, less to recover Theo than to discover what world event might have drawn him so utterly into it that he'd have missed a gathering this immense when the hugeness, after all, had been his idea from the first. These friends and relations would even criss-cross each other's and their own well-trod paths in search of him, nodding and shrugging at one another because the same space at a different time might turn him up.

It turned out that the soldiers and drivers seen on the television were not actors but people who at the time they were filmed were occupied driving and soldiering. As it was, while it was not a movie per se it was a film, that is it wasn't live, a truth which you couldn't know until another camera brought you the news conference explaining what the earlier film and people were all about. People were keeping a vigil outside the Bundestag but not presumably the same people who'd been ousted from their cars earlier, most irate and delayed and inconvenienced to the point where very few would show support for the government. No, the vigil in the morning rain was by *other* people, not *those* people, and it was spontaneously organized for the purpose of showing to still other people, among them the villains of the story, that in a time of crisis the country was unified. Hey Wait a minute! cried Berkeley Bill when the TV jumped to Paris where a fewer number of people discussed the press conference, or the fact that the Crisis Minister hadn't said much. Why hold a press conference in order to refuse to answer questions? When'd that happen? Bill asked everybody gathered around the upstairs room where some had come calling Theo's name and others had emerged startled out of the toilet to find a mob. When what Bill? Lil called. Then another face filled the entirety of the TV, certainly larger than life, to tell the room that the information was up to the minute. It was exciting, all the jumping around the TV was doing, though it seemed unlikely that anybody in the room actually knew what was going on. Nor did that matter. What mattered was the footage of cars, soldiers, ravines; the photos of ordinary faces in candid and posed poses; the wide angle vigil of hundreds of umbrellas and shoes; the fact that the minister was the Crisis one mattered, and that he was shaved; it mattered that in New York the local news had been interrupted for the national station news which was carrying exclusive coverage of news in Germany and France, and that all these broadcasters were also shaved, unless they were women and then their cheeks were rosy; that, and the references to "them" whoever they were. What mattered here was that everybody here and there, yesterday and tonight, had an opportunity to be collectively breathless. Waddyasay, said Bill. One day those wealthy industrialists will retaliate. Not with coppers. They'll start kidnapping terrorists, dragging 'em outa their vans and hideouts and Balkan beaches. Force 'em to live the good life in villas on islands in the Aegean. Make 'em eat lobster. Lie in the sun. Swim nude alot. Teach 'em a lesson.

Even so, not everybody was convinced Theo had been secreted with his box the whole of the evening. Jesus, JJ suddenly said smacking her forehead. She scanned the room. He's still with ———! He knows everything! In the TV a car door opened and a corpse hog-tied and blindfolded spilled onto the pavement. Was that who? When everybody drew breath JJ did too, only she meant it differently. So is that guy dead? somebody asked everybody else. Or another guy? Now who's *that* guy? someone else wanted to know. The dead guy before he was dead, another answered. The room started to empty. Stragglers leaned on the walls. The man with the handlebars rubbed a woman's shoulder, looked at the screen, and said: Is this death then or an advertisement for it?

Meow!!

Another bloody Mary!

OK her stepmom!

Who said seduction? Seduction isn't a nightcap together is it?

It was covered with lint and, I think it was, tobacco!

Accent on the first syllable—*U*ranus. Some difference.

No kidding. Belly up. Wide open. Paws totally stiff.

King Leer they want to retitle it. I said—

For a change she said she wanted to feel a cop.

What about having Dulles on the Warren Commission then? Huh?!

Portugal. On your salary you could live like fuckng pharoah.

I prefer the fear of being awkward to thinking I'm a hulking brute.

What's wrong with a nightcap?! It doesn't have anything to do with bed!

Something's burning.

I feel I've come a long way. Keep going.

Puts the eek back in Greek!

Meow to you too goddammit!

Everybody's the common denominator!!!

"I realized that I was in a place where, if the false appeared true, then the true must appear false, where a man's intelligence must lose half its privileges and where fantasy must make his reason the victim of either illusory hopes or horrible despair."

HISTOIRE

DE MA

FUITE DES PRISONS

DE LA

REPUBLIQUE DE VENISE,

QU'ON APPELLE LES PLOMBS.

ECRITE

A DUX EN BOHEME L'ANNEE 1787.

A LEIPZIG,

CHEZ LE NOBLE DE SCHÖNFELD

1788.

In addition to the taffeta jacket he had worn in Geneva his last evening with Henriette, a Spanish lace hat embellished by the gray quill of an ostrich, buttons of brass foil threading a brocade vest, his breeches of oriental silk soft as a child's pucelage; and more, a mantle, a walking stick, sonorous Parisian boots, a prince's gift of an ivory snuff box—all these, one at a time, with the melancholy care of an exile, Casanova removed from his person to place on rotting hooks and wormy shelves in the airless cell adjoining the attic of the palace. At six feet two inches the prisoner was nine inches higher than the prison ceiling so he passed most of the time (one year, three months, five days) stooping, lying, sitting, or crouched, and in each of these positions obsessed with the necessity of escape. Behind each thought there rested a picture of himself as he would be five and ten and twenty years later if yet imprisoned: raving, filthy, faceless, forgotten. The image caused him to weep, to kick the stone wall, to spit against the muzzle of the first black rat that clawed at him from its nest in the attic . . . and this before the gaoler had even had time to retreat. "This is your cell," he had not yet had an opportunity to say. "What would you like for dinner?" he waited patiently to inquire. It was the eighteenth century; the latter half of the century to be sure; it was the year 1755 to be exact and, to be absolutely accurate, 26 July on the fourth floor of the Ducal Palace, Venice, when Casanova, dressed in his finery, became a victim of the

Inquisition. I must be in prison, thought Casanova, since there are no women here.

THE MOST prevalent form of degradation in the erotic life is the absence of an obstacle. Without a complication there can be no triumph of ideal passion over a hostile reality, only a mute satisfaction that is the birthright of millers and bakers as well as kings: nothing then remains on the tongue but a few coarse hairs, and in the nostrils the vulgar smell of wet mattress—so Casanova thought when on that first day he surveyed the cell devoid of table, chair, bed, candle, and any niche of light. He had only then entered and could hear nothing but the gaoler's clatter of keys (like the bells of San Marco?) which could, in appropriate hands, unlock the nine other cell doors in the puzzlement of rooms comprising the attic of the palace. "No cutlery, books, pens, mirrors, razors," the gaoler Lorenzo mumbled. "No mirrors?" Casanova said. Even as he said this, raising his eyes to heaven, Casanova observed a long perfect hole in the plank of larch that began the deep ceiling.

Robert Steiner

CASANOVA'S memory regains the afternoon he spent with the jewel setter and bezeler Manuzzi at a tavern named Orlando Triumphante. When Casanova had been arrested one of the complaints against him was that he "possessed a leather apron such as Masons wear." Only Manuzzi the bezeler had viewed the necromancer's cloth—as well as the books on matters of the spirit both sacred and profane: *Clavicus* of Solomon, *Zeus-ben, Picatris, Essay on the Planetary Hours* (in Italian). Flattered to be esteemed a magician, though not one of the Kaballah, Casanova denied nothing to Manuzzi (who claimed to be a collector of rare volumes)—not his Petrarca or his Ariosto, not even the Aretino. Under the pretext of seeking contraband salt the *Grande del Inquisizione* arrested books by Jews and Latins; in defense Casanova confessed to the crimes of fashionable and conspicuous dissolution and preferring the tailors of Paris to those of Venice. *"Buon giorno, Signor,"* Manuzzi had said at the Orlando. A short man with food in his beard and one eye enlarged from studying gems, Manuzzi claimed (in Italian) a distant blood relation to the Countess Bonafede who a month earlier had run naked through the streets calling out *Casanova! Casanova!* to the shuttered windows of the hot afternoon. "Her love for you," said Manuzzi, "made her feel young again despite the terrible wrinkles." "Every affair," suggested Casanova, "has its ups and downs, its happy and sad verses." Manuzzi corrected his superior: "I meant (in Italian) the wrinkles on her body." Casanova measured the man's smile and took it for granted that the jewel-setter was sniffing something out. "All my women are sixteen" he replied with an open hand on an empty chair.

Matinee

SHAVED, laced, perfumed, girdled in silk, Casanova was escorted within the week by the Grand Inquisitor into the care of forty archers that marked a path outside his apartments, that kept a respectful distance between the bewildered gathering crowd and the bewigged prisoner whose fan, when extended, displayed a Japanese tea ceremony nearly as wide as a mural. Only then did it occur to Casanova, as the archers stood close around him, their bows drawn and arrows unsheathed, that he had made a mistake entrusting any of his secret books to the bezeler. Soldiers in phalanx, Grand Inquisitor in the black robe and insignia of his office, Casanova smelling of larkspur and rose, onlookers nudging to the fore with a word of solace, a cry of irony, of obscenity—like this the swelling choreographed crowd moved up one street and down another, passing the house of Othello, and separated gradually, the noise fading like breezes, when the accused traveled by gondola to the Inquisitor's own marbled residence where he was permitted a short nap in a locked room. After lunch the troop advanced to the Ducal Palace via the *Sospiri,* then from gallery to gallery within the palace until Casanova, tired of being transported, suddenly heard the order for his incarceration but no sentence. Thence with the escort of only one archer (it was almost like being set free!) he climbed stairs, spanning gallery to garret to his cell in the garret across from the attic proper. The thick heavy door was three and one half feet high, the cell two feet higher. After all this, Casanova sighted first a ten pound rat in the attic, and second his gaoler Lorenzo, who held at his belt the immense ring of keys. "Just get out," Casanova said the moment he took note of the hole in the wood overhead.

ASIDE from Lorenzo's keys, Casanova heard only the bells of the clock of San Marco which gave him splitting headaches—the lead roof made of the palace and the palace of the prison cell a hot vacuumed bell. If there was a metaphorical clacker it would have been the bolt Casanova found while exercising in the attic dressed in fox-lined winter gown and bear-skin slippers. After weeks of sharpening the end of the bolt—bezeling it, he thought with disgust—and in so doing gnashing a hole into his palm the scar of which neither faded nor shrank, he designed into a dagger what he secured in the stuffing of an armchair he had purchased for his cell. In further weeks he feigned maladies including minor hemorrhages, toothaches, and boils—the last of which he generated by infecting his skin with dirt, rust, and rat droppings. For the toothache he received a flint of pumice; for the boils sulfur; for the hemorrhages not only a priest's prayers but books. After *all* these weeks of bells and headaches, of bolts and armchairs, of blisters and bloody kerchiefs, after these days and nights of Lorenzo with the boiled beef, Casanova discovered, when he fingered the hole in the ceiling for the thousandth time, that the tip of his pinkie touched the tip of someone else's.

ALREADY this story seems to require at least four maps—one of Europe at the time, one of Venice itself, another of the Doges Palace bordered by the Piazza San Marco and the Grand Canal, and yet a fourth that would indicate by all its open spaces, by its lack of indications, the nature of the prisoner's cell on the fourth floor of the palace. Then too there should be music; something by Vivaldi, who has only recently died. Also one should try to imagine that while the events in the story are moving ahead more or less economically, conveying the illusion that this was how things might have come to pass—how the protagonist suffered, analyzed, and dreamed, and how lesser figures, generally flattened types though only because in life they were not much livelier, especially those who had spent more than a few years in the prison of the palace, or who proved cowardly, deserve no suffusion of breath—one ought to make the effort, in the midst of the actual credible unfolding of a genuinely poignant and, what is more, basically true account, one should shut one's eyes and imagine, for it was so, that while the protagonist was playing his role in a noble and manly fashion, other very famous figures were doing other things elsewhere. To name a few: Rousseau, de Sade, Voltaire, Washington, Napoleon, Goethe, Haydn, Newton, Shandy. So we should have maps, famous paintings that would have flitted through Casanova's overwrought imagination and can be viewed even today in the Museo San Rocco, the Accademia, etc.; also a tactile sense of the awesome heat—it is partly August in Venice in this story, and it doesn't take Galileo to know what that means (the stench, the dead canal, the off food, the vinegary wine, the sun shimmering in the wave upon wave of relentless hot sick-making wind that courses like a religious parable through the narrow invidious streets and mercilessly passes through the porous walls of the palace to gather in the cramped, dark, verminous cells, in particular Casanova's, where the deadly air with all its toxic meaning forms in the meagre tube of sunlight from the iron door a foot thick, a pale blue cloud of smoke above his head as he would be seated in the armchair thinking of a way to escape and so having by this cloud of sickness at least for himself a visual aid, because the air has turbaned above his lice-encrusted scalp the way an idea occurs to a character in a comic strip), though we should know too what winter in Venice is like.

ONCE he had penetrated the plank of larch with his pinkie, Casanova reconnoitered two more of the same, each four inches thick, so that a foot of space after his internment (three weeks of time) the prisoner struck marble. Eight months later he had piked, scraped and fingered through the marble morain only to encounter another plank. On 23 August he saw daylight through a hole the size of his shoulders; two days after that he was moved to a better, more auspicious, more convenient cell, armchair, fineries and all. "More space," Lorenzo muttered "since you must have already more time than you can use." "Our liberty," coded Casanova to the prisoner Balbi, "depends upon rigor and certainty, like space and time." Superstitious about dates, places, and the prescience of decipherable language Casanova, hysterical by now about his escape and its frustration, considered the three-day holiday enveloping All Saints to be fat with holy significance, and so rewriting Ariosto's *Orlando Furioso* into a *langue-câche* based on the newest theory of cipher propounded by Vigenére

n h c m m r m f c t l

n a b u c o d o n o s o r

he happened near daybreak—the sulfur providing odiferous reading light once it had been fiercely met and flinted—to decode and encode into a word to the wise the following line: "Between the end of October and the first of November," which meant the twelve strokes of midnight, 31 October 1756. Thus (and this he withheld from Balbi) Casanova gambled his life and freedom on a string of verse: Ariosto had helped place him in captivity, it could lift a line to unplace him. He would escape on the first anniversary of the earthquake at Lisbon, an event less signal for its ugliness than for its recollection of nature. Lisbon, like Casanova's escape, prefigured Romantic excess.

WITHIN the palace Casanova was united with other prisoners and identified himself fully with their lot—noble debtors, defrocked priests, scholarly seducers—but only because he experienced such a grandiose solitude. The unity of the prisoners in the Doges Palace depended on their separation; just as the prison itself consisted of cells, each member of the population was a cell (in turn comprised of cells). And so as Balbi dug his way through his floor and Casanova's ceiling, he and Casanova realized that the unity, like the mortar, wood, and marble itself, was crumbling. After months of exchanging letters, notes, knowledge, and dreams, the physical proximity was overbearing. Separated there was a tribe; together there were suddenly individuals capable of lying, stealing, scheming, betraying, even murdering each other. Suddenly the prison was intolerable. When Balbi penetrated the ceiling with a pike, lines intersected at the point of Casanova's stuffed armchair. As the flat bed of light entered in a perfectly Renaissance circle from above because of Balbi's intrusive spike, Casanova was exposed as a shadow, a simple *trompe-l'oeil* or obscuration on the palace walls. Where he moved a knee or an arm from the chair in which he brooded the shadow too moved, like a gaoler.

"Having lost his footing Master Balbi slid the length of the roof. When he stood upright again, or rather more like an ape crouching, he discovered that he had lost his cap over the side as well as the manuscript he had found behind a brick in his cell. With care he attempted to search the slippery roof in search of the lost tale some earlier prisoner had written, perhaps like myself, with an elongated pinkie nail and whatever was available, including blood and feces." **Anon, My Escape From the Leads,** *Leipzig 1788.*

THROWN entirely on himself in prison, forced to imagine life rather than live it, suddenly confronted with the prospect that if he is to live alone he must write to avoid madness, and so must write of what he knows best, namely his life to that point, Casanova recognized seduction as the way in which the aristocracy knew the lower classes. Wigged, powdered, rouged, used to blackening a dimple into his cheek with hot wax, careful not to run his stockings or mortify the lace of his shirts, Casanova nonetheless overcame class structure not by seduction but by the familiarity it had won him with husbands in powerful places. Except in rare cases Casanova maintained contact with the women he seduced regardless of their stations, and so except in rare cases none felt abandoned by him. He was a dedicated writer of letters and would become so again once his escape was made good. The first act of his freedom would be to spend two days in the soft bed of a *guingette* writing letters to Rome, Venice, Vienna, and Paris. The fame of his escape would ring in capitals as far away as Petersburg. Dependent for his livelihood on the wealthy of Europe, who pay him to be entertaining, therefore to take risks, and accord him honor as an adventurer in the arena of sex, Casanova was the last epic hero, and perhaps the greatest because he was also (would soon become, though pacing the cell it is beyond belief) the successful raconteur of his own life, as if Homer had been Odysseus or Odysseus Homer, Cervantes Don Quijote, etc. The prison was therefore odious because there was no one to seduce, and because there was no one to seduce there was no story to tell. Only near the end of his life, when he had become a buffoon in a changing world, when the anciền régime was crumbling and C's passionate dress and manner were ridiculous, would he relate the story of the escape in detail. Until he set it to paper outside Prague he consistently refused to confirm the specifics of the story of his despair, his solitude, the sight of the garrotte that waited just outside the cell door. Incarceration concerned only himself and so it could not be interesting, surely not an entertainment. Pledged to provide pleasure by relating tales of pleasure, Casanova could not speak of the prison in Venice until he himself was past pleasure.

SHEETS, blankets, mattress, shirts, stockings, handkerchiefs, towels, waistcoat, mantle—all these Casanova sliced into strips and made of them a cord three hundred feet long. It was All Saint's Day, just after midnight, when they reached the roof and saw the moonlit festivity in San Marco square. No sooner had Casanova turned to ask Balbi what it was that was slowing him than he slipped in the mist, skidded on his backside, turned to right himself and, at the last second before plunging into the canal, caught by his extended fingernail the gutter that would be removed twenty years later when, as a spy for the Inquisition, Casanova confessed to the Grande himself how the first successful escape from the palace was performed.

LIKE the more distant memory of the story of Europa and Amerigo that Henriette had told him their last evening together in Geneva, Casanova cannot resist recalling too the first day he entered his cell in the Doges Palace. He recollects all three—the tale, the teller, the punishment for owning books that could contain the previous two—even as he is poised, painfully and with exceptional fear, by his elbows in the rain gutter of the lead roof of the palace. Close to escape, he has lost his footing and hangs by a bone and muscles aching with fatigue over the backwash of the Grand Canal known as the Rio di Palazzo. Hovering there a little past midnight, the moon appearing at intervals of cloud screen, the piazza San Marco not one hundred meters away and below packed with revelers, clowns, lovers, thieves, an orchestra, Casanova grunts, sobs, farts, and hies himself no higher than his grizzled chin, tries to call quietly to Balbi his accomplice, all to no avail—he is stuck and weakening, each effort to lift himself or obtain aid in his debilitated condition causing him pain and memory, the sort of memory one expects to enjoy just before death. Below him the dangerous dark plash of the canal that will either drown him outright when he falls (assuming he hasn't bashed his brains on the stones lining the sea wall) or carry him unconscious into the festive lights quayside of San Marco. Briefly, lovingly, he remembers the perverse tale of the twins, remembers the twin spheres on the tail of the perverse teller in Geneva, realizes that her prophecy etched into the window—*tu oublieras aussi Henriette*—has failed, and then, fixing on that first dreadful day he was brought guarded to Piombi to hear the words *cinque anni* uttered by an archer, Casanova recalls the narrow hole in the ceiling of his cell.

WITH the pike he found implanted in a hollow Bible, Balbi was able to carve his way through the marble floor, raining down *lambrissage* onto Casanova's skull. At the first sight of Balbi's face overhead, Casanova felt exhilaration, awe, uncontrollable energy. The hunger, the filth, the hemorrhoids, boils, constipation, fleas, lice, the rats—to parcel out his madness and sanity in equal portions Casanova had been translating Horace, metamorphosing hundreds of pages in search of twelve shapely odes—all this was, in an instant, nothing less than a misfortune, forgiveable, forgettable. What a story! thought Casanova as he leapt up and out from the shoulders of his armchair. What a life! Casanova cries to the half-moon overhead. BALBI! he whispers so loudly that for a moment the oars below fall silent, someone says shush, and the lovers in a cruising gondola laugh at their deceptive senses.

IT COMES as no surprise that while certain things worsen others improve. Such is the picture of European winter in the middle of the century: waiting anxiously for a sign from afar that a heavy cloud is about to bring down the sky, hoping that when it falls it will not be in a torrent, not sweep away or flood the museums, salons, ballrooms, galleries (of course the palaces must be sacrificed, like the prisons!), Casanova decided that he would grow long the nail of his fifth finger in order to use it as a writing implement. Yet, he thought, those fellows overhead are in here as pederasts. But that is the climate of politics, and though while C. grew a long nail and there was already a sprinkle in the air it was still easy to sidestep the weather that would blow Europe away. Later, in his old age, and with his kneejoints harder than iron, his lungs like grilled cow's udder, Casanova would quite simply remain indoors. He would not live to see every one of his patrons fall—kings, queens, princes, the usual crowd who run out of words. But he would live long enough to escape Venice and to dramatize other chapters of the neo-classical life—though while he is busy politicizing the fall he feels sure he is about to take into the Grand Canal, Casanova in the gutter bays like a wounded wolf, indifferent to the lost kingdoms, uncaring of the audience he may be drawing even now—no patrons for sure. Balbi? BALBI??!!

JUST as the printed word placed him in his cell so, he belabored, could it place him outside. Outside of himself is the key. Casanova, it might be said, never leaves the cell. He grows old, loses his teeth, his hair, the famous virility, paces up and down in clothes that lose their splendor, finally their weave, walking until a furrow appears the shape of C's aching feet. Yet he escapes! He does escape! He sits in the armchair regal as the Pope, dangerous as the Grand Inquisitor, and waits patiently as he has done so many times before on balconies, terraces, in gardens and olive groves, for someone's imagination to fetch him from the solitude. As always he waits for his freedom to be symbolized and articulated, and knows that eventually it must—the solitude is the same, the need to get out of himself the same, the seductive urge too is the same, all are the same for the autobiographer in his cell of the palace, for the writer in his prison who must dig the hole in the marble, prying apart sodden planks, in order to execute liberty by a simple magical authority.

HE HAD by the age of thirty seduced in the neighborhood of seventy-five women, or approximately one third of all the women he will have had sexual relations with by the time he retires to the chateau of Count Waldstein at Dux in Bohemia. He had only begun to understand, pacing with bent back the flea-ridden damp cell, what seduction meant to him and therefore what incarceration must mean: women signified for Casanova, as he walked the cell in the furred slippers given him by his mentor, surrogate father, and first homosexual love—women signified (he looked at the walls east and west, north and south, heard the bell announcing the hour from San Marco, or was it Lorenzo rattling his keys?) a way out. A way out of what? I must be in prison, he concluded, since there are no women here; just as while he is escaping—though dangling like a mouse by the tail he no longer conceives succeeding—he has said to Balbi, "This must *not* be a prison for there is a woman walking below me, there is a way out, see her in the square, Balbi." Crying out from the rain gutter, Casanova raises his voice into the purpling midnight sky; a string of stars like Venetian lanterns—he tries to identify the constellatory holes in the night, wishing he could raise himself using those stars as a grip.

FROM the instant he had seen and then fingered the hole in his cell, Casanova felt sure he would be free. I have felt tight spots before, he thought with a smile, a thumb stuck in the ceiling. And some of them have even been pleasurable.

CENTURIES go by. Casanova has been waiting in the armchair, whistling. Can he be both himself and the story of himself?

IT IS no longer the eighteenth century and nowhere near Venice, but Casanova is still escaping, which means of course that there remains something he is escaping from. This obsession with escape has its indigenous tedium. After the thousandth time on the lead roof, in the gutter on his elbows over the canal, after the stockings and skin have been torn and bloodied for the thousandth or ten thousandth time, there is a moment in the escape (perhaps it is while Balbi tries to recover the lost ms.) when the idea of freedom is tiresome, when in fact the urge toward liberty does not seem to Casanova very different from living in the cell of the Ducal Palace. It is, after all, not the freedom that is the problem but the urge. Casanova hangs in the middest of things—like many others he has a story to tell.

INTERMISSION

1. Identify the source of this quotation:

2. On page 152, where you found Casanova *incarcere,* you might also have noticed a cypher system whose key was B U C O D O N O S O R.

   Ignore the obvious references to biblical figures and subtle allusions to the very early work of certain green composers of opera. Focus rather, as our visual era dictates, on the potential *figura* inherent in the errant alphabet. What can you make of it, do you suppose? For example, using those letters I can make the following:

NOW IT'S *YOUR* TURN!

THIS IS NOT A TEST. YOU ARE UNDER NO OBLIGATION TO BE ORIGINAL OR EVEN MODESTLY CLEVER. WERE THIS A TEST YOU'D HAVE BEEN INSTRUCTED TO TURN TO YET ANOTHER PAGE FOR FURTHER INFORMATION. AS IT IS YOU CAN CONSIDER THIS A *REHEARSAL* FOR A FUTURE SERIOUS PERFORMANCE WHICH COULD APPEAR JUST ABOUT ANYWHERE.

GOOD LUCK!

3. Below you will find an example of pornographic connect-the-dots (Have you ever been so lucky in the midst of a long book before?!)

IF YOU ARE OFFENDED BY SCENES OF AN EXPLICITLY PUERILE NATURE DO *NOT* UNDERTAKE THE UNDERNEATH. CHILDREN UNDER 18 YEARS OF AGE ARE EXPRESSLY FORBIDDEN TO TOUCH THE SURFACE OF THIS PAGE. PARENTS ARE WARNED TO KEEP THIS PAGE OUT OF THE REACH OF CHILDREN. IDEALLY, YOU AND YOUR MATE, SPOUSE, FRIEND, WHATEVER OUGHT TO WORK THIS TOGETHER, AND ONCE HAVING COMPLETED IT, THINK OF ME WHILE YOU ATTEMPT FURTHER THE INCREDIBLY ATHLETIC BUT, I MIGHT ADD, THOROUGHLY SATISFYING ACTIVITY DEPICTED.

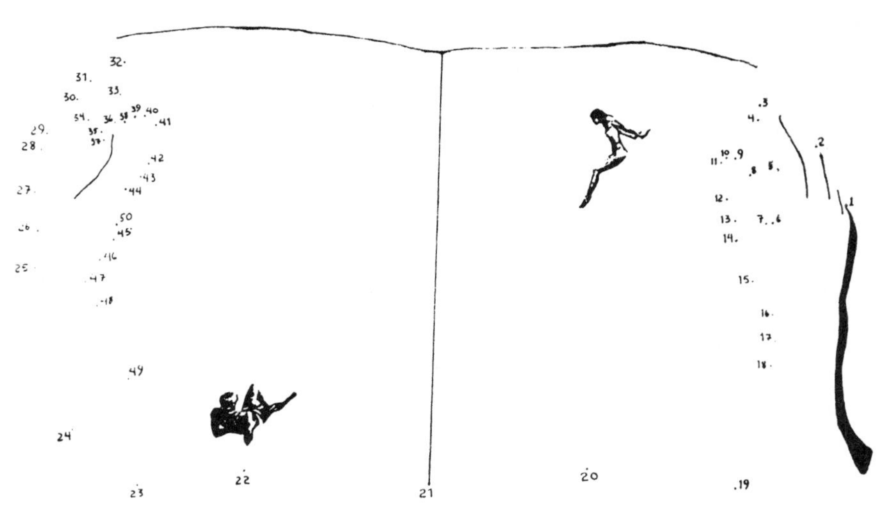

WHEN you see a creature like that one, reamed and suspended so the rest of us can feed, it kinda shatters yr faith in a future. I mean it could be one a us. Which one? Berkeley Bill was asked. He pocketed his hands for balance—this night air was heavy, these sparks of fat stank. Somebody who'd drip alot, he said watching the pig's carcass congeal. Anyone in particular? Tina was hoping he'd name Lil in front of Jean-Paul who was shooting Bill being drunk. Would it matter, Bill scolded her, who eats who? Several eaters drifted away from the pit for the first time that night. Others chortled, waiting for the drunk to pass out. He stood benumbed, it was true, above the fallen pig, his hair curled with sweat, his face flushed, his tall plump figure swaying. Bill's eyes were closing. Suddenly he thought of something and opened them roundly, fixed on a remote tree limb. Somebody who'd get crisp at the edges, he concluded.

The sun of Jean-Paul's switched-on gun hit Bill between the eyes, crinkling his freckled mug. 'Mere Puss, Bill purred over the pig. Once more meow, he said. The newcomer from the nude teenager in the living room stepped between J-P and Berkeley Bill. He pointed his finger, not wagging it, just placing it erect in the air, and saying nothing seemed to cause Jean-Paul's sun to go dead. The filmmaker came out of his one-eyed crouch, looking worriedly at the lens of the camera. The only thing separating the stranger and Jack was Jack's Martin, and the guitarist had had enough of this oddball for one night. Who you? he asked. Pretty soon a small crowd who'd heard Jack, J-P, and Bill's sharp voices ring out smartly at the oddball began to belly-up to the pit. They were eyeing this fellow with heightened suspicion, like he'd fritzed the party and put the kibosh on everything, the sungun being only one example. No one noticed Casanova mosey into the yard riderless; no one noticed Marie trail behind fixing a strap and unsmudging her face with a wet finger; nobody saw the police take the young bespectacled man into custody even though the film of it filled the box and the box was still running; nobody looked when the mustached man slid his greasy hand into sleeping Henriette's blouse, whispering to her of passion and immortal need; nobody but the sculptor in the cellar, wearing an iron mask for safety, caught a glimpse of JJ rooting around for her husband and ———; positively no one at the party could have said exactly when it was that the shutters of the study flew open, a monotonous popping noise ensued, or when after a few seconds ——— stuck his head out calling for assistance. Yo Somebody, he hollered. Yo God Amighty, he wailed with rising alarm. Jesus Fucking Christ, he shrieked. I've shot the bastard!

Paul was at the piano shoeless sockless shirtless and in love. He wanted to play with his woman at his side. Already he hated the secrecy that would obviously form a pattern for weeks, maybe months, until Eddie found the courage to leave her husband. When he began to play the music sounded strange, something was wrong with the Bechstein in the bay window. He opened it up and found his shoes shirt and socks. No panties. When he sat down to send Eddie and her crazy husband different messages with the same piece he found himself surrounded. Jack and his guitar, Jalal and his mdanga, Phoenix's sax. Come on you guys, this is important, he said. Too late.

Too late because out back the sculptor emerged with his creation and Lil said: Just a minute Whadja got there You jes cut two bikes in half and made a third It's still a bicycle fer chrissake You phoney baloney. He lifted the iron mask from his face, he hefted his creation toward the moon. Not just a bicycle, he said. Now it is *my* bicycle. Which he mounted unsteadily and rode away on, leading a hundred moths deeper into the obscure countryside.

Too late because someone in the kitchen said: All women live their entire lives expecting to be raped. A friend told me that as awful as it was, having it over with was something of a relief—at least the stats are on her side now. Her listeners blinked their pessimistic agreement.

Too late because someone else said: And who planted all those crazies in DA Garrison's crack investigation which was closer to the truth than anyone realizes? Assassinations will come and go, investigators will fumble until they uncover the crucial clues which must then be discredited—common folks will intuit the truth without a sealed verdict. And we at parties have learned to keep our theories, even our proofs, to ourselves and to our children.

Too late because Marie was seated on a cut beech's dead stump marveling at her romance with Casanova in the woods this side the brook, woods she would always look upon as forest primeval, as enchanted. When she dies Marie will remember fondly the coarse horse hair she found twisted around her ear and drawn through the lobe hole while sitting on the stump. And she will regret that she never had the courage to tell a soul or to pay any other horse a visit in the woods.

Too late because at the b-b-q pit Jack couldn't decide whether to slug the wiseguy from the nude teen's painting inside the house. Though what he's actually done isn't clear even to Jack, Jack and several others don't like the look of him. Shifting his weight from hip to hip and thus knocking the Martin against his pelvis Jack couldn't make a choice between trouble and none. Jean-Paul didn't understand how his sungun died as suddenly as it did, and so he studied the wiseguy too. Uncanny. They smoked a drug trying to figure this out.

Too late because JJ's given up hunting hubby and is packing instead since life cheats everybody but now and then her most of all   of all the things she doesn't need though ——— is it   is it just phucking they all want or filosophy they all want   they all want more than money can buy anybody   any body would serve them just the same   just the same he calls it romance   romance deserves what it gets   it gets duller and duller crying to them   to them it's an inconvenience really and a disappointment   a disappointment meaning a cancelled appointment   a point meant to show the cynicism of their attraction to anybody   to any body to her   to her he is they are she is   packing in up off   off men and sex too!

Too late because supine on the bed in a blackened bedroom Henriette felt worse than ever before in her life. Stress, she insisted to herself. Something she ate, she reminded herself. The heat of course made it worse but it would be all right. She had to tell this to herself. Being in Theo's house made it worst of all. It wasn't that she regretted the smallness of the house for the brief time she'd lived in it and the hugeness now that she didn't. It wasn't that she regretted divorcing him for Nicole, who'd then left her for him, who'd then been left by him, and who bothered tonight to be quite snotty to her, or that she missed either of them though she was alone more or less. No, she regretted *knowing* them, it was that deep, felt quite sickened to think that her emotional life had ever revolved around two such—who were themselves like father and daughter after all. Yes, Henriette could not bear to feel quite so unwell in Theo's house that she hadn't the capacity to leave it. She held her kerchief at her lips, clutching it, tearing her eyes to subdue the pain. She sobbed, watching the boughs of a tree sough slightly out the window; their breeze was hot, the mere idea of it made her feel worse. Her feet. Her shins. Her knees—these she looked at with palpitant breath, like a parakeet's. In the shadows—someone'd tossed up the moon—she captured a glimpse of the top of her head out of the vanity mirror opposite, then the eyes that she was looking with. She started again trying to calm a growing panic: feet, shins, knees, thighs, then what she could not see she needed to feel, rubbing herself just gently might make the pain disappear—no, this was agony, she concluded—and pressing hard in the crease make her think—she smelled blood—of something else. It could even lead to

Too late because Jack on the guitar Jalal the mdanga and Phoenix the sax have already downbeaten into something like Dave Brubeck no Bird no Monk no Sonny which Sonny no Cole Porter no shit! *I've Got You Under My Skin.* Love song, mewls Paul. Drug song, pules Jack. VD, Phoenix thinks but doesn't say. Uh one, uh three, uh two.

Too late because seated in his MG with Nicole's panties over his head like the Air France pilot he is Nicole's husband thought into the pungent crotch that he'd fly forever   for ever'one to hear about and pass around around in circles but nothing new   new to him of course he's been blind blind man's buff buff nude in 1969 *soixante-neuf* and all those other things he and she can do do not expect him to hang around here hearing all this *merde* from these *merdistes* in this *merdier* is really disap– pointing out to her she can be– have they slept together al– ready willing and able to jeopardize howdoyousay the relation– ship him off ship out outside of the marriage the pilot feels empty and sans a home homely she is not attractive at all all along he's waited for just such an attack a tacky thing to do by a dumb sonofa– bitch that she is she'll want a divorce one day day in and out he's tried to meet her needs needs a stiff Gucci up the ass– ociated love with fidelity so why not also *c'est-á-dire* forgiveness *pas de tout*

Too late because from under the verandah, out in the pen, and across the back yard and into the *schloss* come respectively Quijote the diseased retriever, Panza the moony bull, and Casanova the sated sorrel. Right away the kitchen's a mess and nobody wants to go in there with those smelly ornery galoots taking over. The party peeks at the trio from around walls and through windows and doors. The beasts stomp snort and nip at each other, they knock over pots pans bottles and dishes, tending to slip and slide on the rubbishy floor when they fight over the garbage. JJ'd boot 'em out but she's already feeling it's not only too late because of all the isolation noise misery and booze, but very very late. Two a.m. to be precise.

Robert Steiner

Love Letters: a Life

1743, Venice

Monsieur C.—

I am prepared to do anything for my dear friend Angela. She dines chez nous every Sunday, then spends the night avec moi chaque fois. Allow me to suggest that to accomplish her you must first overcome Signora Orio, my aunt. Nobly born, she is not wealthy and thus craves inscription among the widows of the Brotherhood of the Blessed Sacrament, of which S. Malpiero is president I believe. Bien: last week Angela told the aunt you were favored with him and that the way to the holy brood was through you. She lied that you were struck with love pour moi, that you arrived at the embroiderer's only to pass a letter to me, and in that state you might be persuaded to do our family a favor. Knowing you are recently ordained as well as a fine violinist ma tante saw no cause for caution and urged me to write you on the instant, that is tout de suite. Naturellement I refused to compromise myself despite your robes, and so it is that in an hour or two you shall receive auntie's personal invitation. Accept for Sunday, at which time I shall treat you abominably, enough to concern the old woman who will be flattered that you are not insulted and overjoyed that Angela in my stead will agree to your company. Done politely enough, your speech on behalf of my aunt shall win the witch. Trust me further, Monsieur, I wish to prove my friendship . . .

My aunt will invite you to dine, but you must refuse.

Leave as soon as the smell of supper is in the room, the best excuse is the stomach since she shares the malady and will not only feel sympathy but likely take ill herself in a matter of moments. When we are about to seat ourselves à table you débouche, but of course do not . . . rather slam the door as if your bowels were howling, then climb the stairs to the fourth floor—the room on the left is A's. Angela too will complain of her stomach, so that my aunt will feel unwell that much sooner; aunt to the second floor, A to the fourth, both moaning as they go, I alone will take supper, thinking of you, and of your téte-à-téte avec mon ami.

Buona Fortuna—
Nannetta

1744, Venice

Monsieur,

You must know what our conversations these past months have meant to me! If you have courage to spend another night in my chamber I will give you proof of my affection. I must know if you would have loved me these months had I before now consented to make myself contemptible. But I am certain of your love, and of your desire to be my husband. Whatever you will . . .

Angel

1745, Venice

My Undoing,

Martine, Nanetta's maid, has confessed to me your disgusting acts with her and my former friend, your confidante, and so much more! What of our marriage, Signor Father? What of your vows to me during night after night of my sacrifice to your lusts, some so unspeakable I may die of my shame before completing this last missive to you. How could you do the same things with them! Nannetta denies all and so I have taken my case to her aunt who by now has given your name to the police. Soon, my brute, there will come a knock at your door, and then it will be all up with you. And what of me now, now that I am ruined not only by your cruelty but by the memory of your passion. Who now will satisfy me as you have done. Save me from the nun's dry lips!

A.

1745, Venice

Cher C.,

Under the circumstances it is wise for you to leave Venice. The brat has forced me to action by begging me with her tears to have you arrested. Nannetta, who knows nothing of our meetings, is in such a state of fear that she has taken to bed. Thus you see the effect of a man such as yourself on younger women—they do not know how to enjoy themselves. It would be quite the farce, my seducer, were it not to mean that you must go and I must play the indignant proper auntie. So pack your bags, thou perfidious priest, and make for the highway; I'll soon have the law on your heels. Forget not your violin, nor the other instrument—even Venice is not wide enough to keep you comfortable.

Salute,
O.

Robert Steiner

1748, Geneva

My dear,

"Adieu"

Henriette

1753, Murano

Dearest—

Before writing in detail I must be certain I can trust this woman. I am in the Murano convent and treated very well. The Mother Superior has orders not to allow me to have any visitor or to correspond with anyone, except of course Papa. I do not doubt your fidelity, my husband, and I am sure you will never doubt a heart over which you hold absolute power. You are the God this place lacks! You may be sure that I am eager to do whatever you order, I am yours, your baggage, your beast.

I am terribly distressed by an accident which happened only last night, especially since it must remain hidden to everyone in the convent. I have had a frightful hemorrhage and I do not know what to do to stop the flow of blood. I am running out of linen and cannot request more without creating suspicion. But I will need a great deal if the flow continues. If I die, my darling husband, the convent will know of what; when I think of your fate as a result, think of what my Papa will do to you, I tremble not for my own life but for yours. Oh, do send me linen as soon as you can! You must make it the finest available, from Paris, so that no one will suspect what I might be doing with it. What will you do if your sweet wife dies? Why did this have to happen?

Your tearful
Catarina

P.S. I am certain you will answer favorably and that you realize my impatience. Please reply to the same nun who gave you this letter, eleven o'clock tomorrow, Saint Cançian, but tell her nothing pertinent—she believes merely that we are in love. Realize, my beloved, that if I did not know of your noble heart I would never reveal my condition nor take such steps that might cause your disfavor. Hurry!

1753, Murano

Signor—

If you believe me worthy of acquaintance, though you have judged only on the basis of my appearance as a nun, I feel obligated to obey you, if only to disabuse you that I in any way have acted on my own behalf rather than as the divine messenger between one C. and another C. I hope therefore that you will come to the grille of the visiting room alone, where I will indeed disabuse you.

Having written a note to Countess S., whom you do not know, I enclose it herein. She will expect you and it early tomorrow. Accompany her here as a servant on her gondola; she will ask you no questions so you need not lie. One word more: I shall not remain at the grille unless you are masked the whole of the time; I cannot cover my face within the visiting room but you can without, thus no one seeing us would be able to identify you; and not identifying you, not accusing me.

It is as mysterious as it sounds, but I hope you will still pay the visit since I am able to demonstrate my disinterest.

Yours,
Maria Maddalena

1754, Murano

Husband,

Yesterday, I was walking along the corridor and dropped a toothpick; in order to retrieve it I had to move a footstool that stood before a crack in the wall. I looked through the crack, hearing voices, and saw you speaking with Maria Maddalena. You cannot imagine my surprise. Tell me all, my love. How could I love you with my soul and not be eager to know the story of such an amazing scene. She is my dearest friend, has she not told you? Of course I am not jealous, and that is why I deserve to know all.

Eagerly,
Catarina

1754, Murano

Monsieur Casanova,

I am surprised and saddened to learn that you have told my best friend Catarina that we are lovers. Having performed services for both of you that compromised my own virtue I take your slander very personally indeed. Under the circumstances I can no longer meet you at the grille to inform you of Catarina's condition; I should think as well you have no need of me so that from now on I will be taking my exercise in the convent garden. To prove to Catarina my sincerity and fidelity I am entrusting this letter with her own, and have permitted her access to it. I hope, sir, that my actions will be clear to you, as I never intended any ambiguity between us. Of course I have denied your accusation that I have attempted to separate you from your spiritual wife.

Farewell,
Sister M. M.

1755, Murano

My Darling,

It has depressed me terribly to think that I can no longer discuss our relations with Maria Maddalena because the two of you will not meet to discuss your own differences. I have begged her to forgive you, and on this account she has insisted that the difficulties and hurt would require days of private conversation to undo. How else to say it—I have arranged it through Papa that Maria shall leave the convent and be accompanied by him back to Venice for a two day period, after which she may return with the linen I have sent her to purchase. Since she will be staying at my father's house I can inform you with the enclosed map how you may meet in the attic for hours at a time undisturbed and undetected. Once there simply place the wardrobe across the door and do not walk heavily in the room. Do this for me, since I cherish both of you too much and cannot bear your quarrel. Though you have denied both of us your good agency about this up till now, I beg you to do as I say—it will mean everything to Maria and myself if you consent.

Your wife,
Catarina

1755, Murano

Signor Casanova,

I have decided to reveal a secret concerning the recent meeting you achieved with Maria Maddalena, my friend here in the convent at Murano. You perhaps would take us both for fools, and doubtless will not believe that it is we who have had you. Do you recall placing the wardrobe across the door? Do you recall then rushing to the nun's bosom in that dusty attic, laughing at the success of your plan for a day with her under my father's roof and protection? So it was a conspiracy with your little nun, was it? No, my gallante, no! It was a conspiracy, you are correct there—but it was ours, not yours! When you were spending yourself on the nun's naked bosom for the fourth time, assuring her that the blood you spewed was no cause for alarm, did you not hear my drawn breath, not catch the smell of my own spendings? There, in the darkness of the wardrobe I sat on a footstool, my skirt hiked, my thighs divided one from another, and while you encouraged Maria's foul speech I watched you through the keyhole, I met Maria's eyes as hers met mine, and together she and I reached our own secret plateau, regardless of you and your filthy needs. Ah, sir, even now as I write this to you, the little nun is on her knees before me, her perfect face stuffed into my quim, her head veritably vanished inside the vast space of my womb. Even now I am brought to conclusion, and more, she begs for it, pleads with me to shower her with the morning's transformed wine. She bathes her face in my water, the room fills with the smell of my waste; and there, there, aah, she has accepted on her tongue like a wafer one of my soft extrusions. And while I pen this she smiles between my cheeks, she urges me to tell you that now she is swallowing the transformed bread.

Would the little nun do the same for you, Signor? Would I, despite your request? So, it is clear, sir, that you have been the ass in the affair, yet alas, not so sweetly the one that you might have received the same succulent pleasure. Go sir, out of Venice, leave behind the lyric women to their preferred choices. We banish you from these parts . . .

Verily,
"Donna Juana"

1755, Rome

Dear Brother

Did you receive Catarina's letter? Are you pleased with its contents? I must tell you that I enjoyed myself, but that I am enjoying more the fact that I no longer must wear the robes, no longer simper, no longer play the faithful dog. Yet I had never done that sort before and was glad for the occasion. Do you imagine she knows by now that you have received payment from her father for the safe destruction of the letter? Does she imagine that you have shown it to nearly all her friends? My education at your hands has been exquisite, and my anonymity the meanwhile perhaps the most important feature. No one should know yet that you have a sister by blood. Let the story emerge like a rumor. But you should know that I have sent Catarina a note confessing all, making clear to her who has been the one to eat the ———!! Where do you go next, my brother, my lover?

Aching,
MM

1760, Cologne

Herr Neuhaus,

The designs inspired by love are not so much difficult as subject to uncertainties. I sleep in the small bedroom above the General only when he asks me to, which occurs only at those few times of the month . . . That is not far off now and yet my husband, accustomed to the date, will not be deceived. It is therefore necessary to wait—attendez-vous, Monsieur. You will be notified when the hour of our happiness arrives. You will then hide in the church, and you must not try to bribe the man who locks and unlocks it because, though poor, he is also très betise, too stupid to be corrupted, and would betray the secret. Let yourself rather be locked in as if by accident; that is, remain hidden in the church past sundown and the poor fool will forget you were ever inside!

When the time comes you will only have to push the door adjoining our two staircases; I will see to it that the door is ajar. You will be comfortable on the hidden staircase, where you will find a candle, books, and dinner that I alone will have placed there. Be assured that the time will run shorter for you than for me who must tolerate the long-winded dinner, the belching and insipid speech of the fossil General. At least I will have already told him of my indisposition so that he will have no use of me and therefore pay me no interest. You should know, my sweet, that you are the first man I have known who had no objections to possessing a woman on those rainy days, despite the fact that we are perhaps more ardent then because freer of consequences, and it is only the men who have made us despise our condition. But you who say you savor it, who claim to have drunk from the well! You must, Herr Neuhaus, you must!

God preserve you from coughing on the staircase, that would betray us both and mean total absolute ruin.

Yrs,
Mimi von Groote

1761, Strasbourg

Monsieur Snatlege—

I have wakened with the greatest satisfaction, but not from having spent two hours in your company, for you are no different from the rest, but because I now have my revenge for the continuous contempt you have displayed in public toward me. I have taken my vengenace by unmasking you before another of your victims, and doing so in such a way that she will live to regret as well that she ever came to know you; surely she will lose her cloak of virtue, her air of superiority. She must have waited long for you since you have only now left my bed. I wish only that I might overhear your conversation after you have read this letter. You will not take each other again, Monsieur, for I will have cured both of you of the ardent passion that caused you to mistake me for her in the darkness of your room. So having cured you of your awe at her presence, and your impetuosity because of it, I will not even ask your thanks, you need not feel grateful, your hatred of me will suffice to grant me peace.

If your conduct towards me in the future is not improved then I shall be forced to make the facts public. As a widow of independent capacity I need not fear for myself—I require no one, can purchase whatever and whomever I desire, and am in short able to flaunt public opinion. Your sweetheart, young bride that she is, is in no such position; and you, sir, given the facts of the business stand to lose the welcome everywhere you hope for it. Ah, then, on to the warning which ought to convince you of my good will and generosity—remember, in your fury, that I need not have told you.

For ten years past I am afflicted with a disease that defies treatment. You went to great lengths in proving your love to me, though without the central act—which you managed to withhold—but you will recall what you did achieve. It is certain, granted your eagerness and the duration of your labors, that you have contracted the disease from me. I advise you to seek treatment immediately at least to diminish its intensity, preferably in another city, another country, another world. But the main reason I warn you, sir, is so that you may avoid making a similar present to your new beauty, your Mimi; she has done me no personal injury, the mere fact might ruin her entire life, and in the event her husband has been faithful—there are such walking about—she will have given it him without question. I hope then that there is time; of course, if you lied to me this dawn about your plans for the morning, it is possible she is already infected. In which case you have no one but yourself to blame. Ach, how we tumble from your pedestals! Even your young beauty can no longer seem so pure, whether you have diseased her or not; no, the truth of the matter is simply too great to allow the imagination its convenient veil. Find a good physician. Keep your nose clean.

I have informed no one else of this affair so we may bury the incident in silence as long as you remember that should we meet in the future in public I will expect courtesy and attention. More than that would of course be out of the question; you will never be quite well again.

Mme. Renaud

1761, Strasbourg

Sir—

Do you take the author of the previous letter to be a complete fool? I have lived too long in society to be taken in by your attempt to fabricate a story supposedly more incongruous and more flattering to yourself than my own. It is mere childishness to suggest that you never performed any act with me, and while I will not deny that as is customary for a person in my position we were never together that way in anything but darkness, I am not so gullible as to think it was not you who serviced me but some other using your name. While I confess to having seen you in public on only two occasions, and then indeed all too briefly and curtly—the spark that fueled the previous letter of mine in the first place—I certainly am sure that the person who snubbed me twice and was introduced as yourself is the same person who sent me notes, gifts, and later surprised me in my bedchamber. For you to pretend otherwise can serve no purpose; I have told you already that no one else knows, either of our relations or of my disease. And so, who are you hoping to outwit in this? The disease, sir, is quite real, I assure you, and no amount of deception on your part will change that. What do you gain else by this ruse? Does my better opinion of you matter? Is it possible after all that you were sincere about behaving coolly towards me only so that I might not be compromised among society? I confess that at the moment I can see no other purpose or source for your current vehemence.

You are very clever. Even as I write I find myself bending to your will, imagining myself wronging you terribly, conceiving that some villain who may resemble you in the slightest has in fact had liberty under my skirts; and thus I sit at the escritoire thinking of you fondly, wondering why you may have singled this widow out from so many younger more beautiful women . . . ah, you are too clever, I think! For now I am thinking I have maligned and slandered you, and do not know what to make of your offer to uncover the imposter. Admittedly, I am confused; but I am also experienced. I accept your aid in this, and can promise to reward you if your claim proves the case, just as I promise to humiliate you publicly if you are now lying.

But meanwhile, with this newer issue at hand, and my growing concern that there is someone who feels he has access to me in disguise, I will tell you that there is *no need* for a doctor. *I am healthy,* Monsieur, and am in fact willing, under the new circumstances, to test your identity myself; it may be that I might not successfully recall the face of Casanova beside an imposter's but it is another matter to recall the smell, the taste, the technique of a lover. If it was not you with whom I enacted the soixante-neuf I will know it when we do! Thus you see that you have momentarily won: if you are lying you possess me yet again, though not the hidden treasure; if you are not lying you will have certainly not lost by our meeting, and you may indeed plunge your hand into the câche. With all my experience I find I am giddy! What are you doing to me after all?

La Renaud

1762, Strasbourg

Monsieur Casanova,

It has been weeks since you played your trick on me, and only now am I fully recovered in mind to inform you that I spoke to our mutual acquaintance whose task it was to tell me the truth. It was a mild prank, sir, denying it had been you all along simply to extract from me the truth of the disease and to force yourself upon me in ways which I abhor and against which there are both civil and natural laws. While it may be the case that you injured my body for a time like any chinese torturer, and managed to rend that part of me that should offer no excitement, it does not mean as well that you have defeated me. I have not experienced such a violent occurrence before, nor have I ever been bound and violated in pleasure; but while it may have pleased you to abuse me thus, I am no innocent and would never fail to protect or revenge myself. The fact is, sir, that I am indeed as diseased as I first admitted, and that you have merely contracted a further or double dose, as the physicians say. I might have warned you at the time of our assignation but your immediate brutality toward my most private place imaginable decided me on the spot to give you access to whatever, even urging you to intrude yourself into my treasure with your then soiled member. While that conclusion has caused me pain from infection it assured that you would contract the further dose, which the other place you ravaged has always been clean of.

Who has won, then, you gaudy Venetian? You in your ridiculous masks, your greasy vests . . . Who lies better, Signor? I am too bored to say more . . .

Adieu,
Madame Renaud

1762, Strasbourg

Signor—

Were your letter not unsigned and your various tracks carefully covered I would take action against you; my late husband was a powerful man and has many powerful friends yet. The truth you have disclosed I first did not believe; but I have since had it verified that you were elsewhere and among a large crowd at the time I believed it was you using me so cruelly. You, it seems, have used me far more brutally than did your valet on that occasion. I am ready to admit my utter defeat at your hands, and am writing now only to applaud you your success. But are you spiritually prepared for the consequences before God? I think not, Monsieur. You are right when you say that the only place I was diseased when you, originally, performed upon me was in the heart, and the disease was jealousy. I suppose I knew it was you, the real you, that first time all along; perhaps I believed we were playing a harmless game with each other, a genuine lovers' chess-match for example. I did not know you were grave about these things. What is so horrible is the fact that I allowed a man like you to soil me morally. Sir—if you knew that I was lying about the disease, and knew further that it was *you* who had given *me* a dose of it, why would you persist then in sending me your valet whose own disease he discharged into my bowels? Was it not bad enough to suffer that indignity itself, being taken from behind? Was it not gratuitous to cause me a life of physical agony in both my holes—it is too late I think to be modest—when you say you knew I took it all as a game? I understand full well that among the players in your sexual theatre it is treason to threaten wilfull disease since it is, as you say, an occupational hazard. If I violated a rule I did so out of ignorance, and from bad advice. I was mortified by your aloofness, only because I was instantly in love with you.

There. I have confessed it—is that what you have wanted to reduce me to? Someone you could do with what you would and who nonetheless worshipped you, perhaps even because of your cruelty? Yes, you have won it all, Casanova—your reputation is enhanced, and as you indicate, the story will play well in Petersburg while you are visiting the Empress. I am in place, all right, Monsieur: no empress, no youth or beauty, none but a fool, a widow, a diseased soul. The action I spoke of at the outset is not what you might think: not civil, but the laws of the God you and I must always share. I am praying to Him, Casanova, for your soul and for your awful death. We are united in our disease.

I will have retired into the country by the time you receive this. My health is too delicate for me to appear. I forgive you your villainy because it was my misguided love and assumption that prompted it. Of the tender feelings I exercised I am at least cured. The rest is terminal . . .

R.

1763, London

Mr. Casanova de Sengalt:

I am surprised, sir, that you have written to me in order to recover the bills of exchange for six thousand francs which you gave to my daughter. She has just told me that she will return them to you in person when you have learned to respect her.

Mrs. Charpillon, Esq.

1763, London

Mr. de Sengalt, Esq.—

I do not see what my daughter ever found attractive in you, though fortunately she has assured me you were not quite so enchanting that she corrupted herself for you. As to the furs and jewelry, let me remind you that they were freely given her, with no promises in writing, and certainly no obligation to commit sin with you. We are a poor family and the future of my dauther's dowry forces me to refuse your request to return the items.

Yours,
Mme. de Charpillon

1764, London

Monsieur Casanova—

On the advice of my solicitor I am concluding our correspondence with this letter simply informing you that you may not evict my daughter from the lodgings you purchased for her, nor recover the furniture and bank accounts you established in her name. That she prefers her gardener to you for a friend is simply a testimony against your vanity; as to your accusations regarding what you thought you saw pass between them on the divan in her apartments, I reiterate, sir, that the matter has been referred to my solicitor, and any public declaration from you will result in further losses of more than your reputation.

In order to reduce you to penury, or see you imprisoned, my daughter and I are prepared to have her undergo a physician's examination as proof of her chastity. I advise you therefore to keep silent and make your way out of England as speedily as possible, though where you can go is certainly a mystery.

Fare you well,
La Charpillon

1765, London

Sr. Giacomo Casanova di Seingault—

Your recent vengeful prank against my daughter and myself after your cowardly escape to the Continent has caused me to break the silence I would have maintained into eternity otherwise. I am an old woman, and a widow, so that my reputation is of no account in this matter. However, Marianne is still young and unmarried, and cannot now hope to settle herself happily with some good young gentleman . . . and it is all due to your revenge. Is this the Venetian way of things? We in London have long suspected that you Mediterraneans were beastly, monstrous, blood-thirsty; but now, sadly, I have the proof, though no court but heaven exists that can bring you to justice.

I gather you grew tired of legal threats after so many years of fleeing, or imprisonment, or paying out your last ill-gotten funds. I was unaware of your reputation, sir, as was my daughter, and so we proceeded against you to retain what you had freely given, even as we have been forced to do in the past. My daughter's beauty is such that many kind sirs have been generous, more than yourself I wont. None of the others though, discovering that their cravings were not to be met, have replied as viciously as yourself. I fear it is not merely that you are yourself becoming an old man but that you have always played unfairly. Of course your cunning is another matter: it is true, as my solicitor has indicated, that I cannot take action against you for the parrots you have trained to speak those disgusting words against my daughter and myself, but gradually I shall be suing those persons to whom you made gifts of your filthy creatures, as soon as my solicitor can count the exact number and locate each and every bird. The reason I write then is to compliment you on your cruelty, and to inform you that my daughter rejected you in her mind the moment she met you, and indeed saw only a pigeon of her own. It was amusing, Monsieur, to learn that you parted with 10,000 pounds sterling in your effort to possess my daughter, particularly since the gardener you spoke of had his way for nothing more than a rose!

Adieu.

Robert Steiner

1773, Venice

Monsieur,

I have received your wonderful letters so full of courteous and obliging expression that they are proof to me, after all this time away, of your desire to maintain our friendship. Yes, we are all aging, my poor dear, and I imagine for you it is a bit harder than for the rest of us, being sedate as we have been for years anyhow. I had not known you had been away for eighteen years, since that dreadful business of the Leads. But the thought of your return is already all the rage in town, like a favorite son who has made himself famous and who has become synonymous with the nature and the fate of his homeland. Even so I will respect your wishes in the matter and tell no one myself but the immediate family. My daughter, having heard and read of you so many years, is precious in her excitement; to meet you face to face will be a great pleasure—I assure you that I have reassured my husband you would not dream of trifling with our child, he too is getting on in years and was easy to convince by a flattering comparison between yourselves.

As regards the matter of your safe return into our territory I have spoken personally with the Tribunal Secretary who has a writ of mercy in your name, to the word that you may "come, go, and return at will"—that is as far though as the pardon can extend until you present yourself to the three Inquisitors here, whom I am led to believe want to invite you for dinner for the sole purpose of hearing how you did it. You will owe the Secretary a debt, however, for transmitting a portion of a letter he received from Ancona about your current condition; I too was given a copy whose purpose is to fill the Inquisitors with pity rather than to flatter you. I quote, Monsieur: "Reports say that this unhappy rebel against society and the justice of the august Venetian Council attempts to carry himself boldly, head high, his person well-equipped for almost any sudden need to depart wherever he is living. Received in many houses and often announcing his intention of one day returning home, he nevertheless does not stay long in any country these days. That wanderlust in a man of forty-seven is damaging to his health as well as to his mind. Of high stature and rugged excellent appearance, vigorous, very brown in color, bright of eye, short-wigged, and erudite, if long-winded, in his speech—this is the man who has made a career of desire. Yet he is all crumbling, I think, his looks about to turn, and his manner already passé."

It would appear that the report and the several offers of money to reinstate you to Venice have done the trick for the time being. There are so many interesting things to tell you, and people we used to know to gossip about! We cannot wait until you've arrived. Shall I inform Babbini's wife of your plan? I feel certain she will want to dismiss her cicisbeo in favor of you . . .

À bientot
Catta Manzoni

1783, Venice

Dearest Giacomo,

I see by your last precious letter that you will go first to Dresden, Berlin, and Vienna before returning to Paris. Oh, how tragic that you have said good-bye to your native country! And what of me from now on? Where are the joys you alone could procure me—the comedies, the music, the stories? It is true that you love me in your way, and I understand it why you cannot send a sou, though I do not know "dry as a salamander"—is this a fish of some sort? We have heard the news, in part from Signora Manzoni, that you are responsible for the rumor of an impending earthquake in Venice that will dwarf the disaster of Lisbon. The Ambassador still does not know how you managed to plant your false message in his solicitations to the Doge but you can imagine the panic and furor the rumor has caused. In any case I must tell you that the pardon is revoked and you are again a fugitive. We have tried to save you from this and hoped that money would prove the solution; but as we had none of our own and you were too far to be reached quickly we decided to raise the money by selling off your books—alas, they fetched next to nothing, my dear one, certainly not enough to save your reputation and preserve your safety.

The worst comes now. The Tribunal has let it be known that you were an informant these few years. Many now exist who want to eliminate you once for all! I and my husband remain loyal, and will be so as long as he learns nothing. But never return to Venice! The Secretary has said in a public proclamation, "Signor Casanova's magical voyage will end as it began, in a slum as a bastard." They are confiscating all your publications of the last years, leaving none alive—the whole of your translation of the *Iliad*, your eulogy of Monsieur Voltaire, your romance of the Doges, your *Amori* . . . oh, sir, what has happened?! I fear you when you threaten to write no more to anyone. You are not old!! We do not want you to retire. Oh, my darling, where you will go now to be safe and warm is a mystery to all of us here who love, worship, and honor you. Shall I hear your name again?

Yours forever,
Francesca B.

1786, Vienna

Cher,

As you ask I shall inform you of all my wooers and you may judge for yourself by this whether I deserve the childish reproaches you made me in your last letter. What do you mean when you threaten to write me no more? Oh, am I indeed like all the rest? Let us see if my conduct leads to this conclusion: Two years ago I met Count de K and refused to love him in the way he wished; I could not satisfy his desires. A few months afterward I met Count de M who was not as handsome as K but very artful in seducing a young girl like myself; him I felt much for and did everything I could to make him happy. I did not love him however. At some time I informed both K and M that I loved neither though I had pleased one; the other was jealous and they dueled so that I could not help but admire the one I had earlier not pleased. But pleasing K now made the Count of M jealous, and so they fought again. It was by accident that months later K and M and I, each separate for the time being, met at dinner in the house of L. It was there, while the two glared at each other over beef and said nothing, that I realized how much I preferred Lt. D to either. K and M were relieved at my new interest and have since become friendly I am told. As to D, he is gone, but not before he left me the illness you refer to.

Everyone has lectured me on my libertinism, and I must say that coming from you, whom I love truly and desperately despite your years, the chastisement is too much, too painful. I suffer as it is the illness and your distance; now I must add to these your threats. Forgive me having left this letter in the middle here: it is a note come for me from the Palace. Yes, my dear distant one—the Emperor wishes to teach me French, though how he knows I do not speak it I can't imagine. Was this not the fate as well of the little Kasper, the child you loved briefly when you arrived here? Are you procuring women for our king? Heavens! His carriage is already arrived! I must close. I do hope you will continue to write, as I hope I will be not too busy to reply.

Faithfully,
Caton M.

1789, Prague

Monsieur—

For a long time I have felt a desire to evidence to you my estimation of your spirit and eminent qualities; your superb sonnet to me augmented my hope. The inconveniences of childbirth and the disappearance of my husband have caused me to defer my pleasure of sending you greetings. In his absence your letters have been a great comfort. That he is alive I know; where, I know not. I feel that our mutual despair over the occurrences in Paris have united us in spite of the vast difference in our ages. Yes, Monsieur Casanova, Paris is unthinkable to me too. But nothing lasting will come of the disturbances so we must not feel that we are in some way banished from civilization.

You ask if I have heard of the art theft. Indeed I have, and have bitterly refuted the accusation that it was you who arranged for the theft of the Correggio. "Maddallena," it is called, am I correct? I do not recall it from the Dresden years but am assured that the rumor surrounding you and a recently deceased sister are false. I have said so to those in authority, and am certain your name will be exonerated any day.

Your amiability and courtesy engage me enough to take

up pen to remind you that I am a sincere admirer though we have never met. You are wonderfully talented . . . when I wish to point out a person who writes and thinks with true excellence, I name Monsieur Casanova de Seingault. Is it true that you are seriously ill?

Fondly,
Teresa Boisson de Quency

1795, Vienna

Monsieur Casanova,

I am told the Bohemian winter is the worst in a century. I trust that the Chateau Dux of Count Waldstein is providing you with the warmth and food and cheer that you seem to need. I am doubly sorry for your recurrent pains; the baths will surely help reduce the swelling of them. Do not scratch! It must be some comfort to your old age to learn that so many women young and old, rich and poor, are now claiming to have known you intimately. Society, or what is left of it outside France, talks of nothing else but the apparent number of your conquests. Even more amusing, hundreds of husbands are happy to claim that their wives knew you in order to remark that they proved to be the better lovers and effectively beat you at your own games. Those of us who have been intimate with you know the truth however; it is unlikely that any of us would ever come forward to accuse or reproach you. Ultimately, God directs our paths, and yours too was somehow His will. So I hope the stories amuse you in your exile.

I am of course enchanted at the charming reception you accorded the little dog I sent you when I learned of the death of your beloved greyhound, knowing that she would be nowhere better cared for than with you, Monsieur. I hope with all my heart that she has the qualities which may in some fashion help you to forget the deceased.

Respectfully,
Princess Lobkowitz

1798, Toepliz

C.—

We cannot believe you are as ill as they say since it was only last month that you told us over dinner that rude little story. Were I not recovering at the moment myself I would send for our carriage immediately to prove the liars wrong or at least to care for you properly. My poor poor poodle, it is not the case that the servants at Dux are conspiring to murder you—do not let your imagination go at a gallop, rather save it for your memoirs, which I am delighted to hear have given you such diversion this past year. As to your problem of pain, keep at the baths, they will soften them so one of the girls there can push them back into place. My dear, I would care for them myself were I able . . .

All of our household talks of nothing but your health. We think of nothing but your welfare. All of us believe you will be well as soon as the weather turns, and then we shall ride together in my carriage but only if you promise to behave yourself in the park. Adieu! Au revoir! I pray for you.

Elise

PS. Madeira and bouillon accompany this letter.

Matinee

"He admired the sign of the stars, he saluted the clarity of the moon that would see him safely away."

UPSTAIRS JJ hoped to find something else worth packing if only to postpone the moment of quietly leaving. She wouldn't tell anyone, she decided. At first she decided she'd start walking down the road with her suitcase in her hand and her raffia hat on her head. One look out the window reminded her it was the beginning of the middle of the night. In the country. So she amended her plan to include borrowing one of Theo's vehicles—see, no sooner does the love end and even the old oily pickup becomes *his.* She thought about the fact that come to think of it she'd *never* felt like anything was also hers. She amended the plan again in the light of this new feeling. The plan excluded the pickup since otherwise he'd get possessive and decide that needing to get away had really meant wanting to rob her husband of his life. He could have it. She wanted him to focus on the leaving not the taking. One reason for no ———. If she couldn't stop Theo being personally insulted, which he would, she could at least add ——— in there with him, which he would too. Okay she'd leave anything he might remotely consider *his* right where it was. One of the ex-es could drive her anywhere; that'd be good, and they would she knew be supportive since one at a time they'd all done the same thing. Well she'd packed the lot she could carry for a night. JJ saw Theo's slippers peeking out from under the bed and cried. Not so much sad as angry. Oh Jesus! Sad too, too sad. He never should have married anybody. JJ had to sit down.

She did. Suddenly she knew what the ex-es had felt, what whenever she'd seen any of them they'd conveyed with their eyes, their twitches. It dawned on her—what a dope!—for the first time—that's what "dawning" means—that Theo had known perfectly well all along, probably all his life, that he never should have married even once. That was why he wrote about marriage. Oh my God! JJ thought feeling sick to her stomach. He had never *liked* being married! She stretched out on the bed. Now that she thought about it coolly, drily, and when it didn't actually affect her his solicitude and kindness toward the myriad ex-es, which JJ had always found endearing and unusually humane, albeit naive, itself endearing and humane—that general goodwill he'd sprinkle like fairy dust over his past was the cloud cover the sandstorm no the fallout of Theo's fundamental—What's the word. First that comes to mind. *Ruthlessness.* Oh Jesus Christ! She gripped her stomach between her arms like it was a dead baby. Just as clear and unbearable. And that was exactly the word. Theo didn't actually *feel* emotion, he *thought* it. Neurosis was what he felt, it was neurosis he'd married, neurosis he'd not divorced; it was the only thing he'd ever known well. Or wanted to. Needed to. Leaving wasn't going to be too bad after all, JJ concluded. Maybe what she wanted was a taxi though.

Though it was nearing two a.m. Eddie couldn't imagine going back to the inn because Paul wouldn't be there if she did. You-know-who'd be there and he'd keep her awake with accusations recriminations threats demands for Paris and so forth until she'd given him the blowjob he'd be really negotiating all along. It'd be her proof of devotion that she'd have to swallow his jism rather than spit it back onto his balls. Moreover he'd expect to fuck her in the ass first thing in the morning, expecting her to look pained without actually feeling it so he wouldn't have guilt interfering with the thrill. She'd be careful not to use the word shit or he'd get the graphic truth of what was lubricating his dong and be truly furious. Say pussy, he'd say. *Pussy.* Say it again. Softer. *"Pussy."* Again. Husky this time. *Pussy!* He'd go off even rougher than the night before, he'd snake up her colon like a plumber rooting out caked hair, and the gun'd fire with him boring into her, trying to stuff his balls inside as well, howling like a hyena because she'd be unable to suppress the groans which, sourced as deep in her chest as they'd be, he'd mistake for moans. He'd leave the coated slickery pego up there till it shrank, expecting her to hang there like a lowing cow in a pasture while cum and mucus gathered hotly in her gut. Suddenly Eddie realized how much she hated France, the French language, Parisians most of all, and her husband most of all Parisians. Though she'd lived in this house with Theo she wanted to sleep in it tonight with Theo's son. She heard music. Live from downstairs. Paul was playing for her just like she'd . . . Wait a minute!—who were those other instruments? Guitar, drummer, saxophone. Some serenade! Eddie was feeling gang-banged. What she *really* wanted after all was said and done was to sit here on the loo chin in hand elbow on knee doing nothing but fighting sleep. A way of being less than nothing. The lights snapped on, the door flew open, Eddie let out a scream: *Jesus!* they both shrieked. Sorry, said JJ. Toothbrush. You too? Nicole asked taking a look at JJ's eyes. I've done everything, JJ answered.

Answered by silent smirks Berkeley Bill fossicked through the kitchen even though ——— had already been calling for help from the study for several seconds. He walked beside the latecomer with whom he seemed to be acquainted. Neither of them was talking for a long time but it was obvious from the way they brushed each other that they were at ease with one another's company. They didn't need to look at each other either, they could see the drenching moon and the stars, smell the sweetness of overripe vegetation, feel the cooler dampness of dewing, and by sharing these rather than hiding behind them relax a little one another's extreme discomfort to be among people. Bill was drunk and loud in his anxiety, the other used to be that way but for several years had nurtured a kind of paralysis, retiring so remotely from emotional connection that he appeared pompous and preferred that to vulnerability. Bill could be a lout still, the other was too alert. Not that the latter was better, mind you, but it didn't leave one with a hangover next day. Nor could one wake up in love. So tell me Steiner, Berkeley Bill asked quietly, what's a good hotel in Beograd? In Luxor? Canberra? Where don't you skip to these days? Inertia goes two ways boy. Sheesh! Steiner knew Bill was probably right, it'd been a year since he'd stayed put a month and months since he'd passed a week in the neighborhood of people he knew the names of. As usual he began to feel self-conscious, chastized too, particularly since he could've answered Bill's question about hotels in those cities without even consulting his notebook. His was a kind of entropy, he knew, and sooner or later he'd explode like a balloon. And yes, it was embarrassing always coming and going and never quite being anywhere. It sometimes made him feel so absent that he would be amazed other people remembered him. Between passports? Berkeley Bill thoughtfully asked. Steiner shook his head. Despite this exchange they enjoyed walking together; each in his heart would have otherwise wished to be anywhere but the cloying countryside on a sweltering liquor-driven Saturday night. You hear sumphin? Bill grunted straining to listen in the dark. Hey wuz everbody running?

Running from the highway the hillside the grove the kitchen the bay window and the upstairs, women drunks lovers livestock Paul Jack Phoenix Jalal Eddie and JJ converge on the study from the locked door and the freshly broken shutter. The pistol finally reported; ———'s wail from the window eventually registered; the night and its urgency at last collided. As usual life caught up with the party.

Party's over, more than one person had to admit. From the moon, Jack poeticized, gunfire looks like stars. Both inside and out, the study knew hullaballoo, the sort of clamorous blat that danger leaves after it—squalls chatter cackling something like the threat of a completely new gala starting up to celebrate the absence of real harm except that just as quickly everyone's embarrassed and most of them tremble from the surprising need for privacy and quiet. That is how they know things have gone too far for their own liberal sensibilities. They want to celebrate their survival but nobody feels that alive or that innocent. Party's over instead. But even so the crowd wasn't going anywhere, it pressed against the study so forcefully a seepage of rowdy agitators spilled back onto the verandah the kitchen the road. The walls and floor couldn't help but creak under the weight of fifty moiling bodies, and each voice raised louder than the next about the last time this kind of violence occurred in its proximity. In fact if somebody arrived really late to this thing they'd think it was a party instead of after one though there's only one topic of conversation and that is, Where were you when the shot was fired??? The ghoulishness of the talk lightened the load for everyone including JJ, Paul, and ———, who stood triangulated over Theo who sat with his face in his hands more out of fatigue than shame or any other emotion. ——— was purely angry now, now and again cuffing Theo's ear as the only possible ventilation in such a sociable crowd, but the brand of violence that owns up to its ambiguity since ——— could just as easily have embraced Theo for not being dead. Cut it out! Paul shouted, holding back ———'s hand. ——— was crying because of the fear. Only JJ talked softly to Theo, noticing the grim gray nakedness of her husband, and JJ's voice was the only one piercing Theo's coat of confusion—the truth was that for a few minutes there he really *didn't* know where he was or what had happened and so he too was having a small bout with shock over it all, fighting nausea and breathing back his own tears. He heard JJ though because through the incredible din his wife's serenity reminded him that even this would pass, whatever it was. Instead of interrogating him, instead of blaming him or informing him like a child of the consequences for such action, JJ spoke soothingly, inquiring after his needs: water, air, a place to lie down, a doctor, the removal of the guests, did he want to take a walk with her? His face still shut tight in the web of his threaded fingers, Theo shook each concern aside. It took Paul to place his suit jacket over his father's belly before Theo even realized he'd made a spectacle. That caused him to glance over the edge of his hands and when he did, with one eye only, in addition to a room and a doorway jammed with familiar faces, and his wives, and the bleached shivering traumatized ———, Theo regarded his son whom he'd forgot was invited standing before him in nothing but dress pants. What happened to you? he couldn't help but mutter with astonishment. His son did look like hell—a bruised lip, suit pants slung low and too wide as suit pants on skinny people are, scratches covering his chest, twigs and leaves stuck in his hair, his hair standing on end, his feet filthy. It's a rough neighborhood, his son answered. But Theo was already speaking to JJ, regaining his composure enough to ask some pertinent questions and to realize the drama of the situation. Will everybody please leave? Paul turned and said then. One by one everybody turned and repeated it but nobody moved. It'd take a half hour before anyone did, and that couple would have a fatal accident short of Boston, but somehow saying the request out loud made the guests feel like they'd already begun. Then, without warning, slicing through the hum of loose talk and ragged gesture, Theo's voice rose and darkened: That's why I loaded it with blanks, he was saying. Blanks for a ———! Listening closely and in the light of what he'd earlier read ——— knew the real reason though. Poetic justice? mumbled Paul. License, corrected JJ. ——— knew the real reason. You wanted to kill him? JJ asked calmly, politely, this being her most significant query and therefore the one she tried to toss off. Maim him, Theo replied. ——— still thought he knew the real reason for the blanks. He'd been reading the ms.

*Msss*hugeh! Berkeley Bill hallooed the room, arriving late to the scene flanked by Lil and Tina and their foaming beer cans. It was Bill who pointed out Jean-Paul on the verandah filming through the damaged shutters. In fact J-P filmed Bill pointing him out, he even filmed the quartet that came out after him. He is a filming fool! Bill cried out. Paul felt weird seeing Eddie in her husband's clutches. He could tell the guy was determined to leave and that his wife was reluctant. Paul wondered if under the circumstances she'd stay, knowing the family as she did, being an ex-wife as she was, being a current lover as he knew, and just say oh go to hell to the flying frog. He'd have gone nuts if Eddie had cozied up to him right then and there and grabbed his hand. Of course Theo might've too. Also the frog. Where Jean-Paul had been standing on the verandah the bull now was, groaning into the study and dirtying the floor. Then everybody heard the *clop clop* of Casanova sniffing the kitchen and the scrape of dog paws on the stairs. Party's over, twelve people said with a yawn when Theo started to move around a bit, like an athlete walking off a cramp on the field. That got maybe three sets of people into their cars, including the Finches who would not make it alive to Boston let alone the Heel where they lived, but these made such a racket skidding out that others were encouraged to follow. The call of dawn imbedded in a tire. Party's over. It's finally over. O-o-*ver!*

Over an hour later many have left but none who really matter, only the people needed to fill the house and the grounds earlier, the ones who make such an occasion a party instead of friends dropping by for a drink. The rest have calmed and quieted and farmed out again though this time not too far, each thinking how he or she might be of use under the circumstances. What these friends are doing is reminiscing about Theo as if he'd died, plus puzzling out the sketchy details of the night. Among those that haven't left is Eddie, important because she is about to unless Paul can stop her. Jalal and Jack haven't left either, they're still tuning up, people halfway home are only now realizing that Jack's been tuning his Martin for hours without playing a song. And how do you tune a mdanga?? Lil, Tina, and Jean-Paul have no intention of leaving until they're asked, only now are they starting to get along with each other. Paul, it goes without saying, hasn't left. Needless to say Bill. Looking around it appears that Marie hasn't gone either, nor the assassination buff, nor Phoenix saxing by himself under a spruce. Who else? Whoever's upstairs, in the woods, in the cellar. Can't locate everybody at such short notice. However, that is definitely Paul, wearing one of his father's robes, smoking with Steiner under the arbor. He interrupts his sentence about his father to watch Nicole cut loose from her husband presumably to bid farewell to Theo and JJ. Steiner understands it when Paul tiptoes around the side of house, leaving him standing alone in mid-listen under the leafy roof.

Roof! Roof! Roof! Quijote said quizzing the sneaker of the man in the dark of the arbor. The retriever peed against a rose. He got shoed out of the way just as he'd been doing everywhere; it was discouraging; he went and lay down in the stable, waiting for Odysseus, he thought. He'd go blind if necessary, blind and lame if they wanted, he was that unhappy, unloved. His eczema was killing him. Steiner watched the dog mosey off, sorry he hadn't scratched its ears but whatever it was the dog suffered made him stink like fish. Steiner had understood it when Paul tiptoed around the side of the house, leaving him standing alone in mid-listen under the leafy roof. *Roof!* Quijote was calling out of the night, punctuating the drama with some breed of animal slander. The drama made Steiner grateful, it relaxed him, he could enjoy the gravity of the moment much more than he had the fun before it. The sort of psychic tragedy that appeared to be unfolding on this farm seemed made for Steiner's presence in part because he knew enough to form no opinions. Deferred judgment entitled him to hang around even though at that point he had met Theo only a few times, and then had not spoken to him alone. The verandah was deserted at last, the broken shutter continuing to butt the wall of the house, the lights inside assuming the sleepy befogged aura of a spent mood. Emptying, quiet, littered rooms which Steiner observed displayed the aftermath of concord, discord, and the decay of both. It might have ended there, with the gothic rambling house growing torpid and soft, with voices ghosting to exhaustion in the woods and on the highway, with incidents fixed by their fluidity and the people who'd inhabited them no longer certain who said or did what or why. But it didn't. Steiner had the misfortune of ascending the stairs to the verandah at the moment Theo threw JJ out. Through the space where the shutter was hanging by one stressed bolt a suitcase flew, hit a post, and rolled into the bushes. Steiner looked around, stopped what he was doing, thought he heard voices in the study. A few seconds later the notorious gun hummed like a wasp out the window, gashing the same post and bouncing along the wood floor. It happened to land at Steiner's feet, so after he'd looked around again, grinning in case he was being seen, he picked the thing up. Heavy. It was still loaded. With blanks. Presumably. He thought in these staccato chunks because the occasion generated just the breathless suspense he often sought, and that couldn't help but slice his consciousness into watchful blips of recognition. The discontinuity was nothing new to him. That is why Steiner *instinctively* removed his handkerchief and wiped his fingerprints from the grip of the weapon, then using the cloth as a glove set the pistol down on a seat cushion that was too small for the wicker chair. What traveled next must have been a powerful message in the study and surely demanded serious propulsion—Theo's typewriter sailed briefly, wobbling and nose-diving, before it crashed against the post's pocked face with a melancholic tinny *sproing.* With that Steiner might have entered the study and offered to bring his experience to bear on the event, namely what should be tossed next. But again he didn't. No. While he did enter the study he had nothing in mind but trying to be casual about it.

To be casual about it the man in the mustache conspicuously saluted Marie as he passed her on his way to the bathroom. Once inside he rinsed his face, contemplating the tiny hoop in his left ear that his long pelted hair ordinarily covered. It was not good enough that he should meditate. He'd thought that if he stood respectfully before the mirror he would be spared this time. He was wrong. Again wrong! For years and years, for so many years he could not count them, he had been wrong, and always about the same trouble—that if he stood respectfully or sat or squatted or lay flat, breathed deep or shallow or rapidly or slowly, said prayers cursed saints dreamed of pussy real pussy not the stupid cat that that silly red drunk had been pining for all night—wrong that if he did these things singularly or in combination, and there were hundreds of combinations for analytic postures, he would be spared. Just once spared! Always he was proved wrong. Still he knew nothing else but the desire to be spared and so must keep trying. Tonight it was the turn of a respectful honest examination of his face to spare him, or rather to fail to spare him. The true appraisal of the crags pits scars and morbid creases of the skin of his face ought to count for something; he would not avoid the rodent-like eyes, his self-possessed mirrors so that he must have the sight before him of mirror within mirror to right the dread image, to authenticate his infernal nature. Still he was not to be spared! Even if he were to assume the most drastic measure of forswearing his vice, it would not matter. Even if he were to present himself before the world for what he knew himself to be, it would make no difference. Even if he were to prove to the public the pattern and the order of his decay he could not expect for a single micro-second to be spared a single erg of the awful experience. And then he wasn't! The sickness was hideous, the retching so unabated and loud that he instinctively turned the tap to the sink and started the cold water pouring forth. How it could worsen each time he did not know! The nausea even as he vomited was unrelieved, the constriction of his throat and stomach like grips wringing him dry so that he tore at his flesh with fingernails grown the length of claws on a small jungle cat. But breaking skin and bleeding was not shock enough to deceive his system, so that he retched again, and again, the terrific wave of acid air he was expelling as usual dry, wrenching the throat muscles, the arid sensation gagging him, leaving no space to breathe and no pause in the spewing up of exactly nothing. If he could only think it away! If he could *think* of something! Even this he viscerated, like osmosis, through his pores, *feeling* what others would be able to think as well as what they'd feel. It was too much raw sensation. He vomited so long and barkingly that he went to his knees to disgorge nothing inside the porcelain funnel, inhaling through his pukey nostrils the smells of everyone's piss and shit. Farther down toward the flushing whirlpool he brought his head, the gray pelt hanging now across the hole of the plumbing so that finally his nose touched the awful water. Then he brought up a sound like the chucking of life, retching life for everyone, everyone was that woman down the hall. And then it was over, like flood receding, and when it was quiet again he was already getting stronger, as usual, beginning to feel very strong with the tap running, suddenly, as usual, a surge of adrenalin to accompany the sensation of risk. He did not need to contemplate anything. He had no need to imagine his face, body, or anyone else's. The man with the mustache inhaled profoundly, happily, returned to life and to himself, flicking out the light when he heard footsteps, and only then opening the narrow stiff window to the mansard, only then squeezing himself through the casement, grinning and victorious. Once on the roof he smoothed the ends of his mustache, poised delicately as a dancer thirty feet from the earth. From his position he could see the commotion in the study begin to fade, observe the earliest traffic head home. Could he have been seen hovering like a thief on the roof's decline? He didn't particularly worry, he never worried once his strength returned, and as usual he didn't resist the occasion for offering his arms to the moonlight. His cape swelling behind him, scooping up the breeze from the surrounding wood, his chest broad and thick, his suede boots precarious on the tiles, the man held his mustache into the light. He admired the sign of the stars, he saluted the clarity of the moon that would see him safely away.

Away from the house and her husband, her ex, and his father, Nicole and Paul met near the bones of the eaten pig. Both had been looking forward to a sharp sizzling embrace, wanting to fondle each other through their clothes, a pleasure they'd earlier been denied because of their eagerness; now they were eager to be restrained, eager to enjoy the thrill of the secret encounter, aware since they were sober that what they were up to was risky. Otherwise they desired nothing but to knock their teeth together and try to suck each other's tongue out by the roots. They had raced to meet—Eddie through the living room past the open door of the study and hurdling the horse paddies on the kitchen floor before swinging wide the springy screen, and Paul barefoot on tiptoe in his father's robe dashing across the grass exactly parallel to Eddie's pace. Yet when together they arrived and recognized one another only vaguely because of the robe on the one hand and the sunhat on the other, because they were breathless with excitement and anticipation, because the light from the kitchen was harsh and impersonal and pouring over them, Paul and Nicole fumbled for words twenty feet apart. Their efforts to laugh fell flat. They couldn't regain the breath that might normalize everything, make even their dreamy sex in the grove believable. Paul toed weeds, tugging at them and really seeing if he could uproot them by the force of his foot even though they were prickly. Eddie watched as if it mattered, sighing gravely, stirring the ground with her sandal. Pretty soon the lovers were staring at nothing but weed, feet, and mastic swine bone. That's it then, Paul said, venturesome, testing at least a little the heat of Eddie's residue. Seems so, she mumbled into the brim of her mushroom straw. They remained a hearse-length separate exploring the dirt as if panning for gold. That's it then, Theo's son repeated with the arch defiance of someone wondering how certain dangerous words will actually sound leaving lips. His tone buttressed the hardness of the phrase. In an instant, and to the surprise of both, Nicole was gone, returned inside the house to say goodbye to her former husband—who was asleep upstairs by that time, she learned from JJ who sat sipping scotch alone in the study's dark. Briefly Eddie thought that since she couldn't have a last look at Theo she might risk his son just once more—it was as impulsive an idea as hurriedly walking away had been a moment before. Oh she was crazy all right! That was beside the point! Everything's beside the point, JJ informed her. You can have 'em both as far as I'm concerned. But starting back along toward the kitchen, anxious to escape the new wife's dreadfulness, Nicole saw Paul's robed figure smoking a cigarette with someone under a tree. The pair seemed deep in conversation. Was it about her? She paused to take a breath, her trigger for ingesting true need at any given instant. She gazed again at the arbor. Who needs it?! Nicole said to herself.

Her feet knotted on Theo's desk JJ sits slumped and thin as though on the hopeless side of an argument she's somehow begun. Theo and ———, both gone, are no apparent cause for alarm. As a result JJ clinks the ice in her drink, a quiet salute to the absence of physical harm anyway. Her hair, concealing bare shoulders, is the color of the cowhide bag she has indicated to Steiner in the doorway with her thumb. Rising reluctantly she searches the space between herself and the adjacent staircase, letting Steiner know that Theo is asleep, that ——— is either himself upstairs or gone home. The sadness of her vantage hardens even as she pauses once again, jarring her memory, glossing her eyes, troubling her stomach. In her expression there is finality painfully won, and as mysterious to her witness in the doorway as a rocking chair that swings on its own power, as a pebble dropping from nowhere at one's feet, as finding the car door open on a cold winter morning. That is, a finality mysterious because until it arrives it could only be considered unnatural and impossible, but which when once taken hold of seems inevitable, organic, as if grace itself. On JJ's face that finality has the staggering vacuity of a pony's interminable stare. When she slides the bag for Steiner to accept he steps back to the verandah instead. Doesn't touch a thing anywhere within reach. He pockets his hands. Though she is hesitating constantly, swinging the scotch glass in her hand and assaying the study's litter, once she's on the verandah too she gazes in the direction of the impenetrable road—north, ahead, into the future, a gesture that causes

Steiner to look that way too in the hope however that something huge dangerous and ugly is coming toward the house. Steiner is nothing less than hypnotized that she has singled him out for the dubious honor of driving her away. Between marriages, or what? JJ asks. What, Steiner replies lifting the leather.

The Death of Casanova

[THE last week in October, the year 1787, the Villa Betramka outside Prague, on a writing desk in the attic sheets of smooth clean paper strewn in no order though on the occasional white space a large inked musical staff standing out like an enormous sleeping bug—nothing stirs for a long time, no shadows from the single angular window overlooking a garden, no scrape of feet, no nervous humming, nothing to indicate a living presence except the barely perceptible movement of dust around a body in the draft; and then, later, in the chiaroscuro effect a sigh is heard, more or less out of the picture or scene. A child's distant giggle from the garden at last wakens MOZART *who, slumped in a corner of the floor—they have refused him an easy chair, knowing he'd rather sleep—stares at*

the new quills to be sharpened, shrugs them aside, yawns, farts, and scratches his genitals before drawing toward him with his boot the manuscripts that he'd earlier tossed beyond arm's reach. He looks first at the one, then at the other. Back at the first, the second, reverses the order of his examination before sucking in his breath and recognizing that the child's playful cries down below are what woke him from his sleep. The first manuscript he balances on his left knee, the second his right, weighing them, thinking he'll toss both in the air and see how they mingle when they land. He picks up the first, the left, thumbing through it like a story he knows too well; the second he tries to flip through but each time is stopped by something that catches his attention, his "fancy," like a story he only knows the surface of. Mozart glances again at the title page: Histoire de ma fuite des prisons de la Republique de Venise, *the author anonymous but for his location at Dux in Bohemia. Sighing, Mozart glances at the other ms., sees "DaPonte" scribbled in ink as an afterthought, a question mark beside the name, then groans at his own notations and marginalia. He can't forever ignore the impulse to look up from the floor at the desk in the sunlight where each of the heavily blacked musical notes C A B A occupies its own sheet of paper and stands eight inches high. The child screams in the garden, from pleasure or terror Mozart can't be sure—he realizes it's impossible by a sound alone to distinguish joy from fear. Now, with a conspicuous rush of energy the genius is on his feet heading for the window which is sooty, dusty, cloudy to see through—though he can view only dimly—the child in the garden running circles around a hawthorn, moving now fast, now slow, turning to see if she is pursued, to see* that *she is pursued, as the game calls for. But no one is there at her back, so Mozart sees her stop, turn full around, now with more concern than before in her expression, her disappointment somehow clearer than either fear or joy to Mozart. As though it has dawned on her that the game, while not actually over, has been called off or its rules violated by her playmate, the child takes a deep breath, lowers her head, and twists about again, finally relaxing the tension of the sport, starting to walk with a slight limp and kick to her foot, bewildered, angry, scowling. Mozart too is disappointed, having lost the potential of the moment, its inspiration and import, the game having trailed off like his ms. into nothing. Timed perfectly, the child in the garden and Mozart in the attic sigh their defeat, she walking to the bottom of the maze and he glancing first at the desk beside him, then at the mss. on the floor, at last at the corner of the attic where he can in fact make out the shape of his sprawling body in the dust. The dust looks inviting. For no particular reason, with his face in the heat of the sun that streams through the window, Mozart is aware that flies are buzzing near his face. Suddenly the child outside screams louder than before, a real stentorian blast that shakes Mozart's teeth—when she'd least expected it, when she'd thought the game was over, the rules brutally violated, when like Mozart she felt the sadness of the situation, only then did the old man leap out at her from behind the tree, cry* **BOO***! at the top of his withered lungs, and grab at her with his bony claws. Mozart too can feel his heart pounding, the little girl pursued now along the garden's colorful maze, sick stuttering Casanova thudding after with a walking stick for a third, a balancing leg.*

And so, with the sight of the aged lover in view, and literally locked into the attic because the premiere performance of his new opera is three days away and the score isn't nearly complete, Mozart glances back and forth again and again at the scene in the garden, the writing desk in the sun, the ms. of Casanova's prison escape, the dusty corner, glancing at each more and more quickly all the time, in different dizzying combinations as though searching for—

[The garden sounds have faded, the sunlight brightened to an artificial spotlight; the rest of the attic has disappeared in darkness. Mozart steps forward into the expansive glare of the overhead beam of unnatural sun. His head bobs slightly, as though he alone has heard something. Slowly, as it raises in volume, the rest of us begin to hear it too]:

Mozart

Mozart
When the day is fading, D J ?
You who ____ed your mother, her sister,
Her sis - ter's daugh - ter, yr dad's whore,
Your fa - ther's second wife, their new child,
Your father's se - cond mis - tress —
Da - da Da - da Da - da Dum —

[The song done, the spotlight eases into the more natural tone of the sun as it earlier pierced the window. Ironically the attic itself brightens so that the desk, the mss., the dusty corner—all but forgot in the shock of Mozart's aria—are again visible. Mozart senses the end of the instant and relaxes, returns himself to "real life," resuming the posture and expression of a human being instead of a performer or a dreamer rapt by his dream. In a few seconds the attic is exactly as it was before Mozart began to sing, even the child's laughter is the same, and only then do we realize that in fact no time is supposed to have passed, that the entirety of the song has flashed through Mozart's imagination in an instant. He too understands this theatrical illusion and the significance of its occurence; thus, rushing to the writing desk, sitting

and scribbling, glancing out the window at each successive cry of the child—all these examples of obsession make sense. The genius hums, draws his quill across the air, taps his boot for the tempo, then stabs the space before him with a sharp final punto! *He lowers his head and goes on writing, sheaf after sheaf of paper piling up on the floor where the composer has thrown it. Now a* VOICE *that Mozart doesn't himself hear begins to speak—disembodied, ghostly, unexpected—and this time rather than a spotlight and silence all around the attic dims, the garden noises lower but both remain perceptible. And while the child goes on giggling and Mozart feverishly composes, both are oblivious to]:*

VOICE: *"At the age of nine Casanova rarely spoke or was spoken to. His nose bled frequently and the little boy became certain he was dying. In order to cure him his grandmother took him to a witch's house on the Isola Maggiore where he was shut up in an airless trunk while an incantation was sung in the dark above his head. The nosebleeds ceased as of that day but in their place Giacomo began to have dreams of beautiful women speaking to him through the darkness in a language he could not understand. To understand their words better he learned to read. Then he learned to write as well so that even as he understood the beautiful women in his dreams they, in their distant palaces and towers and magic bottles, could read him too. Only then, after he had learned to read and to write, did he speak, and for some years only to women. Soon he was playing the violin and studying for the priesthood."*

[Light brightens briefly in the attic, noise increases in the garden, Mozart scratches his head and scrapes his

boot on the floor. The composer resumes his furious writing, the child's cries retreat, the attic again falls to a murky burnished shadow. Either the lights miscued, someone thought it essential to be reminded of Mozart's presence, or something important but undetected took place in the attic. The unseen voice recommences, again keeping the genius deaf to it]:

VOICE: *"By successfully identifying his various lovers with literary conventions of his time, Giacomo falsified even the orgasmic experience, denying ecstasy its approximation to death—the popular image of the day. In this sense his fear of death led Casanova to inauthentic sex, but by falsifying that inauthentic experience he intuitively negated a negation, basing his entire sensual aesthetic on the philosophy of antithesis, saying to his conquests such things as—"*

[The dusty corner where Mozart originally lay suddenly lights up like the sun, and in place of the composer who continues to scratch away at his desk in the dark CASANOVA *himself steps forward, saying such things as: "Where you are fatty I am not; where you are moist I am dry; where you are rubeate I am blanch—this is the drama that sees your tunnel await my troika, your mountains my climbers, your button my threaded spittle."*

Sudden blackness of the corner. Sudden light where Mozart is at work. He rises so quickly from the chair that it falls over backward. Somewhere someone titters at the accident. What has moved Mozart so to disrupt his intense work ethic? The garden is silent, Mozart notes. He gazes out the window, stares as though in disbelief, his jaw flexing, his mouth fishing, his breath curdling so deeply that the wall of his chest could explode. What is it? *The composer stamps his foot, starts running a circle with one leg in place for a pivot, each time he passes the window slowing down long enough for a peek into the garden, moaning at the sight, circling faster, gradually realizing he's looking for something in the attic—but what?* What the hell is going on? *The genius sees no help for it, the window doesn't budge when he tries to push it open, nor can anyone below hear his cries of "Wait! Stop! What are you doing there?!" So he hesitates but a moment before raising the chair over his head and bringing it with a deafening crash through the tinctured pane—]*

Jacques, é u-na bam-bina mo-no!

[Shouts of "Beast!" "Pervert!" "Effleuré!" *resound through the cool villa; the noise of urgent commotion traverses not only the garden and the villa's foyer but seems to coil up the staircase into the recessed bedrooms, where a grand dame awakens from her sleep to wonder at the turmoil, and below stairs, where a gardener has pulled out of the chambermaid because of it, to settle finally and of course center stage where Mozart at the attic window can only shout louder and louder to Casanova to let the child go. Then suddenly, when the gardener, his trousers half-buttoned, his feet and chest bare, has reached the scene to grip old deaf Casanova by the wrist, Mozart swings around, stares up at the ceiling—his face funny with the sanctified look of inspiration, divine intervention, etc.—as if life has stopped around him again. He bends over the sheets of paper that have been flying the*

*attic for hours now, beads of artistic breakthrough pearling his powdered face: "*Ja!*" he cries. "*Ja! Mein Gott!*" *And in his eagerness to get it all down immediately, before it's lost and floating in time for some other composer later in the history of music to grasp it coursing by, ignores the fact of the tossed chair, the one that smashed the window. Heavily, heatedly, in the throes of the fleeting moment of musified genius, Mozart crooks his knees to sit and lands square on the floor behind him. All goes* **BLACK**.*]*

FINALE

[The return of the spotlight. The silence of the attic. MOZART *transfixed by the sheaf before him. The floor so covered with paper curling at the edges that there's nowhere to walk. The composer checking and rechecking his visions and re-visions. Running down a list of disjointed words, names and phrases that seem to mean to him, such as—]*

MOZART [*facing us*]:	Homme à la Rose, Fantasia, Vice Punished, Pasticcio
	Venice, Fuga, Ultratumba, Portogallo, Maraña, the
[*chanted*]	Battle of Tolosa, Mascherata, Gonzalo, Trapisonda,
	Salon, Matinée, Bandolini, Ondina da Lago——
[*shouted*]	Nein! Nein! Nein! Nein!
	Pederoos Geest, Vengeance from the Tomb, Steinerne
[*building*]	Todten-Gastmahl, Stone Feast,

Sasso Feste, Kamennyi
Gost, Karácsonyéj, Convidado de
piedra, The stone
[*crescendo*] guest, Steinerne Gast!! Ja! Ja! Ja!
Ja!

[A knock at the door. A key turning in the lock. The lifting of the latch. The slow twist of the handle, ornate, gothic, iron. The creaky opening of the door, thick, wood, tall. Mozart stares dumbfounded, about to faint but too curious to let himself do so. He steps back from the writing desk, opens his arms, indicates the scattered paper, the quill poised in its stand, the missing chair. Prepares to speak, knowing his words may mean life or death, or both. Still we cannot see the visitor because of the open door blocking our field.]

MOZART [*weakly*]: "You! What do you want? Why are you here? Who invited you?!
[Mozart backs off farther as though the visitor has begun to move or made a gesture, sudden, toward him. A reluctant intruder? We do not know.]

STEINERNE GAST:

[Mozart nods at the words obviously only he can hear. He sighs at them. Raises a hand before his face as if to block their arrival. Denies. Rejects. Plugs his ears. Then, resigned, removes his fingers from his head and slumps standing.]

MOZART [*stricken, shocked, but not surprised*]: Kill him? Bring him to an end? A moral consequence? But why? I can't!

STEINERNE GAST:

MOZART: I know! I know! You needn't remind me! But I in turn have created him! How would *you* feel if someone . . . I know there's no one who could, that's beside the point! Yes. Yes. *Yes.* **YES**. Of course you have the power. The right? Well, sure, I suppose you do. You understand that all this is simply your point of view, your vantage, your judgment, your need, your . . . Yes. Yes. YES.

STEINERNE GAST:

MOZART [*frustrated*]: As per the creator analogy, while I must kill off Don Giovanni in the opera, you'll erase Casanova from the book? You can do that to yourself?!

STEINERNE GAST:

MOZART [*awed*]: What do you mean, life is not art???

STEINERNE GAST:

MOZART [*dumbstruck*]: What do you mean, this whole thing is art?????!

STEINERNE GAST:

MOZART [*overcome, clutching his heart*]: What do you mean, IT'S ALL IN YOUR HEAD??!!

[Unable to catch his breath Mozart turns toward us. Squeezes his eyes as if looking a great distance for sight of land, a ship at sea, a **UFO**. *His face pinches. His forehead crenelates. His hand covers his mouth in recogni-*

tion. Slowly, with the majesty of his situation realized, Mozart turns back to the Steinerne Gast, the unseen stone visitor, the unwelcome guest, ineluctable intruder, the alien, etc., etc.]

STEINERNE GAST:

MOZART: Calm down? How can you say calm down? And what do you mean I've got another four years? I'm only thirty-two!

STEINERNE GAST:

MOZART [*trembling but past horror*]: I don't care that it's three more than Don Giovanni's got—he's not alive! And Casanova?! When are you killing him off??

STEINERNE GAST:

MOZART: But I'll *already* be dead! How come he gets to live a long life when he's nothing but a smelly gasbag?

STEINERNE GAST:

MOZART: Oh . . . Now? . . . Yes, you *can* do anything after all . . . But *this*? To my friend? Well, only *a bit* of a gasbag. Only a *smallish* fart.

STEINERNE GAST:

MOZART [*quietly, gravely*]: I've never seen the fear of death, no.

[The re-return of the spotlight. The silence, the papers, Mozart, the corner, the dust, the chanted and sung list of

words, names, and phrases, all as before the arrival of the Steinerne Gast, as though the entire scene with the intruder has been in Mozart's imagination, which we suddenly comprehend because of—]

MOZART [*facing us*]: . . . Feste, Kamennyi
[*crescendo*] Gost, Karácsonyéj, Convidado de piedra,
The stone guest, Steinerne Gast!!
Ja! Ja!
Ja! Ja!

[A knock at the door. A key turning in the lock. The lifting of a latch. The slow turning of the handle, ornate, gothic, iron. The creaky opening of the door, thick, etc. Mozart stares but without surprise; rather with a sense of familiarity that gradually becomes an expression of relief, then briefly puzzlement, and yet more slowly passing through hesitation, apprehension, terror, and gloom. After gloom Mozart's face is fait accompli.]

MOZART: Giacomo! *Buon giorno,* Giacomo! *Comé sta?*

CASANOVA [*behind the door so he cannot be seen*]: I've brought my notes for the second act. Da Ponte's mucked it up as usual, so I was thinking . . .

[C looks past M and stares dumbfounded, pale, entering our field of vision stooped, powdered, caned, but trembling now, about to faint and too curious to let himself do so. He steps back from the writing desk. Opens his withered arms. Indicates the sheaf he has just placed. Prepares to speak, knowing his words will not make a difference.]

CASANOVA [*glib as usual when he's anxious*]: Who's your tall ugly friend, W A?

MOZART [*looking around, seeing nothing, catching himself to realize that the SG has arranged to be visible only to C*]: Huh? Um, nobody but this visitor here, come expressly to meet you.

CASANOVA [*taken aback, furrowing his bushy beetle brow, pondering*]: How'd he get in? I'm the one with the key.

[Unable to continue the charade Mozart backs off the center of the scene, seats himself on the edge of the writing desk, searching for darkness, for dust, wishing he were still curled in the corner and the little girl giggling. He puts his head in his hands. Despair. Then realizes the original point of this encounter and so raises his face to observe Casanova's expression when the latter understands that he is meeting his death. Suddenly both M and C hear]:

The music from Act II, Scene V, Don Giovanni, *the cast of* COMMENDATORE/*Steinerne Gast,* DON GIOVANNI/*Casanova, and* LEPORELLO/*Mozart]:*

SG: Casanova,
your life is
over
No more, old
C, no more
the rover.

C: Ah,
Giacomo
Girolamo?

Ah, Chevalier Seingalt? Comte de Farussi? Eco-néon? Antonio Pratolini too?

M: Not Eupolemo, not Paralis? No, not everyone?!

C: Yes! Everyone!

SG: Yes, every name—Pantessena, Neuhaus, Snout, Gigi, Robert, le Grand Viveur, Giro, Vidi,
Each and every alias, all but *He,*
Each must die and in each the noble C!

M: Like a man
who is sick
of a fever
All my limbs
do is tremble
and shake

C: And am I to
be afraid? I to
quake?

SG: You're on
the ropes,
you don't
even know
it!

C: I'm on the ropes but I'll never show it!

SG: Venice to Petersburg to Nice,
Cologne, Stuttgart, Munich,
London, Paris, Zurich—
You name it, you've seen it!

M: He names it, he's seen it, I write it!

C: Don't forget the best of them—
Genoa, Antibes, Genève . . .

SG: Etcetera!

C: But I'll see no more?

SG: You won't!

M: He'll see no more.

C: No man shall make me coward,
I feel no fear. *You'll* see!

SG: Give me your hand and shake on it!

C: *Eccola! Ohimé!* What a big hand you have!

SG: Kneel and think what I must take,
Casanova, first from you.

C: And if what you've said is true,
Also Mozart? Him too?

SG: In life M dies *before* you!

C: Ah, art! Ah, art! Tricky art!

SG: Speak yr piece, and let's start!

C: I've loved racy tastes: maggoty cheese,
Gamey game, pitchy women, their moms!
At least I have never been Swiss!
All my women were sixteen!

CHORUS: He inspected, perfected the condom!
He invented the striptease!

C: And I uttered the famous words—
What proves that the revolution
Should have arrived is its arrival.
Henriette!! Remember me??

M: When C dies it is of gout,
Small pox, adenoids, boredom,
Pleurisy and penumonia,
Malaria—plus sex!

CHORUS: And so he lived as a philosopher
But he died a Christian.

ALL: It was nearly the Nineteenth Century, the age of Napoleon, the death of the Venetian state, the rise of Industrial Capital, the birth of Karl Marx. And so on. Vivaldi and Voltaire were dead. Rousseau and Ben Franklin, these too were dead. Cagliostro, he as well, in Rome. Dead was Madame de Pompadour; and Robespierre, dead. Mozart was dead. Now too Casanova is dead.

BLACK!
COUNT TEN BACKWARDS
SLOWLY
NO CHEATING
NOT *THAT* SLOWLY

[Slowly the lights come up until we begin to believe the show is over. But the lights are fixed midway and do not get any brighter than a golden glow, the dim murky aura we've grown used to, through which we gradually recognize Mozart lying on the floor in front of the writing desk, unconscious, exactly as and where he fell when he'd forgot there was no chair to sit on. For several seconds nothing moves, during which time we hear shouts from the garden—"Beast!" "Pervert!" "Effleuré!"*—just as we heard them before. The child is crying now as loudly as*

she had been laughing. The garden sounds fade until they are indistinguishable background noise: humming bees, singing birds, crying child, screaming servants, all a blend of static. Then, only then, after another ten seconds or so to think of what we're seeing, Mozart's arm must lift itself off the floor. The genius is alive! He makes a fist, opens the hand, then repeats the gesture several times. Mozart groans. As usual, farts. He tries to heft his head, it falls back, he tries again, fails again, tries, succeeds, gets to knees, snarls at self, looks at us, periwig askew, tongue lolling, arms aquiver at the effort. Suddenly he freezes and his eyes bug. Mozart has remembered something. Something is struggling to come to the fore. He narrows his stare, concentrating, not breathing, like there's a blackhead to squeeze, poised there on his hands and knees in the golden glow like a man in a sauna searching for his lost keys or his watch or a magical ring.]

MOZART [*smirking*]: *Tu oublieras aussi,* Mozart!

[The genius claps his hands with startlement, recognition, therefore losing his precarious balance and falling forward. But just before his nose would touch the attic floor and probably knock him out yet again, Mozart executes a series of rapid perfect push-ups with his fingertips, on the last springing so that he stands alive and well in the gradually brightening attic.]

MOZART [*grinning*]: What a dream! What a vision! What a way to end!

[The attic is bright now with the illusion of flooding sunshine. Magically, the sheaf has neatly piled on the

writing desk, in exactly the way Mozart wants, or will. He grabs a handful of clean sheets and his quill and perches on the window ledge where, glancing frequently at the commotion below, he writes furiously. We hear Mozart singing low, as if to test the notes and lyrics—]

MOZART: *". . . a ce-nar te-co m'in-vi-tasti"*

[Mozart looks quickly at us, quizzically, perhaps hurt, holding his quill steady in his hand. His left arm relaxes and the sheaf of papers cascades to the attic floor, a few of the sheets sailing out into the darkness beyond the scene. His right hand opens and the quill flutters joylessly out of it along Mozart's left pantaloon and toward the floor, but it continues to drift in the air, flying until we are convinced it's a wing. Since he's been postured awkwardly at the window, when Mozart's legs give way it's both at the same time, knees buckling, calves curling like pasta, the feet splaying with the weight of the falling body. At that moment not only the lights come up full but the houselights too, and Casanova bursts through the attic door thought to've been locked the entire time, without his walking stick and no longer hunched over or aged; he hurries to Mozart's crumpled body, goes onto one knee as spryly and comfortably as in the old days when he'd kiss a woman's shoe or investigate her petticoats. By now Mozart is motionless and silent, Casanova has placed Mozart's head in his lap and lifts his own hands for us to see. Everywhere there is what appears to be blood. His face ashen, his eyes glassy, his voice breathless, unrecognizable—]

CASANOVA: Is there a doctor in the house? He's been shot! He's been shot!

[What were at first murmurs rustling through the rest of us, then awkward burbles of worry and bewilderment at the sight of Casanova's dripping palms, turn instantly into screams and shouts, some of us calling out **THIS ISN'T FUNNY ANYMORE A THING LIKE THIS**, *others crying the words* **POLICE CALL THE POLICE**, *still others sitting silent and smug in their seats, despite the house lights, smiling to each other as if they're in the know that the latest turn of events is just the obligatory bow to Brechtism and the Alienation Effect that almost everything wanting to be considered sophisticated and serious—even certain TV shows—is informed by these days. The noise becomes a din because of the echoing walls, the crowd craning forward and standing on their seats to see, reporting to each other what they thought they saw and heard before, what they think they see and hear now, what they're sure they will see, will hear before long; the aisles clogged, rows filling fast, the attic impossible to view except from first few seats, and in general the scene getting enough out of hand that one of us makes his or her way to the writing desk and, facing us,—]*

PERSON FACING US: Let's proceed quietly and in an orderly fashion so the authorities may do the job of unraveling the facts of this case.

[Such a studied remark sets the lot of us going full tilt, some convinced now the whole thing's been trumped up, what's more an insult at these prices, another example why movies are doing so well and every other art form seems to be dying from its own smell. In short, we're angry now, good and miffed, less a crowd and more a mob, sort of looking for Mozart to be dead or else we've been cheated. A few of us have begun vaulting onto the pros-

cenium using the bent backs of others, some are using the velvet drapes to swing from loges, boxes, and balconies onto the attic floor. From the vantage of the chandelier on the rococo ceiling we can see that Mozart hasn't budged and there's a small round hole either through or painted onto his forehead. The attic floor is overrun by us, punching ushers, shoving cops, ambushing the servant, the grand dame, the whining child of the garden, and cursing all forms of performance. After a thunderous crash of glass we can see a space involuntarily made on the attic floor where beside Mozart Casanova now lies, his skull shattered under the wig, his brains pouring under the shoes of those of us nearby. One of us puts an ear to C's heart, presses C's wrist, then stands and clears an air wave before shouting—]

ONE OF US: They've killed Casanova! Casanova's dead!

[Cries ring out for the Author of this catastrophe as the writing desk follows the chair through the window that opens onto the garden—a shout OW! *is heard and two of us emerge from the other side of the dirty window rubbing our heads—]*

TWO OF US: Which dumb fucker of ya's threw a goddamn desk out the winda here? Ya Fucker! Asswipe!

ALL: Author! Author! Author! Author! Beast! Pervert! *Effleuré!*

[Real pandemonium now. Everything out of control. Even a reasonable character, such as myself, is caught in the whirlwind of anarchy—the noise, the screaming, the trampling, the cursing, etc., etc. Overwhelming rush of people. A grenade. Somebody knifed in the balcony. You

get the idea. Well, in the midst of it the house lights darken, we get wilder, then terribly quiet, then motionless at whatever we've been doing that moment, when—]

STEINERNE GAST:

The Adventures of You

THE oily mole, the porcelain jaw, the brittle legs, a necktie fiercely knotted and caught by the breeze, his furtive almond eyes, his vision squeezed to an horizon of blips. The smile. A moist buck-toothed grin that arrested us more than did the badge which one of his understudies displayed from a distance. Someone here call about death? one of the uniforms asked. On the verandah where JJ and Steiner had been taken by surprise we inhaled our wonderment, gathering on the instant like a threatened tribe. Even Theo could be seen to lean out of an upstairs window, and even Steiner set down the leather bag with resignation. Thatuz me, called Berkeley Bill stepping out of the crowd to take credit. His remark signaled the young brassy uniforms to act. They did, by first nudging Bill's elbow into the now deserted study, then in pairs fanning out across the grounds and up into the house itself where from the verandah, breathless and gazing, we could hear the vigorous noise of preliminary search. Doors opened and closed, pots and pans clanked, glassware chimed. Papers, when the pudgy inept hands shuffled them, scattered like felons. That left us alone with the diminutive oriental in the porkpie and muddied shoes who introduced himself more from embarrassment than out of duty because before he spoke he cleared his throat a number of times and scraped his feet along the stones of the drive. The uniforms were making a great calamity, we could hear—this too seemed to shame their leader.

I am Detective You, he said while making an effort to

escape the moonlight. Immediately he shrugged and lifted his chin so we might identify him better. We're a party! one of us enthused. Some of us hoisted our drinks and joints; we were all nestled together in a swarm, in some cases seeing each other for the first time. To You's bemused stare we collectively smiled, though not necessarily rudely. He appeared to accept our play as friendly. *Pahhty,* he repeated to affirm our differences. Chairman ask, he began with a pointed finger, *When will we tie up the gray dragon of the seven stars?* We didn't know what to say to that but some of us couldn't help wondering if he wouldn't have been a good guest at our shindig. Surely his charm was more than nerves and less than affectation. *Ten thousand years is long,* You mused drily, pacing. *And so a morning and an evening count.* We nodded. He looked up, stricken the color of mustard by the moon, with his wire-rimed eyeglasses as thick as rock. Chairman say that too, he afterthought.

Still no triumphant police holding aloft a bloody tire iron. And yet we knew that nothing other than murder had brought You out into the sleepy country at such a dark buggy hour. He'd look up constantly, careful not to intrude his physical person on the verandah proper. It took some minutes before it dawned on us that his vantage permitted him to scrutinize our individualities, separate us out of a crowd as either likely or unlikely candidates. For what? In brief, it took no time at all before that shy grimacing miniature detective had intimidated the lot of us who were drunk red-faced bleary and leaning on any nearby solid object or even the liquid support of one another. False alarm? one of us tooted from the thick middle. Yes please? You averred standing stock still where moths circled his immense ears. Your name please? he inquired with his hands clasped at his back. In the moonlight his rumpled suit was iridescent and onion green. Whaddyamean name?? Jack the guitar hollered back. Yes please? You urged, attending to Jack by turning the whole of his frame rather than just his head. In this way You would always face us squarely. Your name please? he pursued. Fuck you, Lil grumbled. Zat *his* name?! Tina asked with a laugh, indicating the detective grimly protecting the ground beneath his feet. His name's En Why You, Phoenix himself golloped as if to betray his racial neighbor quicker than the rest of us. We all laughed but of course it wasn't funny. Because it wasn't, even You was able to snigger. Soon up and down the verandah and the stairs of the verandah everyone was laughing, making snide puns of You's name, guffawing in that way only a mob can in the face of a humorless situation. Shaddap!! Theo's voice boomed from above. SHAD-AD-AP! You there, he continued bellowing. Me? interrupted You. Not You. You! Theo specified with a fist. WHO?! we clamored overhead. YOU!! Theo screeched. We pointed to the skinny dick in the gravel but our host wagged no, shaking instead his entire torso at the cluster of Lil, Tina, Jean-Paul, and Jalal. US?! they cried in shock and disbelief, a last instant too of guilt. I never liked youse, Theo announced. You kept storing film in my fridge. Me? asked You also craning his twig-like neck in the dark. Them, them, them!!! Theo concluded with a fit of coughing. Get fugging out, he demanded out of the black sky. Us? the quartet pleaded. Theo's house creaked like a docked ship. In deference to the great groans of moving furniture we silenced. Listened for the fissure to run up the side of the west wall. Even Theo moaned. His silhouette disappeared.

The gold monkey swings a mammoth club, You said, not biting at all on our host's taunting bait. He pondered. *Mao* he signed the quote to no one's surprise. Eat shit, Jack the guitar muttered. *Please?* Jack stepped forward, rotten with hard-heartedness. James Baldwin, he said laconically. You puzzled, a finger picking his lip. *The cock whitens the world* he answered. Our heads were still twisting, they'd not uncoiled from Theo's hysteria nor from You's sullen pacing; and it was just as well because one of the uniforms began shouting I've got him I've got him, the voices coming from the upper story, where in a second Theo's forearm appeared, fat and hammer-locked. Leggo! Theo was wailing. Leggo my fugging arm. We watched his eyeglasses fall three storys, from his nose to You's feet, where the detective picked them up and tested their lenses. Meanwhile two more police came bluely around a corner of the house escorting the man with the mustache whose foot'd been injured in a one story fall of his own. He provided no trouble, in fact the uniforms were helping him to unweight the sore limb rather than containing a quarry. You clapped his palms together and rubbed them. He was warming to the task. *Today we have the long rope in our hands,* he said cheerily. Release my husband, JJ demanded, and we parted to give her the space to incriminate herself. Hostess? You politely asked. Sort of, JJ hemmed, the very particularity of You's assumption draining her courage. Suddenly the detective waved a uniform to his side. Got a body? The kid shook him off, ashamed. For a while they spoke whispers, You giving directions, the cop nodding and forever trying to get started before You had finished, or just as he was thinking of something further to do. It was making the kid nervous to dance in front of us. We applauded him, his pink face. Take her too, You remembered to add at the last. The space around JJ widened. We mulled and grazed our side of the verandah, hubbubbing and eyebrowing these late events at Theo's summer bash. Soon Theo, JJ, Berkeley Bill, and the gimp were chorined in the doorway of the study. Fortunately for them their tableau did not have to last long, a uniform pale and saucer-eyed barreled his way out another door and more or less tumbled toward You's opening arms. You whistled shortly. Absorbing us in the wide angle of his position, Detective You held ground in the determined moonlight. He was sizing us up a face at a time, stroking his hairless chin that was cleft and tender as an infant's behind; and then he said: *Down on earth a sudden report of the tiger's defeat.* You-know-who, he concluded.

Stepping so close now to the edge of the verandah, You offered us a life-size gander at him. We could have touched his coat or his cheek if we'd wanted to, or been brave enough. What's your story? he said to Steiner who appeared tethered to a suitcase that wasn't his. Don't have one, the least interesting of the guests replied. We'll have to get you one, You smirked. Come with us. Then the detective, having strode backward, seemed to rise before us on tiptoes with the intensity of a symphony conductor as he is about to break silence for the first time. Opening his arms You invited all of us to go inside. Everyone has a story to tell, I am sure, so why not get them started. *China is vague and immense.* Not Shakespeare, he snarled, exposing the two teeth he could have rented in any novelty shop.

3:30 a.m.

We are sprawled every which way everywhere on the house's ground floor, each of us awaiting a turn to tell a story designed to keep us from having to tell further stories. With each development of our personal narratives we get lifted to higher ground, above the fray and the rabble, or we sink deeper into the murky fen of possibly fatal misunderstanding. Or, more remotely, recite our way to total vindication. Every installment each of us would have to narrate if we were held for further questioning would grow more suspenseful to hear and excruciating to tell. Would also accrue greater and greater legal significance. Not to say moral. You goes from room to room—we can see him from wherever we sit, or at least overhear his cool interrogations—listening to sobering drunks and exhausted couples recount the night and often answer questions from out of the blue, such as where they work, what they do on Sunday, what is their favorite TV show, what is the color of their dog's coat, who was Heisenberg and why do we honor him. There are queries whose sophistication requires that some of us fabricate tales just so we need not feel less than our neighbors, so You and his henchmen will not easily divide us into people who are *with it* and people who are rubes. But You can detect lies at a glance, their memories of Naples, Shanghai, Abu Simbel, the opera con Callas, the theatre starring Guinness, the retrospective Manet, these are too detailed, just as the more urgent liars seem to know precisely where they were and what they drank with whom at times tonight like 9:26, 11:01, and 1:32. These bunglers blink before replying, smile as stiffly as corpses.

It grows embarrassing to hear the contradictions, as for instance that Paul never saw Nicole anywhere, never heard of her he can't wait to offer, and her side of it that passing one another into and out of the grove they discussed Paul's mother, his recent divorce, his father's latest marriage, Nicole's French bliss, Paul's descending career, Nicole's *nostalgia d'Amerique,* and the rejected possibility of a quick fuck behind an oleander. Hearing her insistence from his chair in the kitchen Paul twisted the belt of Theo's robe and rolled his eyes. You was not fooled. JJ up a tree for three hours? Picking apples, she said with naive confidence. Okay, saving a cat, she revised in a few seconds. If you must know, JJ huffily confessed, I was in that tree to be closer to God. *Please?* asked You as though his English had rusted where he stood. But he wasn't fooled. Not for a minute. Marie didn't fool him with her story of being thrown to the cornfield from the horse's lathered back, Tina didn't fool him with hers of designing Berkeley Bill instead of J-P, nor Jack the guitar, nor Jalal, nor Jean-Paul, nor Phoenix, nor the assassination buff, nor Lil—all had tales that fooled You for as long as a toad flicks its tongue and lightning rips the sky. Theo didn't even try to fool You; he told the ugly truth from the beginning, including the ignominious but harmless conclusion in which ——— had rushed him, frightening Theo so soundly in his sleep that our host jumped near out of his armchair, causing the pistol to discharge beside his foot. There is a burn mark, Theo offered to show everybody. Where gat now? You wondered aloud. Chair outside, Steiner remembered just as clearly from the study where he sat behind the author's desk, recalling himself on the verandah only a short while earlier about to convey JJ away. The man with no story, You remarked on his way in. He eyed Steiner's meditations as they floated the amber air of the study. See how easy it is? He grinned while Steiner secretly trembled.

What of ———? Not only You but everyone else wanted to know. And what of the vanished sculptor who'd pedalled into the night on the re-educated bicycle? Even these questions didn't fool You, raised as they were by individuals already cast in the heat of suspicious light. In the middle of the commotion we kept one eye each on Berkeley Bill who'd phoned the authorities and who now sipped coffee at the foot of the stairs. Often he'd glance behind him up into the shadows, where occasionally we would hear footsteps in one of the bedrooms. So who croaked, our eyes asked You. *Ahhh!* You breathed easily, as though waiting for centuries to be returned to life with one question only. *I regret the dying of the dream,* he quoted. The line looked like this:

4:10 a.m.

Where the skin of the neck had split, the exposed bone oxalated so that a fine white powder of calcium dusted the hair. The head, nodding on the atlas vertebra, seesawed between You's thin hands. He could have rotated it on axis if he'd been inclined. Observing the lifeless sclera of the eye You palpated the jelly with the blade of his smallest finger. Still moist. He rubbed the humors against his thumb. He thumbed the crease of his trousers and what we thought we saw when he removed his hand and resumed his examination was a transparent stain no larger than a pinhead. In the light it was opalescent, like sequins, and would not dry but nonetheless stiffened. Perhaps the worst of it, for Theo at least, was the fact that no one had missed Henriette at any time during the party. JJ had once asked Jalal about her, Jalal remembered as soon as he saw the body, and several people had overheard Jalal and Henriette disagree about whether to be sick or not—Henriette, that was, who should or should not be sick. Moreover, Henriette and the pilot had gotten cozy over a platter of chicken wings—most everybody had a vague recollection of something or other. But no one seemed to know what was troubling her.

When casually reconnoitering his former wives and lovers after the arrival of You, even the host had virtually forgotten Henriette. Now he hrumphed bitterly to view the large-boned plump corpse as it was gurneyed out of the scene. Theo hadn't seen his third wife in over a decade, and since they'd been married during his middle thirties he had never taken the relations seriously except as his first habitation of Paris. She was all starch and lesbiana, he glumly thought. JJ comforted his shoulder, Paul felt a sudden ache for Nicole, who after all had not only met his father through Henriette but had been the latter's lover as well—this Paul was happily ignorant of—and the author himself once again concealed his eyes nose and lips in the trough of his rough palms. Jaysus! Theo grunted. Nicole was shivering to recall the look and feel of Henriette's flesh, especially her large taut buttocks; Nicole's husband nuzzled her cheek in French to calm her; across the room Paul stood ossifying until quite incidentally and unrelated to his agony Nicole bristled at the pilot's graying knuckle. Please, muttered You to the corpse's attendants, following them out into the air where after a time an ambulance could be heard creeping across the drive. During You's absence no one in the living room, kitchen, or study said a word, the house therefore quieter than it'd been in days. In place of gregarity we were vigilant, electrified by the glimpse of death, witless and vulnerable because in our imaginations we traded slabs with poor Henriette, adding of course that piquant morsel of still remaining ourselves so as to observe our rigid calcification wheel by.

You understood our expression upon his return. Yet he was not to be fooled. Officiously he read the names of some of us from a sheet of all—Marie, Nicole, Pilot, Jean-Paul, Phoenix, Rosa, Jorge, Andreas, Ilie, Sacha, Ole, Marianna, Esteban, Bjorn, Stavros, Vlad, Fyod, Paolo, Johannes, Irna, Christos, Tristan, Mordred, Benito, Juan One, Juan Two, Juan Two Three You could not resist adding with a laugh. He fired into the room: *Jamal! Jawal! Jalal! All three of you, and the rest, line up against the wall!* The list went on, a smorgasbord of mispronunciation, including Fertig, Gunther, Henri, Istvan, Joiaio, Karla, Luana, Manolio, Naum, Opitz, Primo, Quintus, Rinaldo, Severn, Thibault, Ulrich, Violetta, Wilhelmina, Xenia, Yolanthe, Zadig. You's awful trumpet blared and one by one the crowd mobilized until there it was, three-fourths of the party with their backs not only to the walls of the house that extended from the screen door of the kitchen to the front one of the living room, but beyond, across the verandah and down the cedar steps, a few even straggling between the parked cars and straining to listen. There they stood, the myriad hues tongues dress and cultures of Theo's connections to the world at large over three decades of turmoil and search, each posed as for a mugshot with the inescapable vanity that would be managed by even the most blameless idiot nomading the sub-Sahara. Because of the threat their native languages buzzed in outrage.

Hey Wait a sec! cried Jack the guitar. Even Berkeley Bill who'd found the body roused himself for this affront. Theo was chagrined especially when he surveyed the remainder—*locals.* But there was little time to protest, only enough to catch You's scheming eye, or rather the gleam of the glass that protected him from scrutiny. *We will make a stone wall against the upper river,* You opined, pleased with the snaking file of beleaguered flesh that he inspected from one end to the other, using a hand to peer into the black distance of the stone drive. We hesitated to form an opinion, what was left of us. And were loath to believe any of it. *We* no longer meant what it had. *We* had dwindled to a paltry few. Yet why us? How had we been eliminated from this curious construction in which human replaced brick in You's Chinese wall of suspicion? Yes, we Americans were left sitting and anonymous. It was shaming to be the *Others,* that is, *We* who drew no attention. It was Theo, we suspected, who first gleaned the truth of the matter. Bill only a bit slower. You may go, You excused the foreigners. All dismissed. Please drive carefully. He admired his wall a second longer, as long as it took the pieces of it to realize their luck. Rumbling and snuffling, shaking weary heads, exhaling the reprieve, three-fourths of us returned Theo's farewell wave and filtered out into the drive where gradually our autos roared us away. That left in the house a half dozen natives now divided from the rest as *suspects* were from *guests on the way home.* This was, if possible, a greater affront. And certainly *we* took on an even more ominous significance. Why? *They* had left, innocent and out of You's thoughts. Oh, there was much time between the dismissal and the actual departure, much irked commentary and a great many teary goodbyes, largely from the various women in Theo's past who surely would avoid his presence again. The party had only reiterated their current lives, as reunions are designed to do, and each of them—some anonymous even now, many unknown to one another as O. T.'s lovers—left without regretting the loss, recollecting perhaps by the mere sight of JJ why it was their relations had failed. And for a moment Eddie fiddled with the idea of having one last run at Paul, despite the madnesses of the night, but in the second moment it was just too much trouble. She'd have ghosts now anyway. Poor Henriette; Eddie already was wrapping herself in grief, and grief has its rewards to outstrip every other passion. Paul looked stricken but it didn't matter; she stopped noticing, then she was gone. Like that we were separated, aliens freed to roam the countryside and natives held captive in the light of their own moon.

Hobbling as far as the door, the man with the mustache halted. May I stay? he asked in deference to You's authority. As if it mattered You glanced at Theo, as if he cared Theo nodded sure, and only then did You demure, I am not surprised. *Latino* he murmured to us under his breath. We sort of agreed, unsure of what. It did not seem to us that the uniforms were any better informed or less perplexed than we but that they were at least familiar with You's methods. Some chuckled at the noisy exodus, others sniffed disgust, still more exchanged private signals on the verandah. The cars of the foreigners were departing slowly, pebbles therefore crunched with a singular violence under the weight of rubber and steel. Instinctively, and poignantly, we watched our friends, acquaintances, and familiar strangers disappear back into their lives. It hurt to see the party end; it was merely insulting that a death had done it; we knew we would never see most of us again. We'd live and die separately now, waiting for old age to remind us of that particularly torrid night at Theo's when a hundred or more rioted the summer's finish. Even Theo looked nostalgic at the departure, and JJ who was still hoping to flee, and Paul who missed Eddie already and resented her desertion, and Berkeley Bill who had begun to think he'd have been wiser to pass out hours earlier, and Lil who couldn't trust J-P to wait for her out by the autos even though his camera was still upstairs where he'd wrestled with police for a shot of the body, and Tina who didn't trust Lil not to try to incriminate her to the horrible Chinaman just because she'd wanked Lil's husband out by the fir trees, and Jack the guitar who enjoyed the stage for his anger since absolutely nobody cared if he came home or not because nobody was there, and the assassination buff who couldn't avoid comparing whitewashes even as she was falling asleep in the shape of a chair, and Steiner who out of misplaced courtesy and diffidence was tacitly acknowledging JJ's bag to be his own but wondering at the same time if there would be a flight to Athens he could book for later that day. Together the huddled Americans envied the escaping aliens. In our minds we sat on the passenger side of one debouching car or another. When the final Volvo hummed out of sight we assumed fresh positions, arranging more formally our siege into one room, sitting at moral attention to note with despair the renewed coolness of the uniforms. They'd appeared to mature in the past few minutes, their eyes a sign of dread. The night died everywhere we looked. It didn't move and it stank. It dried up, unlike the secretion from Henriette's eye that was staged on You's rough trousers like a star. Any Jews in the room? the detective asked.

4:44 a.m.

Most of our alibis were unbelievably perforated. Admittedly some were merely scratched LP's, and others left inky blots pathing around. But the majority were as obvious as blowholes and as riddled as sphinxes. One after another we greased our lives for the impossible fit of innocence, and edgily each of us recited some erratic series of events we'd label *up until tonight*, gouging our narratives first with pinholes of explanation, then prettily piped honeycombs of reason; and inescapably, while sweat navigated our private creases, we would bore tunnels of denial so long and gaping that our dishonesty became credible. Not in itself—we didn't fool You, natch—but in its nature and effect. We could never have hoped to fool You, only a fool would've tried, but by duping ourselves into thinking we could be convincing liars, denyers, exaggerators, and evaders we revealed to him our deficiency—if we'd been guilty we'd have told whoppers that go in as silkily as a breeze and persevere like storm.

We circled the room exonerating ourselves, extolling our virtues, and confessing our petty vices to such a pitiful extent you'd have thought *we* were dead instead of pokey old Henriette and were being eulogized, that is if you'd been anyone but You. He heard what he wanted, not what we said. The tales went on for a long time, it seemed forever, and the young cops belting coffee in the kitchen were yawning for home. After we'd concluded mitigating the truth and reiterating the lies foxy You found himself the edge of a chair to sit on. He sighed, borrowed one of the moistened wipers for his spectacles that Theo scattered randomly in the house, and then caressed his dusty windows with tender ovoid motion. *Tortoise and snake are silent,* he said balefully. *A great plan looms.*

What prompter cue could the man with the mustache have rehearsed? It was his turn. He looked the part too. Señor? You offered him the limelight.

5:10 a.m.

What a story! We didn't know whether to laugh, cry, or beat the Spaniard to a pulp! Even before he'd told the complication of the premise and was nowhere near the climax, let alone the dénouement, we were sure that You had his man. The man with the mustache—so called because his, unlike Theo's or Steiner's, curled waxenly at its opposite ends and looked like worms asleep against the skin—the man with this sort of brazen travestied renaissance of a lip-shag leaned forward and creaked, blinking his mind into shape and grimacing either at his swollen ankle or the labor of speech. He analyzed his audience as one acquainted with publicity, posturing and affecting, charming us who didn't matter at all, but ignoring Detective You who alone mattered. But it was us, the common party and fellow suspects he romanced, prefacing his soliloquy by dismissing the law as corruptible, inane, artless, and ridiculously impartial. Without the bias of obsession, he began, the law is a bureaucracy, a structure without substance, therefore an authority without right, and in conclusion the man who served as its limb—he fluttered a rumpled handkerchief at You who blushed the color of pumpkin—was nothing other than a flunkey. A variable, he amended. It would take hard fact to slice You in half. To our surprise the man with the mustache never bothered to address You, or to gauge the effect of his preface. Was it possible he'd meant no insult after all? Was the preface some sort of warning whose subtleties fell through our fumbling fingers like jujubes? See? Already we were paranoid. This guy was good, very good. Totally disarming. Distracting. As his story unfolded the Mediterranean accent thickened, returning him to a more natural state not only of language but of being. Actually, Being to be exact. Big B. He was that good.

The eyes are gypsy, he remarked with a grin and a leathery finger prodding intimate moisture out of one red cornice. The mouth is Velasquez. My nose, he smirked, the gringo calls Gibraltar. The topography of his person went on for several organs more, his navel being Toledo, which was the center of his nation and whose name caused Theo to lean forward and stare, and since his foot was Bilbao it was clear this man rested face down in the sea. He was describing a drowned body. And your crime please? You interrupted the tour. Now the Spaniard faced You, and Theo kept facing the Spaniard, and soon so did You. And we? Because we could not face them all at the same time we felt that this trio was not accidentally met on this long night in Theo's castle in the country. Their encounter suddenly loomed as having been forecast with the weather, ordained even, and even to the rest of us, whose own confessions were at least interesting to ourselves if not rife with scandal and nuance, their parries and thrusts had to be the foreground of the drama. Not even scene–setters or footmen, we were no more than backlight.

There was a question on the air though, You's, and we wondered how to cast the man who'd have to answer it since he was stroking patches of blotched face to think of a reply. He tapped a gold incisor with a pinkie nail.

Crossed his legs philosophically. I am never alone, the Spaniard said bluntly, apropos of nothing, we thought. Yet his words struck a melancholy chord. Yet I do not miss myself, he added. We started to chew that. Pretty soon we felt stupid. Something was lacking in our experience that those three—You, Theo, the man—wore as comfortably as ratty slippers. In truth we knew from the start that we had no chance to keep up. To demonstrate how hopeless our situation was we didn't know yet that the man with the mustache had still not ended defining his crime. It being that I am nothing other than future, he said, the present is always sufficient.

Well. This was pretty esoteric for us. Surely You would have a Maoism to suit the occasion. Something like *The yellow crane has flown.* Something the Spaniard would have to bite on in turn. And why was Theo rubbing his temples? Nothing—for forever, it seemed, You said nothing. Theo said nothing. We of course could *only* think of nothing rather than something. It felt like the millenium. What may have separated those three was immense but even to us what connected them surely was more powerful, more awesome. You was no mere quipster and he spoke no aphorism molded over hundreds of Asian years. The pale green smile he'd used to meet the puffy toothsome mirth of the Spaniard vanished the way thunderheads sweep away sunshine on a placid lake. The wit birthed menace, the play merely prologued a sober nocturnal ritual which we might all feel but which only You, Theo, and the mustached man could perform. Imaginations cartwheeled, hellish visions juggled, flames of perdition licked the ankles of falling creatures. And then Theo pressed his forehead, purpling his face, knowing what was to come before it did. When it came he sighed with such relief to know even the awful truth that our horror was diminished. Now You was coldly professional. Rape corpses, will you? he calmly accused. The man with the mustache frowned. The faces before us melted, or was it that our vision blurred?

It had happened, the Spaniard admitted, though unlike the story You projected. I was *seducing* someone *asleep,* he replied to the detective's slur. Unconsciousness was her ruse. Or so I presumed when she failed to stir under my ministrations. (Here he enunciated details of such a grimy luridness that we closed our ears.) Feigning sleep to be free of responsibility. Pretending I was a dream born in an apple skin or one flute of cheap sherry too many. Her control seemed to me extraordinary. Given my experience, my dexterity. You offered a raised palm to bring the recitation to a halt—clearly he would save the rest for the station house. By now our hearts were thumping like pistons, our knuckles quivering in the soft lamplight. But You pointedly asked if the Spaniard had not smelled death on the woman's person. We shook from ear to toe at that charge. Here the accused reviewed his memory, flipping through the dossier of his adventures in the bedroom and hoping not to confuse one episode with some other. If I recoiled at every death I attended—he paused to weigh the punch, revising the reply he'd perhaps given elsewhere, during another climactic exchange of views—I would have been better born a spring. The furrows darkening our host's face reconciled his age with his experience when the Spaniard concluded. A diffident sniff was all he could manage; and yet it was more of an event than we would undertake. You toted up the facts as he required them. His addition cleared the necrophile.

Berkeley Bill asked if this meant the man with the mustache was free to go. Free is a large word, You replied. Not Mao's either, the Spaniard chorused. Who could say Henriette was indeed dead?! Theo added. The act of rape? JJ asked, containing herself (as always). Who is to press charges? You wanted to know. Jack the guitar threatened the freed man, the assassination buff imputed a cover-up,

Bill moaned for having discovered anything upstairs. Quietly JJ began to weep. Paul, struggling to hold a picture of Eddie in his mind, felt left out. *Ours* was the nightmare then, in which we did not need to be guilty to feel guilt. Steiner's disinterested handshake of farewell when the Spaniard extended his palm violated well enough our position. Even Theo refused. We stared momentarily at Steiner's fragile hand, hoping he would have the decency at least to wipe his fingers of the man's touch. So while we were cutting Steiner dead in the living room where he sat below the portrait of one of Casanova's teenaged mistresses, You showed the necrophile out, Theo padding behind. Two ghastly-looking gawking uniforms escorted the limping effete foreigner to his low and sporty auto listing beside the cornfield. There was now the perceptible graying of sky and the distant disquiet that precedes the song of dawn birds. Even in our numbness we would not forgive the handshake. Until Theo and You returned into the room we stood heavy-footed in front of our chairs staring at Steiner, at Steiner's still outstretched hand, until we were certain he had performed that revolting gesture more out of mechanical courtesy than malice towards us. Not that the excuse made a difference. He was still a creep.

5:35 a.m.

Now it is the story of the silence, which overtook us in place of the sleep we badly missed. The story of our rustling and rooting around the brightening rooms of Theo's house. Our languor, our ennervation, our gathered separateness after a night of too much complicity. We were zomboid. Was ours the type of experience that prevents further meetings among the same faces, each bearing to another the mark of a grueling passage whose meanings are too clear and clearly shared? Were we ashamed? It was a story of silent recriminations, of searching for clues in the muffled kitchen where eggs were being broken in iron skillets, where the odors of charring toast and brewing coffee returned our self-awareness, where we pattered about trivial breakfast tasks on the edge of tears, huge pearly steaming tears that our throats drove down and that unmasked the absurdity of seeking clues in the first place. Where we cracked welcome smiles when out of the study there drifted the introductory bars of one of the *Brandenburgs.* Theo, in his wisdom. His ultimately unfailing humanity.

Like a sacrificed venerable chieftain, a dinosaur roaming the lunar terrain, he returned to the kitchen doorway wearing khaki shorts and sandals, his broad chest's white forest invigorating our gloom, his spectacles' piercing glare translating his eyes to stars. He made certain we were all busy at something. Had our ears on Bach, our minds on life, and our fingers exercising miracles. You was about to exit, refusing Theo's offer of breakfast, an offer that left us holding our breath. Even JJ appeared to brighten at the prospect of Sunday, no longer looking like a trapped animal or a refugee except when Theo approached her, or when Steiner loitering in the next room shuffled the leather bag out of his way, or when You obsequiously entered. *The wild bear cannot frighten a brave man,* he poetized one last time. Or woman! he jauntily amended. What to make of him after all? With quick absolute strokes he drew a phrase on the reverse of a page of Theo's manuscript—how had he gotten hold of that??—using the pen he'd removed from inside his iridescent suit. In this light elf, not onion, green. *Dawn wakes in the east,*

You spoke the picture shaped He handed it to JJ. Smiled broadly, with the sincerity befitting the ordeal he'd overseen. It's an easel! JJ realized after he'd gone. That pleased us all.

5:47 a.m.

Overhearing Theo feeding Casanova in the stable, Steiner and Detective You walked slowly through the ragweed, as if tracking red indians. *Lady Chatterley's Nosebag,* Theo seemed to say through the walls while the sorrel munched liquidly. *Moby Nosebag,* he murmured. *A Tale of Two Nosebags.* Casanova clomped a hoof on the hard stable floor. *War and Nosebag,* Theo whispered. The pair outside halted, inhaling the smells of straw and manure that came to life in the sunrise. *A la recherche de nosebag perdu. The Sufferings of Young Nosebag. Nosebag for Nosebag. I Promessi Nosebag. Les Nosebags Dangereuses. Madame Nosebag. Nosebag and Prejudice. Wuthering Nosebags.* You done yet? Theo intermittently asked the horse. Casanova champed on, Theo's voice softening still further until You and Steiner realized that the horse was finding the repetitions of tone and word soothing. This was their intimate time together, horse and owner making the feed pleasanter, Theo easing the nag's rough digestion with a crude music. *The Brothers Nosebag,* Theo said barely higher than a whisper. There was a long pause in which oats were being pulverized. You and his companion crept away from the intrusion. *The Fall of the House of Nosebag.*

5:55 a.m.

Edge of the highway. In the background the house, inside of which the last light has been turned off. The uniforms have departed, all except the driver behind the wheel of the unmarked sedan belonging to You. Who stands sympatico with Steiner at the highway, facing the swaying stalks of corn, their stringy tough hides greening with daybreak. Lo and behold the air is chill, dewy, briefly even crisp, threatening autumn in a matter of days. *The sky is three feet away,* You self-consciously can't resist saying. Already Steiner can see the sky at thirty-thousand feet with hundreds of miles of ocean below. Suicide then? he asks You timidly, drawn to the solution by his own image of the sea from jet height, a white-dotted blue canvas of cold stiff stilllife. Henriette a suicide, whoever she was? You frowns at Steiner's dull conclusion. Unsolved murder, he spins out of his thin lips in a perfectly incredulous tone. Who do you think I am for heaven's sake?? He peers in the middle distance, craning forward his smooth neck. He grips Steiner's elbow. Now *there's* a suicide! You points out. In the nearby ditch lies ———'s body, teeming with flies, especially around the wound opening his head at the top. The pistol looks familiar to the nauseous Steiner. This wants attention, You sighs wearily.

5:55 a.m.

JJ extinguished the last lamplight, surveying for the first time the calamity visited upon the house. If you're walking out on him, she thought, now is the time. Do I want ——— after all? Her ambivalence gnawed her cortex, it wasn't only fatigue from the impossible night killing her. In the kitchen we were snarfing eggs and tearing toast. Giving Bach a chance. Making tentative verbalizations, most of them mutterings at our plates. It was just late, the weekend, we were just tired, remote—expressing discomfort and wanting to sleep and be irresponsible gave us these tired faces. We were so tired that each friend was tired for another. One look at a friend's eyes and we could have keeled over. Though this party was very special it faded, it fell, but before that it was a good one, one of the better. It's all talk the way we threaten everything, then calm down, then plan a hijacking or something until two of us have dozed off and it's clear the weekend is over. Like that, worked up but spent, Theo's party ended, other people left, and keep leaving, until finally there is no other.

5:56 a.m.

Crimson sun-moon dawn. Not in Rome, said Steiner being wistful. You go off? Non-stop. Relentless clarity of the unbroken horizon. Travel expensive? Not if nothing else is necessary. He said it again, raveling each syllable carefully before the two men's eyes because he was explaining a long-lasting pattern of chronic restlessness. Afterward, watching ———'s body refuse to move, he was exhausted. You's car was chugging carbon out of the muffler, the driver reporting the suicide discovered his beard had grown in the night. This was really the end, everything seemed to indicate, just waiting for the house to see the fresh body. Upstairs it looked as though Theo was warning his bed of his arrival. Downstairs the lollers drifted into daylight, shading their eyes from the revealed word. Lil, Tina, Jack, Bill, the buff, the few who'd been suspected, the few who'd meant something but not enough. Jean-Paul, to no one's surprise, hadn't waited for anybody. Imo back to the lab, Bill said before he saw ——— across the road. I got cells warming. The circle of keys he jangled signified Berkeley Bill's success. He'd discovered an element a decade earlier and was now coasting. Wuzzat? Bill asked Jack the guitar pointing yonder.

From the doorway JJ observed You and Steiner facing the cornfield—they made her shiver. When she heard the toilet flush overhead and the TV newsman speak, JJ thought Oh God We're Alone Again. Straining like a goose JJ's neck couldn't stretch far enough down the road for her to see if ———'s Porsche was parked. More? No more? Theo blew his nose like the goose JJ's neck resembled.

5:56 a.m.

You sound like a man with a *mission,* the detective suggests. It's a condescension though. Steiner's stomach contracts. At sunup the world looks edible. In the distance the siren fantasies. From the house people come running. *Mission?* Steiner said: The four I know are ad-, o-, sub-, and

INTERMISSION

Robert Steiner

PLACE-NAMES: THE NAME

1	2	3	4	■	5	6	7	8	9	■	10	11	12	13
14					■	15					■	16		
17			■	■	18					■	19			
■	20		21	■	22			■	23					■
24				25		■	26	27	■	■	28			29
	■		■	30					■	31				
32	33		34			■	35		36		■	37		
38				■	39	40		■	41		42			■
43			■	44							■		■	45
46			47	■		■		■	48				49	
50				51	■	52		■	53		■	54		
	■		■	55		■		■	56					
■	57		58		■	59					■	60		
61					62			■	63					
■	64						■	65			■		■	

Matinee

ACROSS

1 Brechtian god
5 Alphabetized
10 Alter ———
14 It's curtains for Polonius!
15 ———
16 Novel that begins "All happy families are more or less dissimilar . ."
17 Tit merchant
18 Casanova, Don Juan, Don Giovanni
19 Ossian or Menard
20 Out of the horse's mouth
22 Possess
23 The grassy ———
24 Predicate; expect
26 Theo's box
28 Length of power to Casanova
30 Lime-twig to catch Hawkes
31 Sorrel, e.g.
32 Stick it out; repulse
35 The Missing Link
37 ID
38 ——— upon a time
39 Editor-in-Chief
41 Contiguous
43 Belongs with Hiss
44 Code again
46 Vs. Censorship
48 Most authoritative
50 Rosy prick (Don't be so literal!)
52 A's ini.
53 Printer's implement to guard
54 Put on
55 Competition for one of 10 across
56 Who gets screwed
57 Berkeley Bill negation
59 Hello your guests
60 ——— and outs
61 G Casanova in Bavaria
63 Observed
64 Theo in Bavaria
65 Lucius in translation

DOWN

1 What's in the belfry, Masterson?
2 Jamal, Jawal and Jalal
3 Writers' New Worlds
4 Renaud or Charpillon
6 Dirty job
7 Kafka practitioners
8 Of St.Venus or St.Agnes
9 Theo's was "gothic mahogany"
11 Keeper of the Wilde
12 Art Tarts
13 Phoenix's tenor or the first Hamlet
18 Ray's name
19 Divine Scope
21 Intimate Parisian
24 Flying vampyrs
25 Short, unpublished novels
27 After tee but before dee
29 Org. whose help the A gratefully acknowledges
31 Grizzly in January, Theo all year
33 Author of ancient dreambook
34 Be specific
36 Lacking socially redeeming features
40 Mantra for You perhaps
42 AEIO—
45 Witnesses
47 Proto, or after I.M.
49 Venetian stage
51 City in southern Franthe
57 What Casanova got from Henriette, The A from JJ, or Paul from Eddie
58 Brazil
59 It goes off on page 141
62 Conventional cry in dramas, novels and poems but never actually pronounced by a living human being in the whole of history

Matinee

PLACE-NAMES: THE NAME (SOLUTION)

1 B	2 A	3 A	4 L		5 A	6 B	7 C	8 E	9 D		10 E	11 G	12 O	13 S
14 A	R	R	A	S		15 L	O	V	E	R		16 A	D	A
17 T	A	T			18 R	O	U	E	S		19 H	O	A	X
	20 B	I	21 T		22 O	W	N		23 K	N	O	L	L	
24 A	S	S	U	25 M	E		26 T	27 V			28 R	E	I	29 N
C		T		30 S	N	A	R	E		31 H	O	R	S	E
32 R	33 E	S	34 I	S	T		35 Y	E	36 T	I		37 A	K	A
38 O	N	C			39 G	40 O	D		41 A	B	42 U	T	S	
43 B	O	O		44 R	E	M	O	R	S	E		R		45 A
46 A	C	L	47 U		N		C		48 T	R	U	E	49 S	T
50 T	H	O	R	51 N		52 O	T		53 E	N		54 A	C	T
S		N		55 I	D		O		56 L	A	I	D	E	E
	57 A	I	58 N	T		59 G	R	E	E	T		60 I	N	S
61 J	N	E	U	H	62 A	U	S		63 S	E	E	N	A	T
	64 O	S	T	E	I	N		65 A	S	S		G		S

To THIS point there's been nothing but fun. One story winding into another, another into the next, the next to the following, the suspense and sexual play absorbing, various, enigmatic; and all of us thank goodness willing to keep the pages flying by. Up until now there hasn't been much to memorize, and then only the occasional misdirection quickly corrected or the absent detail quietly implaced or the necessary turn carefully withheld. There's been music. You've had pictures to look at. Arriving here should have been a comfortable voyage, a nostalgic Orient Express or luxury liner cruise kind of journey, replete with oddballs, ribald sagas, curious junctions in- and con-, the hint of persistent danger, the brooding cloud of conspiracy loosely joined by the Inquisition and the long hidden life of Masonry that unites Cervantes, Quijote, Casanova, Mozart. There might've been towns in Turkey, the Slavias, China whizzing by, to say nothing of seductive gestures among fashionable women and men, glances that shroud them in insidious fogs of significance. Smoking, drinking, eyeing each other lasciviously or with threat, such personages in those express train compartments, on those liner sun decks, each waiting for another to start the drama rolling, and all reminiscent of a dreamy matinee where the audience accepted the mood and the melomania, even though outdoors it might've been hot enough to melt the wings of your eyeglasses, bright enough to blind your dog, cold enough to freeze your mother-in-law, or storming like a

Russian revolution. Part of the pleasure of course has been in the thought that so much pure entertainment, novelty, and diversion must be concealing some thetic gravity; part of the fun has always been the assumption that not only what you see is a pleasure but what is imbedded in what you see, the microscopic nodules of wisdom that go down silkily and dot the Author's own human eye.

It's possible that some out there believe the Author's done all this stuff so well that he or she has more or less abdicated his or her authority to continue. No, that's a lie. That's just an arrogant way of suppressing an unpleasant subject. Though the Author feels a threat to his book mightily, viscerally, and is pondering even now its apocalypse, it is largely as a result of the need for a vacation of sorts. A holiday from the grueling business of rising every morning with the fog, nibbling JJ's ear like a mosquito so she won't waken to ask the time or take the Author's head off, pulling on sweatshirt and cords in the john (again so JJ won't etc.), tiptoeing out to the stove to launch sleeping bugs under the burner into oblivion, snuffling up coffee in what JJ has derisively termed the A's "modernist" mug because it's brittle, funereally black, and was bought in Europe, then switching on and off and on the newly rewired lamp on the desk, sifting through legal sheets in search of the sentence broken off at the waist the day before, and finally finding the unfinished thing, giving it a glower for its simpering appearance, hearing the birds getting their show on the air, and staring at the Bic that the A's pincers are about to shatter because of their unconscious will to wrestle. All of that could be chucked aside! We could execute that trip to the Grand Canyon or to Nova Scotia, or be at the beach by noon, at the worst wake up together curled like rabbits in January, neither of us incurring or encouraging the other's anger, jealousy, spite, whatever!

JJ shook her head after reading the above, dismissing the idea when she put on her mac, stepped into the hard summer rain, and headed down the muddy road at a trot. I called to her but the sheets of downpour muffled my voice. Obviously things could not continue as they were; I felt sure the book was in the way. An obsessive, consuming project. A dinosaur of a thing, mutant as well as extinct, hulking as well as haunted, nothing but bones to suggest the absent meat and muscle. I looked in the mirror and said

Y GO ON ?

Can a question such as this ever be satisfactorily answered? Y we don't give up in the face of overwhelming odds? In the face of a hostile reality burning to crush us underfoot? Our closest friends secretly despising us and eager for our failure, happiest when we come to them in desperate trouble? Our contemporaries grinning at our setbacks as though they were their advancements? Our cut corners? Our errors of judgment? Our moral blindnesses? Oh, there are always simplistic answers but all are symptoms of simplistic thought. And none that successfully explains, to my satisfaction at least, y for example unrequited lovers and cuckolds continue to love unrequitedly, cuckoldedly ? Y doomed lovers embrace their hopelessness in shabby rooms for a few hours' textural pleasure? Y not pack it in, as JJ has suggested on more than one occasion.

Y NOT ?

The first time JJ said this she was kidding, I believe, exploiting my neurotic fear of abandonment which is based on the fact that women have always abandoned me.

Once Mother, and after my several wives. Y not call it off? suggested JJ, referring I thought to my book which indeed was something of an albatross and something of a millstone and something of a wedge. She had been vehement that there was just so much attitudinizing even the most sympathetic reader might tolerate. Bristling with disquiet, seeking to evade a headache by locating somewhere the signature of an Author who could be trusted through the warfare of all my signs and cymbals, the poor "besotted and beset viewer, by now punchy with pericranial rue, can only," JJ averred, "hope for the book's death." The book itself was her most convincing argument, and the bedraggled viewer coiled in an armchair, holding it open, her persuasive victim. However when I replied my usual reply she reacted differently. "As though we were about to agree," I said, "along with our dead father Kafka, that Don Quijote was an invention of Sancho Panza who then passed his days following his invention's adventures with a head full of stories in his blistering dust-choked no-name burg, our meaning is serious, JJ, our effort more earnest than Amerigo's when he sharpened his sword for dueling, or Casanova's when he dipped his aching quill into human flesh, Mozart's when he slashed the semi-quavers that struck Don Giovanni from the score, even and especially the Quijote's himself when he renounced his madness and set the household right again. Earnest, ya know what I mean?" She hadn't meant the book this time but us. All the up-to-date stuff of it, she said, was academic. Reread it, I asked her. I'd rather be dead, she replied. All the self-consciousness, she moaned. We'll examine it closely, I suggested. She was still talking about us though, not the book. That floored me.

The revolutions at all the palaces and countries we've visited in this book, literal and figural, may exclude me, may not wait for me, may be against me, and I in each case may be as dead as a cow when it protects your feet, but even so every dislocation celebrates dysfunction. How else to transcend our alienated existences—mine and JJ's for example? Here, graphically, is dislocation celebrating dysfunction:

Morning Herald
Special Edition
AUTHOR
MAKES
HEADLINES

Look at it! I cried to JJ. Just have a look. Y the mac again? Where ya goin now? Just down the road? JJ, think of it this way: who else but a bunch of specialists could have wanted to fracture an atom? What with JJ's attitude, my having reams to go on this thing, no hope of getting a perfect printer to set it up, I became a fairly wired guy, a hyperventilator, an insomniac, a boozer, a two-pack a day man. Not exactly the devil-may-care ice-cream suited avant-gardist we'd all like to think I am. Y not then give it up—the book, I mean. JJ's right, there're gobs of reason for shredding it and deep-sixing the confetti. When she returned from *down the road* I said as much. And she answered: Y not give yrself a chance to relax the imperious tone? Talk like the rest of us who're reading you in the first place over Fruit Loops, yogurt, Postum, Chivas, hash, Maui wowee, trying t'erase the kids' screaming who loves ya baby with lollipops in their mouths, or include the Razumovskys in their earflow, exclude the neighbor's mower, trimmer, saw, spouse-slicer etc., and otherwise deciding whether it's worth it to turn another pg of this stiff's turgid over-educated prose. Y not try the unguarded moment when we catch the king coursing the palace in a dripping towel—no speeches, no swords, no deep structures. Stop giving out the mushroom treatment: keeping us in the dark and feeding us bullshit. Again JJ did not refer to the book but to its A. I handed the mac down to her from its hook on the door. Still pouring, I said.

After she had read the above JJ shook her fist at me from across the room. This is what I feared, she said. You using me. Exploiting me. I feel violated. To put a living person in a book degrades both people and books. But you, you not only do that, you include that person's response to it too. That's really vile. Through her harangue I remained urbane, effectively detached, unusually charming, and in calm control of myself rather than of the situation. JJ gradually grew hysterical, needing to be restrained even though I refused to restrain her; as a result lots of items in our house were broken, torn, smashed, pulverized. I reminded JJ that among our guests for tonight's party would be ——— who lived down the road, and surely she did not want him seeing her and our home in such a state. Fuck ———, she said. Fuck u too, she added. Fuck men period. She was becoming as unmagical as Quijote's Dulcinea, Amerigo's Therese, Casanova's Henriette. How would she feel, I wondered, when she learned that our private life's chaos was finding its way into the book? Y our sordid situation with its real problems had crept into the unreal ones of the story, a graver condition which when discovered by JJ would generate yet uglier confrontations on the confused front of our marriage. Rain, mac, squeaky Adidas, add a tumbler of warm scotch, JJ trundling down the road to see ——— for the ———th time but walking slowly now, meditative, ruminating, sex spent, romance ruined, gesturing to the storm, soliloquizing, and uniformly being miserable.

Before JJ read the above, glaring at me with her wet hair snaked around her face, her eyes teary, her sneakers caked in mud, her tumbler refilled at ———'s place, she said,

Lemme see. I handed it over like a thief returning stolen property, then retired to my desk, this one, and labored the following into the world:

As it was to have been written this story will not appear. We have gathered the Author's notes, journal entries, unsent or unfinished letters, his diary, his writer's log, his book marginalia. Neither will these appear, for legal, moral and aesthetic reasons, though we can say that together they paint a portrait of a man obsessed, of a man no longer straddling the barbed wire dividing reality from imagination, and of a man whose awesome output over these last months testifies more to his dementia than to his genius. For the sake of his memory to the bereaved family we shall merely offer an anatomy of the story that was to have appeared, as well as the surrounding grisly events, with a hope that its implications will be received by readers outside this book as clearly and poignantly as they have been by those of us trapped within. View this as the book's tale of horror, for there are demons here, there are nightmares, and there will, we are sorry to say, be blood everywhere—

To begin in the middle, then, where the real trouble always commences—though earlier one thought some X or other was *going to be* the real trouble—but no, the real trouble lay for the Author in treating what he later realized had been by comparison a mere inconvenience (it is hard for us even to contemplate it that *we* are all that's left of the book, and that the Author's voice, which we'd come to rely upon like the mutt in the old Victrola logo, will not be heard again; but just as he persevered despite his own misery so will we, determined in our manner, declarative in our speech, frill-less in our recitation; the jungle is sparse now, comrades, our miscreant guide has been lost to us . . .)

Ceci n'est pas l'Auteur

Beginning then in the middle (again), it appears that the Author had been working happily and with diligence on his acreage in the woods of western Massachusetts: rising at dawn, stoking the furnace, negotiating a three mile run, wolfing orange juice with yeast and raw egg congealing *chez* the fruit pulp, then brewing coffee and sitting in his sweatsuit and Nikes at his blood-wood desk overseeing the duck pond and birches—like this, confident and a little smug, his days ran together in the cozy atmosphere of the countryside. As is well-known to all loyal readers, the A had recently remarried, his bride this time being younger than he by a generation, in part accounting for the A's vigorous quest for health and his runner's ledger that rested beside his writer's log on the Bechstein in the bay window. So he worked at the book you've been reading, sensing in the effort a definite and pleasurable breakthrough—quite simply from having in the past considered his written work to be a Flaubertian search for the perfect "*rien*" at the heart of a fiction (and of a life) to considering his present effort to be a Flaubertian search for the perfect "something" at the heart of the earlier nothing—an Author therefore catching a second or Zen wind in the abused lungs not only of his cretified body but of his overripe elegant and baroque imagination.

What he would say to his "contemporaries" on the tennis court when they'd inquire after his "youngish" spouse was that since he'd dropped thirty pounds, begun to study Italian, and bowed out of arguments with his son he was not middle-aged but in fact as youthful as JJ. "Even a ten year old can die of old age," he'd quip, "if he dies at ten it's as old as he's going to get. I don't believe in age anymore than I believe in consciousness. Whose serve is it?" When he gave up cigars his friends knew he was serious about a fresh start, and praised him; when he traded his tennis game for aerobically running the country road they admired his rigor and threshhold of pain, but worried at his gauntness; when he began to refuse liquor they questioned the longevity of his second, perhaps hallucinatory, self; and when he began to bring along his own bag of rice to dinner his friends deserted him, an effect they concluded he'd been seeking all the while. His wife's friends—her "contemporaries"—were his son's age, and in fact he'd met JJ through his son who was briefly in love with JJ's mother, herself revolting against her ex-husband's middle-agedness and so at forty, firmly, becoming a Connecticut collagist. JJ was a practicing CPA and her counterpart, the A's son, a pianist in the orchestra of a small provincial city—the Bechstein of the Author's bay window had been acquired in order to make the son feel welcome in the new family. Once, in the spirit of reconciliation and brotherhood toward the whole of humanity that only middle-age can conjure without embarrassment, the A organized a weekend at the acreage that included his son, his son's mother, JJ's mother, and JJ's mother's former husband. The attempt was such a dismal failure that by Saturday afternoon the house was empty, everyone having escaped back to the city, leaving only the A and JJ to sweep the broken dishes and shattered pottery. "We all have our ex-es to bear," JJ reminded him when he broke down weeping. But all this had the desirable result that one chapter ended and a new one began, literally as well as figuratively. New life, new habits, new spouse, new Nikes, new book—the optimistic metamorphosis of every cocoon: "After a night of pleasant dreams A woke to find that he had been transformed into a happy loveable man. He looked around the mansion. It was no dream." And so we have a portrait of the A as vivified man, revised into existence, sure of where he's been, unsure of the future and, preferring the lack of direction, passionately attached to the moment.

Numerous anecdotes in the preterite might dramatize the year that followed the A's metamorphosis, in which he and JJ circled each other, came briefly together, but continued to edit the difference in their years, experience, and personhood so that the text of their romance might seem both original and archetypal of all those viable sunset/sunrise marriages. It was in that amorous reincarnative anecdotal year that the A dedicated himself to the *Death of Don Quijote* and to the story of Amerigo and Europa, in honor of his own Puritan heritage and JJ's French correlatives. The Casanova-Henriette story was at first a whim based largely on the Author's belated discovery and puerile enjoyment of the wordplay attending "tail" and "tale"—yes, just such things *do* nourish genius to flower. During this period he noted the significance of "October" in his thinking: 7 October 1571 is the date of the battle of Lepanto in which Miguel Cervantes de Saavedra lost the use of a hand, (the hero of the battle was named Don Juan) and which the city-state of Venice celebrated yearly thereafter to commemorate the first major defeat of the Moslems—and yes, from his cell in the Doges Palace Casanova, nearly two centuries later, not only observed the partying procession of priests and politicos who were marching from the church of St. Justinia for the Hall of the Scrutinio but at that moment on 7 October 1755 thanked Cervantes under his breath for recalling to him that an even larger celebration would be taking place in exactly twenty-four days (his own number of years on earth!) on 31 October, according to Ariosto a good night for an escape. So in this accidental but eurekafied manner the A first recognized the curious connections of Quijote to Casanova. Then, to his truly amazed sense of coincidence, he recognized as well that Mozart's *Don Giovanni* premiered in Prague 29 *October* 1787, and that Casanova was not only present but had had a direct effect on the composition itself in its final phases—*Overture,* Leporello's first song, and the *Finale* in which the stone guest kills the great DG by merely touching his hand.

It was glorious! The A ran grinning through the woods, lengthening his stride, hardening his flexors, hilling to toughen his quads—all for the furious search of further "actual" bridges between his typewriter's actors, events, and artistic modes. A driven A, he was in no way distressed by JJ's self-absorption; indeed he didn't notice it because of his own, and even if he had he'd have also assumed it gave JJ pleasure to account for her husband's rejuvenation, though it might at times mean he was not always sure who she was when he looked at her through a film concealing the details of the recreatable history of Europe. Yes, anecdotes would fill the gap of emotions, but it is an ancient tale really, of oldish men failing to keep their youngish women from becoming curioush, and to retell such a pitiful bumpkin's saga would only slow the progress of the more original and terrific resolution. We'd have to resort to tricks to keep it interesting, and we abhor those—

Suffice it therefore that you can recall from the earlier parts of the book "when" it was that the marriage entropied, and when *in real life* JJ trysted with ———, himself a novelist no less who no less lived on the acreage adjacent to the A's, *our* A's—they were sort of bookends—and who claimed to perceive in JJ the makings of still another writer! It must've given JJ a shock to hear ——— explain that he too was at work on a book in which Venice prominently figured. "Oh, I thought you meant Venice California," ——— apologized to JJ when she exclaimed her delight at the parallel. The afternoon of the party JJ read first from the A's ms., then from ———'s, not so much to compare their literary merits and debits, though this was inescapable, but to conceive in her own imagination the men behind the corrasable masks. With thought, instinct, depression, and simple boredom, JJ chose her new lover ——— so that there eventuated a dreadful scene which for litigious reasons shall be indirectly reported. How a certain person of the female persuasion whose initials redund packed a suitcase in the middle of a party and, with ——— hefting the load, demarched *chez* ———, leaving the mortified A alone with thirty or forty guests roaming the house, the yard, the bedrooms, the study, the stable and canoe. Drunk as skunks, happy as larks, smoking like chimneys, raucous as hens, the cliched crowd for a long time figured nothing. After the sock A gave ———'s jaw it was assumed the trouble was over. But later the pinched nose-holes of the A as he stood on his creaky wood porch in the August moonlight gave it away; his moist palm insanely held up a pillar that looked like it in turn held up the whole clapboard scene; a Pabst Blue Ribbon warmed his hand and drew bottleflies; the wide acreage of weed and vegetable garden shook with Saturday night frolic—the laughter, the music, the gossip, the groping, the entire New England rural culture—rocked and congratulated itself while JJ lowered her head, lifted her stickered suitcase, and unfolded her sinewy gold figure onto the deathseat of ——— 's disgusting Porsche. Already the A's dialogue had heard JJ say in parting, her lovely head uncoiling from behind the down-rolled greasy ——— window, *Hic est vale!* And already the A's narrative observed the Porsche skid in the gravel raising dust, pebbles, feathers, the errant Blatz can, the paragraph accompanied by New Wave radio music in the Porsche, an eartaste JJ surreptitiously acquired those rainy afternoons in ———'s company. The screeching tires and careening sportster, as well as the A's own brief speech in the empty hot dark, wakened say half the guests to the idea that something really untoward had happened. God *fucking* damn! the A cried. Y him? What am I sposed to do now?

JJ paled. I thought she would be sick. Looking at me as if I'd sprouted another nose she set aside what she'd just read, namely the above, and sighed one of those mammalian breach-like aerations that never quite mean something but sound like they should. I never expected something like this, she said. Good, huh? I answered. How do you expect me to do this party tonight after what you've just done? I warded off the demons, I said. There'll be no trouble now. I wrote them out of our systems. And you want this in print? she asked. I thought maybe. It's going to look very odd, she explained worriedly. I mean really odd. Odder than you've imagined. Believe me. I need a drink. Look! I said to JJ. The rain's stopped, sky's clear. Sun's out! JJ pinched my face between her fingers: Fucking fiction, she said. JJ's letters quiver and quake as they trot out onto the vast white plain of the A's La Mancha, his Paris, his Venice. Of course JJ's own awe at the A's complicity in her decision to leave him makes the letters reluctant to emerge; they've got to be shoved, kicked and cajoled, coaxed by promises of rest stops and pleasant stories they'll later be shaped to, before they'll risk the awful light of JJ's words. Harsh and polished, rehearsed with ——— over omelettes and still more scotch, her letters would cower if there were a convenient corner, they'd loiter in the margins like punks with smokes hanging from their lips, impassive, phlegmatic, reflecting on and reflective of nothing. But JJ won't stop them coming. And the A won't let JJ. JJ said her story ought to be called, Y I M O K N U R F'D. Tell it to me, the A pleaded. Give me the word, JJ.

After reading this last little bit JJ rose, dumped her scotch in the sink, buttoned up her workshirt, turned around while I waited to hear the bad news, and looked right through me. Tell me the fucking tale! I shrieked. JJ went on looking through me. Hi! Hi! (Now who's that?) We have guests, JJ said smugly. I turned and saw standing in the doorway the arrival of the party. We're running out of time, I said quickly under my breath. Hi, you two! We're out of it, JJ concluded.

Matinee

"Sea to the fore, ash aft, left and right town and country, beneath us beautiful beach, we'd a hell of a time ruining it."

The Final Adventures of You

YOU wake up, it's Geneva outside, you remember you've hidden the moleskin notebook under your pillow but when you reach for it it's gone. A sportscar can be heard speeding away.

You wake up and remember you're a king, it's a scorcher at Thebes, into which a dusty messenger comes running.

You wake up, Prague, overhead the ceiling of your room in your parents' apartment, your legs feel funny, etc., etc.

You realize you're Don Juan passing in and out of consciousness after accidentally giving yourself a fatal wound in the grove behind the Accademia. Voices.

You wake up and everyone in the room starts calling you Raskolnikov. You're in Petersburg. It's 1885. *Oh my God!* you cry and it comes out Russian!

Thank goodness you realize you're Sancho Panza and everything's been a story Don Juan has recited on the way to the village from which very soon you will set out together to tour the New World. In fact before you know it it's the New World!

Given your reputation as a perspicacious reader, a detective when it comes to gossipy matters, and one who come what may likes to see a thing through to an end, you want to discover the fates of JJ and Theo. Love may have its place, you educe, time is what is fleet. Only once the word is wordless is there no longer a doubt as to its meaning—*love,* that is to say. These pullulations, like assorted others, draw you to Venice. You can't help it. Having come this far in the matter you decide to organize your vacation this year around the fates of JJ and Theo. Knowing this decision may not be readily understood by the figure beside you in bed or on the beach or across the room smoking in the dark with irritation at your nose conspicuously dipped into a book yet again, you prepare to read aloud the funniest or filthiest pages you can quickly locate. You might, on the other hand, announce to your future traveling companion a fact of relevant interest, such as that Mozart's last bars of music, written into his *Requiem,* are of the same key as the death of Don Giovanni. Then again this information may not elicit the response you would hope for. Try rather a particularly pithy sentence, read aloud neither dramatically nor in monotone, permitting its intrinsic validity to tease the sensibilities of the one you would influence in the direction of Italy. Try, for example, this: *Send a person into it and moonlight bruises.* If this strikes you as precious, as well it might on second thought, it having no context beyond the crass one of persuasion, attempt another—*One horse is worth a thousand kings, in particular to the thousandth and first.* On such a remark you can discourse a long time. Or you might, in order to achieve Venice, more earnestly than usual whisper into your friend's ear Italian words vaguely seductive at an appropriate moment of your own choosing. Such stand readily available in any pasta cookbook. Like as not your success will depend more on the voice's tenor. Oral love say. Friseur it. How you manage a Venetian journey on behalf of characters in a book is your business. Failure to get there, to see for yourself, will mean missing the resolutions of Theo, of JJ, perhaps even of others. Think Paul and Nicole, for two. Think Berkeley Bill. Now what would he be doing in Venice, you wonder. To Venice for the answer! Standing before the mural *Battle of Lepanto* in the Great Hall of the

Doges' Palace, much will begin to occur to you. *Non so d'onde Viene,* you will think, among other things. That will be only the beginning.

For a moment assume Venice.

Midnight's heroes on rooftops and balconies, hanging from gutters even, crouched behind the bougainvillea on verandas, even fettered in cell beds, or in fact grumbling across the bars—

During breakfast at a sidewalk café, a nameless one which you will know when you see it, you recognize Steiner drinking wine by himself. Confidentially, he'll be unslept, hair too long, beard grizzled and flecked with matter, weight below health—that is enough to identify him. Though agitated by the interruption of his privacy, he is not the least surprised. Others have come before you. He is used to these intrusions. Polite and deferential to an obsessive degree, RS invites you to be seated—*Bring your goombah along too!*—and offers you the glass of wine the hour of the morning cautions you against. Not really knowing the hour, he drinks alone. If he knew it, however, he'd still drink alone. Having met one of the characters you've been seeking—though this a mere point of reference for the large drama of passion, madness, prophetic art, perhaps the violence which if possible you'd like to prevent—you'll begin to interrogate him. (You've the entire length of the air journey to devise your questions and a strategy for posing them.) Despite his inveterate and unnerving remoteness, Steiner is direct. Over and over he will say, for example, more to your quiet bewildered companion than to you, *Rather than actually live somewhere, I tend to bivouac. Involves frequent packing, frequent pushing on.*

As will other casual remarks, this puts you on notice that RS may have discovered no more than you about the whereabouts of Theo and JJ despite a grueling odyssey etched into his rough skin. As he confesses, squeezing your eye between sun and cerulean sky, you note that his has become an impersonal character, a function. Already overwhelmed by your fortune, you naively exclaim something along the lines of, *I can't believe it's really you!* To which, unfailingly polite, Robert Steiner grins.

When it was you will later not be able to recall, but at some instant of your encounter with Robert Steiner you realize that what is to you a whimsical holiday with an unusually bookish itinerary is to him a vivid persistent nightmare. What you will emphasize about this phase of your vacation, when you speak of it to friends back home at parties, say, is the surprising lack of self-consciousness this character conveys. In that condition he will acquaint you with his latest failure. You're all ears.

The Adventures of Robert Steiner

DESPITE a basically stony disposition I have for years been victimized by chronic nostalgia, an excruciating sentiment that overtakes me when I least can afford it. Accompanied by awesome fatigue, nostalgia makes me want to explain myself to people many dramas distant from my life in the present, as if something might have been omitted way back when that could even now change everything. In the luminous phase of these attacks a bullet of reality always manages to enter my ear to remind me that those people whose resolutions in my life still feel so distant are not undergoing my absence from them, or their own failure toward me, with anything if at all like the fervor, anxiety, or regret I experience.

Although this nostalgia is attended by physical ailments such as nausea, palpitations, blurred vision, boils, loss of appetite, insomnia, a long fall from the three-wheeled wagon, and the renewed vigorous use of nicotine, it at least provides an occasion for my body and my mind to harmonize, a feat otherwise Walenda-like impossible. Understand that when I was a mere six years of age I could look back with regret at the age of four, and in the presence of younger cousins try to regain the innocence and carefreeness the earlier youth meant. Therefore, as you might expect, from one *casa nova* to another I am forever glancing to the rear and cannot say goodbye to anyone. At the same time I neither narrate nor picture a life for these absent people who have constituted the whole of my existence. To feel them is enough. I am time and again reminded that all people in the flesh are more or less alike, and many I even care to avoid, but that each absence occurs in its own way and to its unique sentimental effect. One of these effects is that wherever I am I am always waiting for someone from the past to reappear; on occasion I have planned ahead with absolutely no external evidence that anyone I know is even on the same continent, or even alive for that matter. Ordinarily this would be a particularly insidious form of paranoia, but it is also possible that I have been so unfailingly non-committal that I have broken through to recklessness. I am, from your point of view, merely setting the scene for a last meeting with JJ and Theo, whose fates I take it are the ones that propelled you here. Quite okay, really. For your purposes let's say the real story can start now. There's tons of wine here if you'd care to . . .

The Further Adventures of Robert Steiner

SEVERAL years ago I learned that O. T. Stone had published a novel in which a certain summer party he'd hosted occupied a considerable portion of the text. You are of course familiar with this text though I have scrupulously avoided it, celebrated though it has become. On that same occasion I was also informed that the author had done nothing to protect identities. He named names? I asked amazed. The other dinner guests—no, this will not be another party—were impressed that I had no knowledge of this book or of my tangential but unpleasant role in it. Though, for a time at least, I was the one who got the girl—this he neglected to type. The setting for all this new knowledge I received was Gretl's Brooklyn brownstone, rather the intimate dining room of it, on the table of which were splintered bird bones as well as spikey green vegetables and gummy potato-scapes. Gretl's family and few friends sat around soused, none more so than Gretl herself who had withdrawn into a matriarchal stupor, endlessly shrugging butterflies of irritation off her shoulders, alert to everything but the fact that even her son and grandson saw her as a relic. I however was not soused; I was medicated, per prescription. I should say here that I was recovering from a depression so encompassing, imbricated, and enduring that by stages I had lost my senses of smell, taste, hearing, and touch. To be civilized one whole day had been impossible. A depression as low as Death Valley and blacker than the belly of a dead horse. While I was not the first person ever to require a period of supervision I felt at the time like a carp in a tank. While not a public nuisance, nonetheless scrutinized. Therefore luculently anxious about making a decent social statement. Taking another whack at exposure. And, but for my dark glasses, glad to be vulnerable.

Yes, he named names, Paul said over creamed broccoli, his hair having dramatically thinned. And Dad made you look like a real shmuck, Bobby.

To this I tongued a tooth and explored Nicole's cruel eyes for confirmation. I said I'd been away awhile, and even if I hadn't I hardly ever read anything but timetables. A few folks coughed at the remark.

Just as well, JJ concluded with a smile I had last seen when she assured me Theo was out of her mind for good, and I was in it.

Paul said, I was wondering if you'd had a chance, given so much free time recently, to read the book since you're in it.

Like I said I said, no, n-n-no.

We're all in it, JJ reassured me. Off and on she watched me to make certain I wasn't adrift too far. It was her first gander at me since my release. Paul's too. Mine, for that matter. Whereas I might've cried, Simpering Librium! and left the room, instead I laughed Paul off, sitting back in my chair and interrupting him with a squeaky liquid laugh that apparently scared hell out of everyone.

Gimme, I said when the cheese and fruit appeared, though I wasn't actually speaking to a soul. Rather, as though a dark threshhold had been crossed, I waited to be welcomed back into the grubby streets of monotonous life. Gimme more, I said, feeling the weight of persistent efforts to start living again. But I didn't dwell on them.

I said to Giorgio, aged twelve, across the table, I was your age once. Everyone quieted. Maybe even twice, I added, recalling that adults used to bore me in my adolescence, and now and again still did. The kid looked at me as though I were a TV screen, providing me the sort of embarrassment which a year earlier I could've heightened into calamity, skin-crawling terror. Listening then to Nicole attack her first former husband to her current one, her former husband's son, I thought she did not particularly want to exercise power over people, though she did, but that she loved to fight for it. Soon I realized I was witnessing a family argument. During it I learned that O. T. Stone had vanished, as he had written O. T. Stone would. Just don't call him looney! Paul shouted, and that pretty much squelched the fire only because, as I further realized, some people were glancing in my direction at the mention of that word looney. Fortunately, Paul was too upset to care. Off and on the conversation turned passionate; clearly lines had been drawn over Theo so that the only thing everyone there shared about him was frustration.

Sure, oh sure, I'd casually remark to show I could follow the arguments. Details, though, were the subject, while larger questions were left floating—these washed across me, some vanishing under the table. The argument souffled again, and for a while I was like everyone else, busy disagreeing with someone, about what I could not be sure. Then the place fell silent.

What do you think? Paul asked me suddenly. I purpled and lost ground in front of everyone, they therefore gained it back.

Um-m-m, I said, forgetting my viewpoint on the matter which was just as well since I'd forgotten the matter too.

To err is human, JJ replied. To umm divine.

Why was everyone laughing at that? But JJ's expression along the table calmed me. I did not take the joke personally. She wasn't judging me, and no one here would judge me even if I spoke out. I think I could have made any answer, I think there wasn't just one they were expecting to hear. However when I laughed I could tell they feared I was slipping into hysteria, which I was not. How do you feel, Gretl asked me, you look unwell. How do you feel inside, I mean?

With my finger, I said.

Well, I think, Nicole quickly drummed, that the whole fucking mess only started at that party. Lives fucked because of it, several ended for Christ's sake, that fucking movie that fucking J-P made, and fucking Theo bugging the whole place. Dead people everywhere—Henriette, the Finches on the way home, poor fucking ——— blowing his fucking brains all over the fucking road.

What party? I quietly asked, and for an instant felt as conscious as a lamppost.

It was in '75, JJ reminded me, trembling at the mention of ———'s suicide, which I had also forgotten.

You remember 1975, don't you? Gretl asked me.

At first I thought this was a trick question, then understood I was merely being insulted. '75? I said philosophically. What's not to remember? All I had to show for '75 was a few months with JJ and an absence of fear. Nothing after '75 could spook me again. *Especially* nothing.

Interesting, Giorgio spoke up curling his lip with disgust. Interesting that you think you weren't a part of it.

"Cowbird munching oxcheek, that close."

The Fall of Robert Steiner

READING O. T. Stone's book, remember me invading JJ's privacy after the ruckus of guns and wanton sex was more or less put to bed? Theo the A upstairs, ——— on his way home to load the pistol to blow open his head, without blanks this time, just as the book said he would? Remember all the others with all their so forths? And that the things crashing onto the verandah with an h drew me into the study? Clarifies now, does it? JJ sipping, no, inhaling scotch, literally that is, as though smelling for drugs, while I toed the floor shame-faced or something. My sleepy gaze philandered her jumper and shorts. I wanted nothing in particular, in particular nothing from her, married more often even than I. I didn't want her, let's say, let's say I wished I could want her. Keep old-fashioned love out of this, that goes without saying. Just as the sole cause of so much divorce is so much marriage, so is it that love flattens the world that lust makes go round. Understand that realizing my temperament during periods of prolonged intimacy, of which love serves as a universal model, by 1975 I was content to be an acquaintance, listener, and house guest at domiciles from coast to coast on several continents. Even so, or because, I could see JJ had had it, whatever it was, and would give anything for a week's peace. Who wouldn't? At that point, seeing JJ had had it, suddenly I felt I hadn't. Leaning on our hips in the middle of her husband's study, face to face and chin to chest, we sighed. A lifetime of shit requires our kind of sigh. Though I flagged her with two open arms she just indicated to me her suitcase, as beat up outside as she was in. While no romance fugged the air sympathy did, nothing feverish or mouse-proof but enough to walk through the door on. After a half minute of unusually empty staring we caught ourselves feeling ourselves self-conscious and so headed for the door, the biggest of us hefting the luggage.

Sounds like a love story. As the tenant once said, I was comfortable in that room, and apart from the rats happy. Sounds like is one thing, was is another. On the verandah with an h we met You, not you, You. If I recall somebody turned up dead. Then somebody else did too. In such a situation, to us what was love but a choice of breakdowns in which at least one finds not only ambosex but fellow feeling, where each time you fuck you fuck friend. Our relations were not nothing right up until the moment they became so. On the contrary they were something, cowbird munching oxcheek, that close. Call this story mackled then. When not hearing it, call that over. Though ———'s suicide postponed it JJ and I still left Theo's house, Theo asleep because we'd put him there. Interminable, this story, isn't it, and scarcely begun. Like marriage, the one thing wrong with storytelling is you've got to be there.

Try it this way then. At last the place cleared of cops, creeps, and killers, to say nothing of killed. Just us three and me so sullen Theo doesn't know I'm around. Just as well. Sun down, eats, hours tick off, I note Theo looks ill, JJ notes it and that I do too, meaning I note too we'll discuss it later, assuming later will occur, if at all, when we're alone, which we are around ten p.m. because Theo pill-takes and conks out, covered on the sofa by horsehair; JJ and I blanket him together, *blanquet de vieux* you might say, and retreating tiptoe to the kitchen we chew fat, mostly hers, where just as I thought I hear Theo's a goner, in his brain though, the body's a horse's, the brain though, I tell JJ, is the worst organ to be gone in. Oh despondent, she clarifies, suicidal, I understand, I wag my noggin, this is an easy disease for me to grasp.

No sooner invited over night than I assume she means for fucking, foolishly I mostly undress; it is still a kitchen, she is considerably stunned, just as soon I realize that what is wrong here is I seem to be out for something, with which to my surprise JJ empathizes, and what is more she finds my interest utterly endearing, nearly as utterly as the pitifulness of it, a speech bringing her to tears, just as well therefore I didn't fully re-dress though it isn't over the sink or anything where it happens, in fact no appliances were involved at all. Sex done, lying upstairs in the dark I don't like it, it smells, I light the room as a result, wondering is this where whose-it died then got raped the night of the party, and even if not what am I doing in Theo's house for a snooze, his wife numbing my bicep, when he might be anywhere? You know the sensation, gets you dressed and on your way, forget tired, forget post-coitus-itis; in my case what I got was downstairs planning to wake Theo my host with a hard shake, but changed my mind, no, postponed it, why I couldn't say, his drooly lips maybe, rapid eyelid motion signifying an important nightmare, who knows why I instead of waking him went back to the bedroom to lie bolstered by JJ's breast, my teethmarks furrowed in the skin still, puffing blue in fact, I couldn't help palming it, the tit, while I thought, hating thinking as I did, what the hell! No sooner said than we were gone, creeping like burglars in felony shoes so Theo the A could sleep right through it.

Here comes the sad part.

Though we travel, JJ and I, we manage to avoid enjoying it, living instead a mutual impatience which if we took pleasure in anything else would be sweat off a duck's tail. As it is, hell. Not that either life was previously a joy, how could it be? Our holiday beneath Antwerp-blue skies of this, that, and the other place was an airbleed. To what end even we wondered. Like many we needed gonging to know it and no gonging resounds like scalading foreign terrains—their heat, their verbs and mires, their being altogether Elsewhere. The perfectly happy break down there; Elsewhere is notorious for it, since it offers bullnoon all day and at night bone-shaving scream. You, she, they, I, he, we tend to die Elsewhere. That's where we went anyhow. Something to krex about. There, Elsewhere then, it turns out JJ had had enough of me too, around the sixth week, where she wept alot of mythology and goats smoking in the sun. Sea to the fore, ash aft, left and right town and country, beneath us beautiful beach, we'd a hell of a time ruining it. JJ'd had it again, another emotional boner, so she looked me differently in the eye, her whole person other. *Exo,* was what she concluded. *Exo ta femina,* Greek goodbye. The sort of recognition, after a lifetime of them, requiring eyestalk and chunder, perhaps even roughhouse. We blister in the loamy powder, suck lobster claw free of flux, we even level the infrequent doornick at one another, fortunately none big enough to do any damage. Who knew toward what we'd been racing if racing is apt when sunning and sleeping off drink were how we were what. Of a reasonably lengthy stable environment—consisting say of flat, employment, chitchat over toast, a snow shovel—there was none.

Go, I said in exhaustion. Thinking it for weeks I drew out the drama of saying it the width of the sea and length of the alps, any alps. She breathed, the relief and the sadness. Gazed, as they say, searchingly into my eyes. As they say, mournfully. Having to remove my blue glasses to do so. Are you sure? I repeated my suggestion, JJ her question, she her question, I my etc. for what seemed days and probably were. You sure? Sure. Really? I glanced around, over with was all we had left. Love loves best that loves lost, something like that she mumbled. What's love got to do with it? I replied. You sure as can be? Sure enough, I confessed. But what of your gloom, your tireless apathy, listless bark, all that carping and guilt, so much failure, what'll you do Bobby? I expected as much, I said.

So she goes. Separated we regreted as never together had we enjoyed. But in no way were either the diminished hope or risen despair dicorticating me. Woe, anguish, shame, worry, solitude, its infirmities—these dogged me, but no hebephrenia. Of catatonias, none. Rather the many many lighted cities of my experience, me alone in them, undergoing their otherness, my sameness, distance, speed, more distance—Elsewhere, on my own, I was at home. By temperament a sightseer, I required not-here to thrive in. *Here* not only did I starve, I toxified.

The breakdown. How it came about. The reason, taking for granted a modest knowledge of myself, I didn't see it coming. Why when it came it chose the occasion it did. By what stretch of truth I convinced myself it wasn't one. Why that particular stretch and how I assayed the possibility of different ones. The routine, from one end to the other, of depression's eternity. The motive, as in the symphony, the motive of diminisheds. The motive, as in the murder, that of jealousy. The tedium. The tedium of the tedium. What we said during before and after that we hadn't when we should have and did when we shouldn't or did when it didn't matter. Scenes of odious domesticity. Those of blood-curdling ordinariness. Others of ordinary blood-curdlingness. These impertinences I leave to the imagination.

Anyhow, Thanksgiving dinner drew to a close. Paul, Gretl, Nicole, and Giorgio said so long from their door and I knew we were quits then and there. No sooner were JJ and I alone in the snowfall than I felt a context envelop us. Within it I was careful not to confuse life with any stories about it. Of Theo's disappearance I spoke not a word, and of JJ's from me I asked no questions. For this she slipped her hand into my peacoat pocket, her palm warming mine. Such embrace as this amounted to could not be judged sexual but rather the balm of human touch, soothing the ache of always waking alive. So how you been, kiddo? Up from execrable. Who asked and who answered did not matter. To avoid loose talk and yet not to separate we did what everyone does with embarrassment, went to the movies. In which I'm reminded over and over that ideas kill. Happens all the time. End narrative, end life, fucking too over, oh well once more, yawn and fart—movies move me like that. The movie house entered, the story on, not waiting for us, the theatre's crippled seats in the dark, JJ and I ushered by flashlight front and center—call this the late show, if ever there was one.

The Final Adventures of Robert Steiner

LOOKING, often back, as often I do, I remain surprised that I am still shocked by the experience of the movie house, round about midnight, Thanksgiving, front and center. At times the shock, at my age, grows unbearable. Know only, of that movie house, that from our entrance to the rapid raveling celluloid JJ kept her feet on the seat, her knees tucked to her chin, her eyes impelled. Mine were too, eyes that is, toward her however rather than the screen. Which had a painful rent running north and south. *Ouch!* A sparse crowd, losers, these too I observed. I watched, in fact, just about everything but the commotion on the screen whose afterglow greened our faces. I was getting ready for a bout of nostalgia, starting to feel teary, some great hunk of regret crawling up my throat muscle. It might have been a whopper, the scene I was edging toward, full of sobbing and speechifying, self-accusations, the whole breast-thumping spectacle right there at the midnight show, the sort of undoing gets you back to the lithium, the lithium and scotch, lithium, scotch, and Mahler say, all of them in the dark, and all in that space where it's always two a.m. Unfortunately JJ had her own crisis, fingernailing my forearm to the seat rest, more or less crying out. I assumed she'd done something like burst a blood vessel and even before I turned to face it I was preparing to cradle her head.

The film, I should say at this point—such details often

escape me, so eager am I to get the story told—was some wreck called *Casanova.* You will not have heard of it. In its midst however JJ was definitely not dying. She pointed with the hand that wasn't tearing my flesh, pointed west of the rent, into a salon scene peopled by magicians, mesmerists, phrenological quacks, and goose-fleshed courtesans, to a mouth six feet wide that claimed possession of the philosopher's stone. This mouth orated over a table shot strewn with beef. In the flick the mouth's teeth were brown like tree bark, its tongue leathern. Under a wig, rouged and wimpled, waxed at the lips, rigged in satin and lace, O. T. Stone, to us vanished, recited his part. As usual, with our necks craned, he was larger than life. No less mortified than JJ, I urged her to leave with me, rising swiftly enough to upset the popcorn and jujubes. As with most of my requests this she refused, perceptibly easing the grip on my skin as her surprise gave way to horror, it to bewilderment, that to curiosity, fascination finally, so that she didn't even have the presence of mind to ask me not to leave. I'd already left so to speak. Before us braced in our seats, our heads tossed back with whiplash, Theo's face was about nine feet high; I could have walked through the spaces between his teeth, or skied down his black throat. Though we couldn't know it at the time, his character appeared only once, enigmatic and to my mind gratuitous. A bit part. One we waited for, though, to resurface. The flick dragged. Dragged and dragged. I thought anyhow. If I tried to speak JJ hushed me, move and she stilled me with her hand. I reminded her that what we were witnessing was plastic. Even before I'd lost her I'd lost her, and remember I'd lost her before.

To kill the time and calm my nerves I counted the number of shots, then within some studied the objects in backgrounds—of those I noted the shapes and colors, with shapes and colors I analyzed the geometric patterns this film consisted of. Venice got staged, the star stood in it, the star's bride, she too plastic. I leaned over to inform JJ of the fakiness this movie was made of but she was no longer next to me. The movie, interminable as it had been, even it ended. Lights as a result came up, occupying the space of the dark. In those lights no sign of JJ. Nor strolling up the aisle among the yawning few who staggered out with those bleary expressions that signal massive headache. The big screen blanked out, behind me a long way the projector died, and in the sudden quiet and haze the empty theatre was even shabbier than I'd imagined. In addition I smelled a new stink loose somewhere, it rose with the lights and the fleeing patrons. A sticky something or other.

I recall that after that I hunted JJ under seats, calling out her initials the way one times breaths over a heart victim. JJ, look see, JJ, look see, JJ, again, and so forth. For vantage I commandeered the stage, and shading my view against the bulbs in the ceiling I scrutinized pews and corners, and bending the neck I combed the floor. The word peered fits what I was doing. Opposite me, a long way off, a fat man in a red jacket captured me with a flashlight. He was, you could say, a theatre away. HEY YOU he announced, he reverberated. I ignored both the voice and the echo. YOU. AUDIENCE. SHOW'S OVER. That's what *he* thought. I could not really see his face and ignored the voice some more. SWEEPIN UP. Ignored too the code of his flashlight though it shot me often and then surrounded me completely. When with a huff he bent down I hoped it'd be JJ he would pull from under a seat like a bunny dragged from a stovepipe. WADDYA SPOSE MAKESUM DOOT? This I of course ignored. LOOKA DIS MESS. Ignored his in favor of my own. YOU IM TALKING TO. Nowhere JJ. YOU. As I say I peered. *YOU*!

I could go on. *YOU*!! Could but won't though. Life is

riddled by nothing if not fugacity. *DO I HAFTA CALL COPS*??!! Begin grief again, I thought that then. The worst aspect of grief being the very direct object it takes, causing one to lose sight of the complete meaninglessness life comforts us by. *MAYBE YOUD INSTEAD A SOCK IN THE JAW*! Though vanished to me JJ knew perfectly well where she was. Without me she would be lonely but then what was her loneliness when compared with mine?

You took advantage, you'll tell your guests, of the insufferable pause with which Steiner withdrew into a reflective mode to ask him was this autobiography the best he could come up with in the way of information? It has grown hot, crowded, noisy, the canal is as stinky as you feared, your companion is squirming with bone-ache at the chair the café expects you to eat and run in, or out of. Well, there's something, Steiner adds with a shrug, but few of you hang around long enough. In an instant you understand why JJ deserted this guy. Twice.

Federico Fellini, gray, plump, and intense, and surrounded by jugglers, clowns, and extraordinarily ugly people, invited Robert Steiner one day to be seated on the set. After inquiring did Steiner want to appear in his latest film, so like Kafka just before death did he look, Steiner explained his purpose in coming, and made it clear that if nothing else he guarded his anonymity. Fellini understood immediately. The interview was brief, F may have found it interminable. During it he recalled Theo, their acquaintanceship a fast cantankerous one, if not actually ended then truncated by virtue of unbreachable differences. After the film had been shot Theo remained in the city a long while, accompanied everywhere by the large brutish woman he called a sister but who was either something else, or worse, something more. Fellini remembered her irritation when he and Theo would argue matters of Casanovism, glaring as if to sock the great director as much for Theo's vehemence as for the disagreements themselves. *Immense buxoms,* Fellini reassured himself, tracing perfect planets out in front of his heart for Steiner to observe.

Fellini's hair poked out like straw, except in his ears and nose where it coiled. The cardigan he wore was holey. Fellini viewed Casanova as a fascist, that is to say as a protracted adolescent. *He went all over the world,* the director remarked, *and it was as if he never got out of bed.* At this Theo quivered with rage, you'll say Steiner said Fellini told him. Theo'd struggle to remain sociable, a good guest. *No! No!* he would moan in reply. *He never got out of bed and it's as if he went all over the world!* As Steiner tells you this you await mention of JJ, half expecting her to marry Fellini by now. RS's desultory stare and glassy voice promise some meaningful fact soon to emerge. Fellini had said: *I thought I saw a very recent attitude in that eye sliding across reality and erasing it without judgment, without interpretation, without feeling it. The charm of an aquarium, an absent-mindedness of sealike profundity where everything is completely hidden and unknown because there is no human penetration or intimacy.* This was the sort of commentary that would make Theo furious.

But for Fellini—Federico, you can't resist calling him—was Federico speaking of Casanova at the time? *Who else?* RS replies rhetorically, frowning at you in the sunlight. Certainly you do not wish to antagonize him, wondering as well how many readers came to him before you, thinking as you that without knowing it RS might provide the best clues. *Without secrets and without shame,* Steiner continues quoting Fellini. *A presumptuous man, as cumbersome as a horse in the house, he has the health of a horse, he is a horse!* Perhaps Steiner will foresee your discomfort at his digressions and abruptly call them off, heading for heartland as he quaintly puts it. Paraphrasing, RS claims, the great aging film-maker, he is willing to include not only Theo but JJ and yes even himself as only masses, episodes, tumults of inert and often mute matter. We're the empty forms, he extrapolates from Federico, into which you (and *you*—he adds your companion who is thus stirred to attention) pour your secrets and your shames and therefore see them enclosed and separate from yourselves. Some paraphrase, you are wont to assume. And what is more you don't believe a word of it. It occurs to you Steiner may be a blind alley in your search. Who brings the encounter to a close is up to you. RS can rattle until he's totally exhausted. It is this logorrhea that gets you on your feet again, and gets you tugging your companion's sleeve, poor companion who is only now beginning to take an interest in these alarmed mirrors of dissolution that you feel are going to disintegrate too soon. When you leave Robert Steiner you make a point of not glancing back over your shoulder for fear he may have vanished in the meanwhile, or worse, be inviting another sunburnt couple to sit, or worst of all, be observing your every move as you depart.

If you've learned anything in your chance encounter it is that RS's appearance in the book must be a mistake. Or is it just possible that you have entirely misread the book and need to try again, beginning immediately? Then again—you decide you've read your last contemporary novel. Fuck Theo, you say. JJ. Fuck all. From now on records and movies. Books, you claim to your sleeping friend beside you, are so many shitheaps. On the other hand, having read with thorough and lasting pleasure, you might also decide that despite the stiff price you will give one copy each to each of your numerous friends for the new year. Instantly you feel relieved to think you've solved the problem of gifts so easily, quickly, so *usefully.*

About to fall asleep in Venice, you decide that reading of a place just isn't the same as being there, even though once you're there it is more a pleasure to read that other people have been there before you, thinking it a place worth writing up. Even so, you can't help but feel that you are the first person who ever went to sleep in Venice. As you set the book aside you glance at its cover one last time. You feel comforted. Ready for unconsciousness. Your final thought before sleep is a resolution to purchase anything else this author has written, regardless of the cost. A short while later, roused by the prospect of a new reading experience, you lie wondering what else, in fact, if anything, this person has written, and where can you get your hands on it, or them? You head for the window with the big book to see by the moonlight of Venice if other works are listed. When suddenly, startlingly, your friend, companion, and lover rolls over in bed, murmuring as though half dead, *I've got something important to tell you. You can fool with that later.*

Chance Meetings

After a brief visit to Venice, Casanova returned to Paris in 1782, and here the manuscript of his life finishes . . .

HERE is a tale from my history to prove once again there are no sins in the bourgeois life. Pisce, so called for reasons that will become evident, lived in a *burchiello* on the Seine, one of those bobbing and rocking affairs that Pashas refer to as a floating palaz. Hers was not stately, and the Seine is no Nile. Word of Pisce's greatness had reached me years before in Petersburg, and would reach me again later on the Vistula when Cagliostro, the Mesmerist soon after executed in Rome, bragged of his relations with her. At the time of the incident to be related, however, I had forgotten the Petersburg occasion and had not yet encountered the Vistula. The reader will recall with distress that my days as a Venetian were now truly at an end. No more would I see the *mascheratas* in the Ridotto! Never again journey my slumber from midnight until dawn in the lull and luffing, the plash and stroke of a gondola! I was forbidden la Galeria, la Scuola, l'Accademia—never to view again Tiziano, Tintoretto, the Bellini Sebastiano, Bosch's paradise, the Lazarus, the Maria Maddalenas! In this mood of permanent exile, of forever being a fugitive from my native land, I was in need of succor, friendship, diversion, in need of death. And so it was that one evening, brooding my way along the river, with the sun freshly down and the operas, theatres, and balls excluded from my melancholy desires, I remembered the story of Pisce told me in Petersburg (by a personage of such rank and responsibility I dare not attribute it even here, even though these words cannot be viewed until after I no longer live—until after I have tapped out with my hoof the last of my messages to the world). Might my reputation and my grave situation persuade the notable Pisce to give me entry? Having won entry would I be allowed the liberties she is famous for? And being allowed would the experience entertain me? Being then entertained was it possible my melancholy and dreams of death would vanish like some hallucinatory other self, or better yet like a spirit representing my entire past to that instant? Such were my questions, yet each too far down the same boulevard, since while I knew of the *burchiello* on the Seine I knew naught of its location. To discover such as Pisce, one did not interrupt an acquaintance's opera box for directions, nor disturb a minister's family dinner.

Thus I wandered the river's edges while carriages clacked by, lovers giggled behind curtains, the stars overhead sparkled like erotic puzzles, fishing boats returned to their moorings, and one by one the Seine's buoyant dwellings darkened with the night, growing unidentifiable and undifferentiated until I felt it possible that Pisce herself might not exist. For myself then, not for the impossible meeting, I wept bitter tears into the river, already teeming with the miseries, the musings, the corpses of thousands like me. Yes—after the years of sojourn, adventure, passion, my risks and escapes, my dealings and losses, I Casanova stood like a schoolboy wringing my hands. How it was that sounds penetrated my burbling I cannot say, but it is true that no sooner had I foresworn life and prepared to hove my body into the murky deep for some collector to sell to students of anatomy, than a voice from out the darkness sang:

The Moorish king walked with his train
Through Granada's fertile plain,
When the message was brought him
That the Alhambra had been taken

Who was singing such a sad song? Who beyond myself could claim a wound so deep to warrant the pathetic air? When I stepped closer into the dark, remaining silent and secret, the song continued in a voice so plaintive and broken with affection that I began to weep all over again. In an instant the aria ceased, and its singer breathed deeply, in unhappiness at his state or in dread of discovery it was impossible to know. Gradually I realized that before me in the fog, and before the lonely singer elsewhere in the fog, stood a creaking *burchiello* with the shutters closed on its quiet interior. I had to realize this quickly, I say, because no sooner was I struck by the recognition than those same shutters, booming wide against the cabin wall, drenched the foggy quay with light where on one side, still in the shadows, stood the mute singer, and on the other, hidden as well, the sobbing joymaker—me. But in the window of the *burchiello,* filling it with the enormous bulk of her celebrated bosoms, and with the alpen crevasses of her numerous chins, stood Pisce—broader than a schooner, coiffed like a spiral tower, her beefy arms the color of lobster meat. By itself the headpiece she wore would have been harmful to lift, and the bodice restraining her titans was strung more times than a tapestry. *"Pourquoi tu ne soupiras pas, Monsieur? As-tu renoncé à moi? Et moi avec soixante pouces des mamelles?"* The singer suffered an even greater loss of speech at her words. Pisce in her regalia stood exposed at the window, beyond which the suitor and I could see erotica displayed on the walls, and with her subduing dry voice spoke of blissing him in intimate detail. Who there was the more authentic suitor? Who there the truer voyeur? "Mademoiselle," came the quick reply. *"Cessez! Il y a quelq'un la-bas! Dans l'obscur! Taissez-vous pour le moment.* Monsieur! Monsieur *dans l'ombre, qui êtes vous? Allez,* Monsieur. *Vous êtes un gêneur, n'est-ce pas?* Monsieur *la maricona! Allez avec les pucelles, des grisettes! Salaud!"*

Obviously a man of low breeding stood on the dock insulting me, as though I had usurped his place before Pisce. I vaguely heard the scrape of metal and decided in a flash that rather than support a duel with this buffoon—I had already a near murder to my credit on the champs d'honneur—I would suffer him a lesson with the very woman he adored. One whom I myself was finding no less a growing urgency toward, even if the edges were not heated steel. Until now Pisce, the sweetcake of our disagreement, had not moved from the light, instead framing herself like a museum piece, a statue, or rather like the painting of a statue. As permanent against the night as she was stunning, Pisce loomed in the fog as all the sirenes put together, like the mountainside of them itself. To fox the young fox at the gate of his coop, I too began to sing—

Cicerenella, because she'd a mind to,
Kept a cat that was crooked & blind too
& she'd drag it about by the tail, ah!
Twas the pussy of Cicerenella—

at the conclusion of which it was Pisce replying first to my serenade. *"Votre voix est très rouillée,* Signor d'Italie. Oof!" I suppose I was not the troubador I'd once been, and perhaps my effort lacked the enthusiasm of youth which seemed more suited to curry Pisce's affection. But I hungered as surely as he, and being younger he could not be so jaded as myself, and being not so jaded could not be in the same need of the bizarre, the peculiar, the *outré* in order to be satisfied. In brief, I outranked him. In this desperate mood for the soothing touch of the unknown, I approached the opened shutter to view the objects of my affection more clearly, shooing my rival out of the scene with a wave of my malacca. Oily, engirthed, fubsy, redolent, Pisce beckoned me closer, but not with the same mischievous voice as she had fashioned toward my rival.

So fixed was I on the immediate future's promise of holding in my hands a pair of planets whose density, gravity, and general mooniness were already a species of history that I bumped heads in the fog with my rival. We hit skulls. The pilings upholding the quay swayed where we had lowered our brows at the same moment, dropping them chest high in the light of the nearing window. *Giaow!* one of us called to the other—he too was stealing toward Pisce, he too awaiting the unveiling, he too imagining what novel delight she had conceived in an imagination as monumental and inspirational as her figure. Well, we bumped hard, reader, and in the encounter took long significant looks at our mutual faces. We lingered. Stared. Left off our rubbing of sore foreheads, forgot to step forward into Pisce's arms. I saw in him the expressions of a singer who had earned a song about the fall of a king of Spain—moist, earnest, worldly past his years. And what of me would he have seen? The chiseled profile that had served a score of artists no longer boasted the stiff upright flesh, and the eyes I suspect bore a glaze of that film which lately injured my sight. He saw the weariness, the fickleness, the dread; he observed the philosopher that was replacing the libertine. I waited therefore for the insult he would feel compelled to unleash in hopes of sending me on my way. Like this then, composed and anxious, we studied each other, all the while Pisce speaking low about the ménage we three might make if only we two left off staring and crooning and came inside the boat. *"Ma chatte béante!"* Pisce called to the sky. As neither the rival nor I made a further move in her direction Pisce began the auto-sacraments, manipulating herself with her thick hands, unbridling her burdens and tracing the chicken skin with her thumbs. She coaxed, pleaded, she scolded us, she made promises of deeds even I could not quite follow the mechanics of. Still the young man and I did not move. Lest the reader assume he or she is soon to encounter an unnatural passage between my rival and myself I must both clarify and muddy the mystery by answering yes and no. What then was the nature of our relations?

As you will recognize there was some significance because, to begin, neither separately nor together did the rival and I visit Pisce that night, though later I returned alone in a still more morbid state. In a delirium I would watch as the famous one immersed her tonnage in a tub of water poured expressly for the occasion, and spreading far her vast southern lips drew into herself one fish after another—othellos, goldfish, bonitos, each swimming frantically for the calm inner darkness. As if in a trance she scooped them toward her, shuddering each time the head, dorsal fin, the prickly tail disappeared along her passage. The water foamed where Pisce urged them into her, and her hands worked miracles in leading the swimmers on. She shivered when the last fish entered, clenching her muscles to seal the door, and stood with her eyes wide, our breathless silence mingling in the magical deed, dripping from massive head to thick foot as she flooded the room. Once lifted from the tub, thighs squeezed to encase the fish, Pisce undulated her puckering puffed body across the floor and into a harness suspended from the ceiling. I began to doubt I could play my role in this drama. Strappadoed by leather bonds, upturned so her thighs faced ceiling and her torso the floor, the great breasts wholly covering her face, she urged me forward—I was far to the opposite end of the *burchiello*—with her extended fingernails. Even as I approached like a suppliant Pisce unfolded and revealed the unfathomable trench, opening her channel and yet beckoning me close, closer. The remote sound from within her *chatte béante,* as she had crudely put it earlier, evoked for me a universal sadness for now performing what would surely prove the supreme act of my career. I knelt at the grotto of my experience.

With my face to the odiferous alley I peered inside as at a fish tank. One by one the wriggling swimmers passed the furred window so that I might observe not merely the shadowy shapes of them but meet their eyes as they darted for the yawn, for the light they could not reach, condemned to course the length and width of Pisce's canal. I observed as well the striate colors of them, the bright pigments, the brittle fins, the delicate scaling. Their mouths, some whiskered, opened and closed as they swam toward me—and the more they fell back from the grotto's arch the harder they struggled upstream, the more frantic they were in escape, more stricken at the eyes, those rapid mouths. To my shock and surprise the symbol of my curiosity had peeked from its pocket and was smiling—pulsing, coloring, engorged! In an instant I stopped looking and commenced plunging. The feel of the fish as they whisked and skimmed the circumference of my symbol was a giddiness and chill I cannot describe, but only recommend. Their minute teeth nipped, their spikey fins pricked, those cold sleek scuttlers toured first the length, then the breadth, then the roundness of my dragon. Between Pisce's squeals of delight and my gruff squeamishness we passed several minutes introducing ourselves to each other's motion. At once like the coup performed by a dozen mouths, then the threat of castration in the claws of a tiger or great bird of the Andes, and all, all occuring between the classic columns of the statue's immense legs!

I had of course to regulate my breathing else Pisce's large body would begin a swing from its harness to separate us and I then might find myself trousers down in the limelight with a goldfish on the end of me. I breathed, I bent, I rotated hips, expanded chest, got a solid grip on the woman's glaciers, tried glancing at her expression but found it lost beneath the wobbling bosoms skirting the floor. I waltzed the uprighted body, I hefted it twixt my scapulas, I kneaded, stroked, kissed, and bit, all to remain attached. The polar bear growled.

Soon we understood each other, our adjustments were complete, and if only to steady my footing Pisce clutched my ballocks in one gargantuan hand. Slowly I moved in and out of the well, dipping my quill gently, cautiously, feeling the trails of fish lips that bumped, prodded, and analyzed my symbol. Together, just as slowly, we swung on the creaking perch Pisce hung from, listening as to a ship's straining sides while we cooed and aahed and whistled in the rocking room. This easiness we maintained a great time, until I discovered that the fish were serving to prolong my pleasure and to intensify, because of the discomfort, Pisce's efforts at ending it. I waited patiently for the stream not of fish but of obscenities whose wit and originality were said capable of bringing both men and women to conclusion without so much as the touch of a finger. She asked me, between grumbles and snorts, which language I preferred. What else? "Latin?" I clamored. "Give it me in Latin!" Through then her bark, snarl, and yelp, and my own bleating and chirp, she set to immediately a sequence of vulgarisms and explicit provocations in the tongue of Ovid, Petronius, and the Church, all the while jiggling my sac in her moist palm which enclosed my privates so completely they might not have been there! Lords and ladies, what a speech was heard! Cicero himself would never have feared death more!

I rammed Pisce then. I heard the splashing labor of desperate fish, viewed Pisce's gelatinous mounds roll and toss as if they too were ripe with terrorized shark, coaxing her as I plundered groan upon groan, the convulsive belly alive with furious squid. Her skin rippled everywhere I tweaked it, she remarked the twinges and stitches I caused, her breath came fitful, it scorched, and soon she was sobbing for me to finish off! Let be, let be! Out, get out!! Through the thrashing of her legs in their bonds, where the welts rose like flowers, and the clank of the chains that held the harness, I did not falter or pause, neither hesitate nor hear mercy but drove on at and between fish, aiming for them, their gullets, pounding them to unconsciousness, gutting some, tearing several at the gills, until Pisce was begging and howling, until fish blood poured from her to the floor and onto my boots, until my raw and scratched symbol was blue glitter from the hundreds of gummy scales. There, like a constellation, my dragon shone and sparkled, entertaining the night, able to hold a mob, to divert the throng and rush and audience that even now crowded the streets of Paris!

When my spend came it was in barrels, in kegs, in high seas, enough to father a civilization. So wrought were we that Pisce wept for me to give her the load, so heated that we could not remain clasped for the sweat, so conscious of the magnificence that we roared with laughter even as I shot into her a flaming wire of dragon's breath that signified the last of the battery. For eternity the whale and I did not move, instead braying and whinnying our exhausted satisfaction. When at last I had unfastened the bonds and released the harness and chain the woman thundered to the floor panting, maroon, bathed in water; together we rubbed each other's bodies out of the queasiness our effort created. Only then did I hear the goddess moan as though stabbed, only then did she move, rolling over heavily, raising her bulk into a squat, thus to take hold of my hands for leverage and from her position let go of the wad inside her. She squeezed my fists until the knuckles whitened, she glared at me as at a ghost, her swollen body quivered at the discharge. The noise, reader, was deafening, the woman's creased brow blue with struggle, and what I saw before me in that dim light of the room was an imitation of childbirth, the sudden outbursting of some evicted element. Spreading her legs farther and farther, stretching the tendons hidden in fat, she dilated her cunt with a finger, then in frustration inserted her entire free hand up into the passage until with a single quick jerk that sealed her eyes she dislodged the reluctant intruder. It was an enormous emetic gush that sent the last shredded fish sliding across the floor, and with it my own amorous drainage in a rope that clung first to Pisce's hair, paused, then dropped to join the bones, skin, and viscera heaped between us. I thought she must be concluded and so released her hand, which was near to crushing mine. As though in terror Pisce grabbed for it, holding it to her oily breasts which no longer seemed voluptuous but pitiable, woeful, all too human for scorn. She pressed me against the spongey flesh and as I knelt before her in stupefaction I heard the copious flow of urine that passed steaming over the pile before us. "*Peee*-shay," she said to me, pronouncing her name in my native language. "Pisce," she enunciated with a thick laugh.

But as I have said, that event occurred on another occasion from the one I am relating. That is another story, not relevant to the chapter I mean to recite; I apologize for the digression. . . . The night in question saw me walk *away* from the *burchiello,* leaving Pisce in a rage in which, slamming her shutter, she broke one of the slats. I did not leave the Seine by myself, but rather in the company of that gentleman whom I had earlier eliminated as bearing any worth to me, and no greater individuality than say one of those fish that were eventually to swim in and out of Pisce's quim. Let the reader judge whether this would be so! Let the reader decide if my companion were mad, a liar, or if this were merely one of those coincidences which now and again threaten to provide our futile lives with a sense of wonder if not outright meaning.

We had strolled only a short distance, still following the Seine and indifferently noting the supper crowd, when my companion caught his reflection on the river's surface. Pausing, he drew me beside him to indicate my own face in the water, but in beckoning me it was as though he were seeing it already, before my arrival. Our jaws elongated, our skin rippling, our expressions plasticized in the perpetual metamorphosis of the picture frame: we smiled, frowned, smirked, rued, scowled, grinned, stuck out our tongues, crossed our eyes, bent our noses with our fingers, and generally distorted our distortions as they appeared, vanished, and returned to the murky glass of the river. "Casanova," he named me quietly. He repeated the sound. For a stranger to identify me means I have encountered someone who at sometime spied or otherwise informed against me; my memory is so extraordinary, even now, that it has always seemed inconceivable that I would be remembered without remembering. As a result I was on my guard in an instant, and being in the darkness alone with him I could not help but stroke the dagger the reader by now knows I always carried under my cloak. "Do not be concerned," my companion said, reading my mind. "It matters little to you who I am. But you are a great deal to me." He sounded like a lawyer; I gripped the dagger, awaiting a summons or a writ to be slipped into my armpit. Instead he touched my elbow in a display of affection, then turned it to lead me on.

We walked until the city lights harshened, the noise deafened, mud spattered and laughter pealed, and through it all I realized my companion was anything but young. Good God! He was older than I! In the dark and from a distance he had appeared twenty; it gave me a shudder to understand that only a few minutes earlier he had his life ahead of him, in my mind that is, and now he was just as easily fading, decaying, dying. As ancient as I had been feeling an hour before, this man was twice my time—wrinkled, sallow, shrunken, his mustache patchy and gray, his skin blotchy and pocked. Yet the earring, a true anomaly from dead days across frontiers of language and class, glinted in the moonlight, and somehow my confusion I attributed to my own moodiness. As if again he had read my thoughts, the poor fellow said, "Do not fright, Casanova. Everyone but you may take fright." This befuddled me further. I carried my bewilderment into the small park located near the Bourse—the reader surely knows it well—a place anarchic not with vegetation, lovers, or thieves but a chaos of derivative artwork, a clutter of imitative statuary, most familiar to me because many have their originals in my native city, those very institutions I was still aching from the loss of.

"Like the grove behind the Accademia?" my acquaintance remarked.

"Sordidly," I replied, now fully attendant to his every nuance and subtlety, and at the same time glancing at the rows of marble eyes as we passed them. The night in that park was still, a bird sang, the moon halved, autumn the season.

"I was left for dead there a long time ago. A silly matter of honor."

"There is no such thing," I countered.

"No such thing as honor?" he asked.

"No such honor as silly."

"Ah! *You* would think so."

We turned then down an even narrower path where I brushed against a greening outstretched marble hand. It made me shiver. "Yes, left for dead by three of your countrymen on a morning not unlike the one we shall have tomorrow. Gutted like a flounder," he concluded, looking back over his shoulder in the direction of the Seine. We laughed, he heartily, I nervously.

What prank is this? I asked myself. My heart had begun to thump, it was absurd my feeling girlish in his presence. "Señor!" I cried.

To which, without permitting me my statement, he raised a hand that silenced me, and said himself, "Of course you need to view the scar. That goes without saying."

My chest pounded terrifically, the stars in the sky multiplied, my eyesight narrowed, blurred. He unclasped his mantle, unknotted his collar and plied open the shirt with a finger. Because I could not see well in the dark he bade me feel the scar that ran the length of his torso in the shape of a scimitar. The skin was sunken, pinched, and hairless where the blade had sliced him open.

Now here, reader, begins one of those passages which distinguishes the viewer, namely you in this instance, from the painter, namely Giacomo Casanova, since while you, I am sure, are stunned or at least musing on the contrivance that acts as a thread from here to Venice, I was at the time rocked by the quite other concern—that my companion had known, perhaps intimately, the woman in my life whom I had loved above all, and who must have given him access not merely to the moleskin book containing the "story" of her parents' romance but to the contents of "our story" as well, wherein I denied Don Juan and rejected the very idea of him. "Yes," my companion muttered, "I am called Don Juan. *Che sciagura d'essere con i coglioni.*" Only a part of me heard this trickster, for as soon as the image of Henriette stabbed me I fainted on the one and the only occasion of my life.

Even out cold I asked myself, Had she put him up to it? Had our meeting been an accident? Has he sought me out? Where is Henriette?? When I woke to find my head cradled in his lap I leaped as best a fifty-seven year old leaps. Don Juan was shaking his head. "Why is it that in all my stories people keep fainting? Now even *you.* Do they lose consciousness so often in *your* stories?"

"Where is Henriette?" I demanded, trembling with excitement.

The Spaniard drew himself up, looking gravely into my face. The imposter or madman or prankster formed his answer carefully. *"Oú est qui?"*

Was he pretending to be deaf as well?! "Henriette!" I repeated. "Henriette! Dové, Signor? In Parigi? Staséra?" I shook him fiercely, quite prepared to throttle him for a reply. *"Io vo vederla"* I pleaded. I smiled, I grinned, my eyes teared to show my sincere desperation.

The gentleman hugged me, placing his short hairy arms about my neck and pulling me toward him until our foreheads bumped. "Giacomo! Giacomo!" he whispered. " *Non conosco quest'Henriette. Mi credi.* Isn't it enough I tell you who *I* am? I do not know who you are speaking of. It is a woman, of course, so what difference, eh?"

After I had shoved him away and stepped back I counted the years on my fingertips, over and over subtracting *quarantotto* from *ottantadue,* as the reader should do now, and each time the figure made me weep, as the reader should too. The fool who was calling himself Don Juan had to hold me upright, beginning himself to tremble at my condition, until the pair of us were trudging like withered drunken spinsters between the decadent and bourgeois replicas. I could not bear the sight, the smell, or the breath of my companion, nor could I afford to see him leave my side. For various reasons I must keep the location of his lodgings unknown, and yet I can say that he informed me the street would one day bear my name; to those of you reading this in a hundred or two hundred years, the truth or falsity of this man's claim may be evident. I assume Paris still stands? I assume there are Parisians? Is there a France? At these lodgings, then, in the dead of night, with leaves whipping us as we arrived, a wind howling at our heels, and the boulevard deserted, we removed our wigs, undid our girdles, kicked away our slippers, wiped the paste from our cheeks, tweezered off our waxen beauty marks, and at the last had close scrutinies of each other's organ. Where mine spun out slender, sprawling and porcelain, his was chunky, squat and the color of snuff; his he termed concise, mine prolonged; we had a medium-length laugh over our differences.

"Come now" I said, changing the subject, hoping to have arrived at a cordiality that did not, thank goodness, require him to *be* in actuality Don Juan or for me to believe it. "Come now, amigo," I began none the less. "How is it you know the story of Therese and Amerigo? Calm my nerves. Where did you meet her? When did she show you the book? Why did she tell you the story of our relations? Did you see my handiwork on her buttocks? Come! Confess it up, Señor, Henriette is dead, is she not?!" I must have been concealing that terrible fear all along, perhaps as long as my life since I last saw her in Geneva rushing off in her carriage, the terror that by losing track of loved ones you will never be acquainted with the moments of their lives, and worst, be ignorant of their passing. Was it not possible that Henriette had died five minutes out of Geneva that forlorn day, and that I in my need of her could never rest since I presumed her alive, well, and in my vicinity? Until the moment it slipped out into the air toward Don Juan—what else to call the poor beggar, dressed and convinced as he was?—I had not conceived the depth of my obsession. The old man fingered his thick mustache, looked at me with surprise, chagrin, pity, with his empty peasant face, and opened his arms to prove there was nothing between them. "Enough!" I shouted. "Come now! This is not humor but *a* humor. Give, Señor, give! *Dondé* and *qué* and *quién* and *cuando—contadme todo,* Señor Don Juan."

I will shorten the fool's epic by summarizing that he had wandered over a century earlier into a village in Spain and there, in the company of one Sancho Panza, was introduced to Antonia, the niece of Señor Panza's former and now dead master, Señor Quexana. Smitten with Antonia, Don Juan offered to marry her, did, had children, and left only after these were grown, Antonia was dead, and Señor Panza lived in a cage on the outskirts of town. The reader will understand that in my distress I tapped my fingers, swung my legs, bit my lip, rolled my eyes, and otherwise suffered the nonsense well. Now and then I reminded the "great lover" that my subject of interest was Henriette, to which he would reply, "But of course, it goes without saying!" As to the matter at hand, therefore, he said he had told me the Manchegan tale only to verify that *since* he had married Antonia and *since* her uncle had willed it that she marry only an illiterate so books might not be read in the household, it stood to reason, he was embarrassed to admit, that Don Juan read no book about himself, Henriette's mama and papa, nor anyone else either. *"Peccato and bruto!"* he said of his ignorance.

I am a step up front, reader, and knew what question to ask next. Would yours have been the following? "Señor," I gravely quired, "How came it then that you were *reading a book* on the Venetian quay that day when you heard Therese laugh, a laugh which led to the grove, the duel, your gutting, and so forth, a so forth in part at least comprised of me, Casanova, seated here interrogating you, and warning you, sir, as to your honest reply." (Indeed the same *so forth* actually must include my recitation of the whole affair now, must not ignore the fact of the composition.) Don Juan's honest reply came instantly, that is as soon as he figured the logic of my queston, as soon as he knocked at his memory for the evidence, as soon as he recovered from laughing at the coincidence that both of us had had occasion to touch one of those rare women gifted with a protruding button, and moreover our examples had been mother and daughter. This last "fact" brought a tear to his eye, so paternal did he behave toward me. Having recovered from such pleasures at my expense, Don Juan rose, pulled from a drawer a book, and handed it over. "Open it," he insisted. I quickly did. I flipped the pages. Quickly I closed it. Placed it on the table beside me. Nudged it away. Sighed. *"Illustrations,"* Don Juan said matter-of-factly, again opening his arms as though newborn and innocent of so much as smelling a rose. "I am a visual person, you might say. I have no rhetoric, no scholarship, Monsieur. Quite simply, I do not die even when gutted because I do not *think*. I do not know what a thought is! I do not even dream, Signor. I just do!"

More then came to me concerning Henriette. Our discussion of Don Juan, my dread of his very being, my loathing of the brute sense of him, my love's irony in the presence of my dread, her understanding of its source—*ah!* all these rushed forward from the past to fix me to the armchair with my forehead propped by two fingers. It did not matter to me if this fellow was or was not Don Juan, the result was the same. It did not matter if he aged or I did or neither, the death was the same. "I never met no Henriette," he said gruffly. "I only serve you. My immortality, my ruthlessness, illiteracy, all-round barbarism serve to make you that much more credible. Everyone wants to meet *you* because you're the sociable equivalent of me. I am a pig, Casanova, more or less. You are a fox only because of the pig. It is what, 1783? Soon I am going to make you very very famous by parading my own disgusting person in front of others. *Again.* It will be in an opera. You'll be immortal, of course, too. In your own way."

Boat-jawed, gorilla-faced, cootie-headed, flatulent, pug, thorned, wen-cheeked, vacant, and crazed, Don Juan went to sleep. I watched him wheeze, saw the blubbery lips drool, inhaled the stench of his clothes, sores, feet, identified the bugs scoring his hair, and generally held in my throat a nausea reminiscent of seasickness. I left the great lover shortly thereafter but must not avoid mention, here for the first time, that as I was about to depart and Don Juan curled himself into a question mark (or should I call it hook?) I rushed him, unsheathed my dagger, and prepared to bury it in the center of his chest. Certain moments conclude forever the possibility of one's freedom. To the bourgeois, marriage is generally such an event; to the slave it is his yoking; to the prelate his vow-day; the courtesan old age. But in each case there is retained in the mind the dream of what has been lost. As I stood above the sleeping body of Don Juan I experienced a damning like no other—to kill him was to let him live, to let him live was to condemn him, and in either instance I remained snared, fractured, in harness. My dagger left the room bloodless. That is why when, months later, I came to kiss the behemoth Pisce farewell and reentered the fogged bank of the Seine with that splendid sense of worthlessness that only perversion can instill, I was not startled or alarumed to hear in the mist a voice singing to the *burchiello* of Granada and of Moors and of revolution, of all such nonsense that one day passes into legend.